THE GOLDEN WOLF - BOOK 2

NEW YORK TIMES BESTSELLING AUTHOR

SHANNON
MAYER

Cover Design by Melissa Stevens

GLITTER

THE GOLDEN WOLF - BOOK 2

NEW YORK TIMES BESTSELLING AUTHOR

SHANNON MAYER

To all the caffeine in the world that kept me writing when nothing else could.

Blessed be the stimulant we hide as a breakfast drink.

CONTENTS

1

IF YOU'RE GOING TO GET FUCKED OVER, MAY I SUGGEST LOTS OF LUBE?

For a werewolf, pain is a part of life from the moment you make your first shift from two legs to four. It has been an integral part of so many moments of my life that I'm not sure I could define my journey without it.

"Cin, listen to me. Pain means you're alive, little wolf. When you stop hurting, when the pain slips away, you surely are close to dying, if you aren't already dead." That advice had been spoken more than once to me by Mars. My stepfather, the only father I'd ever known. So maybe it was a good thing my body hurt like hell.

"Just pain, still alive," I whimpered. Just more of the same, as Mars would have said. Except this was on a larger scale. I couldn't remember a time when so many pieces of my body had felt broken, when so much of me had hurt all at the same time. My skin, bones, muscles. Everything had been lit up. Not even when my brothers had tried to kill me, shot me full of silver and dumped me into a river to drown.

"Life is pain," I said through swollen lips, tasting the blood that dripped freely from my nose and mouth as I hung with my arms bound high above my head. The cuffs were silver, of course. The steady flow of liquid dropping into the puddle below me was the only sound in the basement other than my own labored breathing, the burble of blood in my lungs.

I could have stayed quiet, but the sound of my voice was helping me stay alert.

I'd heal if given the chance, but I doubted that chance would come anytime soon. The light hadn't shifted outside yet, but I could feel dawn approaching. Dawn meant it would all be over. Not just my life, but the world and everything in it.

Because of a stupid damn curse and a prophecy that I'd walked into unwittingly.

Okay, to be crystal clear on the curse: I had two of them.

1. The first curse was courtesy of my family. I was a golden retriever by day, and if I was not fucked by a Prince by midnight, I would die. Not good, but not the end of the world. Hang on, that leads me to curse number two.

2. The second curse came from Soleil, when she slipped the bracelets onto me. She'd carried the sun within her, and when she'd handed me the bracelets, I'd inadvertently taken on her curse—which left me being hunted by Han and Havoc. Now if one of them kills me (or I am killed by another means, say a previous curse) the world is thrown into Ragnarök. AKA the end of the world as we know it.

"Damn you, Soleil." the words dripped from my lips with the blood. I'd trusted the girl, and she, like everyone else in my life, had fucked me over. The bracelets she'd slipped over my wrist had slid partway up my forearm. I'd rip them off if I'd been able to and throw them in her face.

One of my eyes was swollen shut, the other was half closed as I moved in and out of consciousness. Waiting for it all to be over.

The bad guys were going to win this time, sorry about that.

Funny, I wasn't even sure who the bad guys were anymore. Maybe I was one of them? If I hadn't kept Havoc from taking Soleil, then none of this would have happened.

"Sorry," I mumbled, my mind fuzzy with pain and sorrow and a good bit of pity for everyone in the world.

Ragnarök was no bueno, and when I died, the end times would be upon us. No pressure, of course. None at all.

"Girlfriend, I need you to stay awake!" yelled Bebe from the cardboard box she'd been stuffed into. My friend was a human, but I'd only ever known her as a cat. She was cursed, like me, only her curse was permanent, and mine allowed me to be human at night and a golden retriever by day. Bebe had been quiet for a long time—asleep, maybe. Or drugged by my kidnapper, I wasn't sure which. Or maybe she'd just stayed quiet during my beatings. "I'm getting us out of here!" She scratched at the box, the sound grating.

"Asshole face taped you in." I swayed slightly from side to side, the bones of my wrists rubbed raw against the thick manacles that had been clamped on me. My feet were bound to the wall too. It wouldn't do to have me kicking the motherfucker in the balls again, would it? I'd managed it once when he'd first caught me, and the pleasure I'd taken in his pain was no small thing.

I laughed and then groaned because the movement pulled on my ribs, all of which were most certainly broken. The gurgling rasp of my breath said yes, all were broken and likely one or two were pressing on my lungs.

"Cin, I need you to stay with me," Bebe yelled.

I didn't think there was a part of me that hadn't been hit with a fist or boot, with a metal bar or the butt of a gun. I'd been stripped to my bra and jean shorts and a quick glance from my one good eye had me counting the slashes that littered my upper body.

"Silver knife, Bebe. That's the thing. He knows I can't heal those wounds, he knows the silver will poison me, even if the wounds don't kill me." And that, my friends, was the main reason I was slurring my words. Silver made a werewolf sloppy, stupid. The first of the wounds with the knife had been inflicted hours before, and they had just kept coming, over and over. "Makes me weak."

Bebe let out a yowl that had me turning toward her box on the table—in as much as I could turn at all. "I don't care if it makes you drag your ass on the carpet like a dog, I need you to stay with me. What do you see? I can't see anything!"

I frowned, but even that hurt. I squinted out of my one good eye. "You're in a cardboard box, on a table about three feet high. Window to my right, high over my head. Basement." I squinted harder. "Two hours from dawn, maybe a little more."

"Shit! Okay. Anyone in the room with us?"

I drew in a long, slow breath that hurt my ribs and left me groaning. "No."

But for how long? How long would I be left hanging here before I was moved to a new location, all to keep me alive just long enough to torture me longer?

A chair scraped across the floor above our heads,

so the motherfucker who'd messed me up wasn't far. I'd kill him given the chance. Or at least I'd try.

"Okay, I'm going to roll the box!" Bebe called out as she did just that, rocking the box until it started turning like a Ferris wheel, spinning end over end. I couldn't see her, but I could easily imagine her little body working furiously to make the box move, pounding at the sides.

I wasn't sure that the box falling would break it open, but it seemed like it was worth a shot.

The box with the cat in it—Schrodinger would have a damn field day with this—landed on the floor with a light thump.

"Damn it!" Bebe screeched. "It didn't break open."

I wiggled a bare foot, forcing myself to focus and think through the silver contamination slugging up my veins and slowing my reflexes. Giving up just wasn't an option for me.

I had about a twelve-inch radius of movement with my foot. Maybe I could get the box open if she got it closer? If for nothing else, Bebe could escape. My life was coming to an end, and with it, the entire world. But if she stayed here, there would be no chance for her survival. I'd fight for her. I'd fight for my friend Denna too.

Denna had followed me all the way from Alaska, looking for adventure. She'd found a bit more than she'd counted on, but that was life when you were friends with an outcast werewolf. All I could hope at that point was that Denna was safe somewhere. As safe as a ghoul could be.

She'd gone with Soleil, to keep her safe. But...well that hadn't worked so well.

I drew a deep breath and focused on what needed to be done. "Follow my voice, Bebe," I said. "If you can get closer, I think I can open the box."

"That's my bitch!" Bebe shouted.

There was a moment of darkness and then Bebe's voice cut through to me. "I need you to stay awake, girlfriend! Talk to me, tell me a story or something!"

A story. I dug deep for one worth telling.

"I never knew my father," I said, just focusing on telling her a story. "I only ever knew Mars, and he was the best father. Strong and smart and kind. Firm, we didn't get away with anything. Not me or the boys. But they didn't turn out like their dad. Juniper began to poison them as soon as he left, before I understood what was happening...I was young. Barely eighteen when it all happened. Shipley, though, I thought he was different. We were friends as children, closest in age, sharing adventures. But he's just as big of a monster as the others now. Worse, because at least I knew that Kieran hated me, even if I didn't understand why. And Dick, he...he tried here and there, but the Ogre beer took him away. But Ship, I thought we were friends. I thought...he would stand with me against them. But he buckled, sided with the winning team."

Bebe was closer, but even straining I couldn't reach her yet.

"Keep talking!" she yelped.

Blood dripped over my bottom lip, sliding into my mouth, coppery and sweet. "Meg, now Meghan, was like me. At least I thought so. My little sister, she turned to me for comfort when Juniper went on a rampage. She was born after Mars left—not his child any more than I am. But Meg looked like Juniper, and I think that saved her so many times. But I still taught her the way that Mars taught me. How to fight, how to hunt and track, how to do some small spells. How to survive."

"You know magic and you never told me?"

"Nothing that would be helpful here, Bebe," I groaned. "Simple spells for surviving in nature. How to find water, revealing footprints on hard ground, that sort of thing."

Bebe rolled the box right to my foot with her next tumble, and I pressed on it with my big toe. "Gotcha," I said.

"Hurry!"

Gripping the chains above my head that were attached to my manacles, I lifted my body a little, so I had use of both feet at the same time. I hissed as the silver-coated manacles dug in deeper, cutting into tendons and biting my bones. Asshole had really done his research to make sure I couldn't escape.

Like he'd been prepping for years to kill me, not just the short time he'd been hunting me.

The cardboard box was tough, but between Bebe and me, we got a hole open large enough that she could squeeze out. A gray tabby with cream across her belly and nose, she peered up at me with bright eyes. "Shit, girl. I'd hoped it wasn't this bad."

"Go." I tipped my head to the window. "Go, while you can."

"Nope, not leaving you."

A clatter above our heads had us both turning toward the stairs. I was more awake now, even with the silver poisoning. Trying to get Bebe out had sobered me up enough to clear my head.

"Bebe, I'm going to die here, and the world will go boom when that happens." I drew a difficult breath, focusing all my thoughts on getting Bebe out. "You can find Denna. Go into hiding. Go underground, whatever it takes."

And hopefully survive. Somehow.

"There won't be any surviving the end of the world, girlfriend." She circled around me. "Maybe I can pull the pin back here, and at least if we're going to die, we'll do it up right. Ice cream, remember? Strippers? Maybe a sexy lap dance."

I sighed, unable to keep the ghost of a smile from

flitting across my face, even though that hurt too. Bebe wasn't going to leave me. I'd never had a friend like her before, and now we were both about to die.

Another crash upstairs, a scream followed by a shout. The sound of doors banging, thumps like bodies being tossed around. What in the donkey's ass of fuckery was happening up there?

A tiny shiver of apprehension shook through me as the door to the basement opened and a flood of scents rolled down to me. The scents were immediate and violent, coated in blood and death.

"Bebe, hide," I said. I could smell him now, closer and closer. They smelled so alike, it was easy to believe I was being rescued by Havoc. Only Havoc was dead. Chopped into little pieces by Kieran.

She scooted behind me. "Keep his attention, I'll break you free so you can kick his ass into next week!"

She was completely overestimating my abilities in my current condition. Maybe if I wasn't injured, maybe if I wasn't chained to the wall, then I could take on the monster coming down the stairs.

His footsteps were light and fast on the wooden stairs, barely creaking under his weight.

I squinted as he came into view, only able to see out of my one blurred eye.

He wasn't dragging his axe, but held it loosely at his side, the edge of it catching the light and glittering. Double-headed, wickedly sharp, and coated in blood.

Bebe shot out from behind me, puffed up and screeching. "You bastard! I'll kill you myself! Oh shit."

Havoc locked eyes with me, black eyes with that fleck of silver in the left, so different from the eyes he had when he was in his wolf form. "I doubt that."

"Chicken!" she screeched.

He didn't even glance at her. "Pussy."

Shock rippled through me. "You were killed. Kieran said he did it."

Chopped up. Those were his words. Maybe I was hallucinating. That was possible with the silver in my bloodstream. With the injuries I'd sustained. Maybe I was seeing Havoc, but it was really Han.

No, my nose didn't lie. It was Havoc in front of me. Alive when I was so sure he'd been dead.

"It happened," he said. "But I don't die easy. You on the other hand, will die very easy."

I should have been terrified. Should have been freaking out. But if he ended this now, then at least I wouldn't hurt anymore.

"Going to finish this?" I slurred. "Get it over with? Might as well, I'm halfway dead already."

"You are far more than half-way dead, Goldie."

With a flick of his wrist, he had the axe up and swinging toward me. All I could do was close my eyes and be grateful it was going to end fast.

2

8 HOURS EARLIER

I stood there in complete shock, staring at Havoc, his hand wrapped around my wrist, the chaos of the multi-car pile-up around us. Black smoke and red gold flames, women screaming, the screech of brakes as other vehicles tried to avoid the mess I'd created in the middle of the highway. I mean, to be fair, it was Loki who'd dropped me there, so I was going to blame him for the mess.

Loki, who'd had an affair with my mother, Juniper, which had started this whole mess of mine. He was the reason that I was stuck as a golden retriever when I shifted.

But that's another story. This one starts with... fucking.

"What did you just say?" I spluttered at Havoc.

He dragged me behind him, south on the highway. "If you don't want to die, and I don't want the world to end up in Han's hands, we need to get fucking."

Yes, I knew that would be the outcome of telling him that I would need to bang a royal of some sort. A prince, a king, maybe a lord would do it? But I hadn't really expected it to happen this quick.

"Where are we going?"

"The back of the SUV should do it," he growled.

"What?"

He didn't even look over his shoulder at me. "Are you expecting flowers? Pretty words? Surely as fuck you are not expecting foreplay. This is about saving the world, Goldie, nothing else."

I grimaced at the nickname, but I hurried my feet up. "I wouldn't think a guy like you would even have a play book, never mind know what foreplay is. So yes, my expectations are low."

His grip tightened on my wrist as he jerked me to the left, around a smoking front end of a semi-truck.

Chaos, thy name is Loki.

He'd dropped me into the middle of the highway not just to find Havoc, but because he'd known it would make the biggest mess of things and not just for me but for everyone on the highway too.

My study of old mythologies had taken me through the Norse pantheon a time or two. I wasn't an expert by any means, but I knew enough to know the major play-ers. So, I knew very well that Loki was trouble.

"Bebe?" I twisted around to see her there at my heels, silent. Which wasn't like her. "You okay?"

"I don't like this. I have a bad feeling," she mewed up at me. I held out my free arm, and she leapt up. I held her tight.

"I just have to get through this. Then we can go from there, figure out a next step after," I said.

Havoc didn't so much as grunt a response to my assessment of fucking him. *Getting through it* is some-thing one might say after twenty-five years of marriage.

But I was nothing if not pragmatic, and he was right. The quicker the better. "Look, Bebe, I've had shitty sex for far worse reasons than saving the world. Think of the story this will be some day. Right?"

Her yellow-green eyes blinked solemnly up at me. "I suppose. It just sucks."

I grinned down at her. "But I won't."

She gritted her teeth and snickered. "No, you won't! And no swallowing either!"

Havoc didn't react to our banter except for a rumble that issued from his chest. Was that a laugh or a growl? I wasn't sure, and it didn't matter. I was going to fuck the prince of the Norse Pantheon, and then get the hell out of here. Run as far away as I could.

Because they were all crazy as far as I was

concerned. Him, his brother Han, and Loki were all certifiable.

We were through the worst of the highway mess, and I could see the black SUV ahead of us now. "Open the back up!" Havoc yelled.

The tailgate of the SUV lifted.

"Oh, what a romantic first time. I'm going to feel like I'm sixteen again," I laughed. Bebe giggled though I could hear the strain in it. An act to help me get through this.

"I lost my virginity in a Toyota," she said. "Almost lost it to the stick shift if I'm being honest."

I sighed. "Dodge truck for me. But that's living in the boonies for you."

Havoc pulled me forward, all but tossing me into the back of the SUV. And he immediately started to undo his belt.

I closed my eyes and went for the button at the top of my jean shorts.

"What in the name of Odin is going on here?" Sven grumbled. "Havoc, what...why? What are you doing?"

"If she doesn't get fucked by a prince before dawn, she dies. Because of Loki's interfering. And she holds the sun in her now, Sven. Can't you see it?"

I opened my eyes to see Sven standing next to Havoc. His wood-like skin was mostly hidden under a long brown robe with a cowl that made me think of a

Jedi master. Or a Sith lord. Depended on the day with him working as a double agent with Han too.

Sven sucked in a slow breath, like the sound of wind through the leaves of an oak tree. "Her eyes glitter with it. Havoc, you can't really mean to—"

"Unless you want to fuck her, old king? Because we cannot let her die," Havoc growled, and there was a definite feeling of possessiveness in his tone.

"I don't think you want to share her." Bebe was sitting beside my head, but her words were for Havoc.

"Bebe, a bit of privacy." I was shimmying out of my shorts, until they were down to mid-thigh.

She turned her back, wrapping her tail tight around her body. "That's the best you're going to get from me. I'm not leaving your side. It's not like it's going to be a gentle, caring love-making session." She paused and tipped her head so I could see one of her yellow-green eyes. "You know what's funny?"

I couldn't look at her other than a quick glance. Havoc had grabbed my thighs and was pulling me close to the back end of the SUV. Unable to look away from him, and yet I couldn't bear to keep eye contact either. That was the golden in me, shame rolling through me, pushing me to drop my gaze. This time, I buckled to it. Let it win.

I closed my eyes and let myself submit to this.

"What's that, Bebe?" I said, as the tip of his cock pressed to my opening.

"Havoc never even questioned whether you might be lying to him to get a piece of ass. He jumped right into fucking you. Which makes me think maybe he wants you more than he would like to admit."

His growl was immediate.

I blew out a breath, prepping myself for a raw fucking. I told myself it didn't matter. It would be over in minutes, and I'd no longer be trapped as a golden retriever. And, more importantly, I wouldn't die, and curse the world to Ragnarök. I could move on and forget this ever happened.

I mean, I'd still have to deal with Han trying to kill me, but I'd survived so many people trying to kill me, what was one more?

Havoc's hands flexed on my thighs, fingers digging into the flesh, thumbs sweeping over the tops of my legs.

I peeked out from under my lashes. Why was he hesitating? Did he want more of an audience? I opened my mouth to ask him, but there was no chance for the words to fall from my lips.

A sudden screech of brakes filled the air, followed by screams from someone in the front of the SUV, and then I was flying through the air away from Havoc, torn from his hands. I tumbled over and over with the SUV as it rolled over the edge of the highway and down an embankment.

"What the fuck?" Bebe screeched as we fell. The

impact of the SUV landing and flipping over and over sent me around the interior of the back multiple times.

A rib cracked. A cut on my cheek opened.

My head hit the side window. The world was full of stars, sparkling and glittering across my vision, seemingly slowing the tumble.

Finally, the SUV slid to a stop, upside down in a river.

I clung to the headrest of the back seat as the SUV floated. It would only last for a second before it inevitably sank. "It's always a fucking river with me," I groaned as I pushed to my hands and knees, water sloshing around me, up over my feet. Icy cold, the river slipped up past my knees as the SUV picked up speed with drowning itself. I grabbed my shorts and yanked them up, buttoning them quickly as I slipped out into the water, wincing.

I touched my head, and my fingers came away with blood. "Bebe?"

"What happened?" she swam toward me, and I scooped her out of the water. I was about waist deep, head groggy, eyes hurting.

Ropes flung out toward me, splashing in the water. In the dark of the night, the shadows along the bank were indistinct.

Someone wanted to help us, but I couldn't see who. My eyes were fuzzy from smacking my head. I reached for the first rope as Bebe screeched.

"No!"

I tried to jerk my hand away, but it was too late. The rope tightened around my wrist, silver woven through the rope, biting into me. I was yanked off my feet and dragged through the water as more ropes settled over my head and around my neck. Over my feet.

"Take her. I have what I want." Han's voice cut through the chaos in my head as I was brought in like a fish on a line, thrashing hard. The silver made it difficult at best to put up much of a fight. I could barely breathe.

"Where?" Shipley asked, his voice cutting me. His betrayal was old news by now, but it still hurt. So it was my brothers who'd caught up with me...my brothers and my mate.

"Here. I have a place not far. I'll catch up with you once I deal with my brother."

I lifted my head and stared into the face of the man who was meant to be my mate. Even now, as he sent me off with my brothers who would likely kill me, I couldn't help but want to reach out to him. To try and convince him that he was wrong to throw me aside. That was magic for you, pushing people where they didn't want to be pushed.

I was dragged to my feet, swaying from the head injury as my brothers bound my hands. But they forgot my feet, the fools.

I snapped a foot out and caught Han right in the

dick. I felt him crumple under my foot as he went to the ground, his face contorting into a twist of pain.

"Might be immortal, but a ball-busting still works!" Bebe screeched.

I kicked back at the brother behind me—Dick, as it so happened. Got him in the knee, which released my right hand. I slugged it into the left side of Shipley's jaw, which sent him reeling.

To my left was Meg, her eyes wide. Another time I would have hesitated on smashing my sister in the face.

Not after she shot me.

I grabbed her by the hair and snapped my head into hers, breaking her nose.

Everything went down in under five seconds flat.

I flung off the ropes and ran along the river's edge without looking back. I knew they'd be on me. I knew there was a good chance they'd catch me. But I had to try to get away, not just for me but for all of us.

I had to survive.

"Run!" Sven bellowed up at me from high above, along the edge of the highway. "Run!"

Yeah, I wasn't about to stop and ask for directions. I'd do better on four legs than two, but until my first curse was broken, I was stuck on two legs until the sun was up.

Bebe streaked along beside me. "They're catching up!"

"Time to swim."

Without stopping to wonder if it was a good idea, I leapt for the raging current.

My arms windmilled as I flew through the air, as far out as I could go. Once I hit the water, I swam hard, Bebe landing in the water behind me. Or so I thought.

"Wolf! In the water!" Bebe screamed from somewhere behind me. I spun in a circle to see her on the shore, her scruff clutched in Meg's hands. My sister's face streaming with blood as she bared her teeth.

The wolf in the water with me was Ship.

I dove down under him, swimming back for shore. Maybe bravery wasn't in my genetics as a golden, but loyalty sure as fuck was, and I wasn't leaving Bebe behind. Not with my asshole family.

I burst up out of the water on the other side of Ship and swam hard as I could for shore.

"She loves the stupid cat," Meg said, her voice thick with blood. She spat to the side. "We have her now."

I lifted a lip. Let out a snarl. As if my love for Bebe would be my undoing, or maybe it was jealousy on Meg's part. I'd fought for her once too—and now she used my ability to love against me, as a weapon.

My feet touched the sand and rock of the shore, and I tried to run forward. Would have if Shipley hadn't leapt on me from behind. Shoving me down into the water. Pinning me there until I blacked out.

Of course, that didn't kill me. The gods were not merciful enough to let me go easily.

I woke up in the back of a van, legs and hands bound behind me and tied together at the small of my back. Bebe was in a cardboard box.

The voices around me told me that they didn't know I was awake yet.

"How do we trust him?" Meghan asked.

"We don't," Kieran responded. "He wants her dead. We want her dead. So he'll be happy if we kill her. Tell him she wasn't strong enough to withstand questioning."

I knew there was no point in arguing with my brothers. So even though I wasn't gagged, I didn't bother saying anything.

"Her heartbeat is up, she's awake," Meg said.

"Awake, Cinny?" Kieran called from the driver's side, using the nickname I hated. He was the only one of my siblings that I hadn't gotten to hit. Where had he been? "You know I killed that big brute you were about to fuck. Cut him into pieces. Threw them into the river. Fed him to the fishes as they say."

Something crawled through me, I wasn't sure if it was horror, or grief, or just the kind of despair that came from knowing there was no one able to save me. If anyone could have saved me, it would have been Havoc.

That had to be why Sven had told me to run. There would be no Havoc swooping in to save me. There would be no prince to give me a royal banging.

The world was over.

"Tell me you aren't crying for him," Kieran said with a laugh.

There was no point in answering. I knew this game of his all too well.

He just wanted a reaction, anyway. Whether or not he had cut Havoc up, he was looking to scare me. To make me feel alone and helpless. That was one of the power trips he enjoyed.

Bebe, stuck in her box, could do nothing but screech and curse at them.

The back of the van was dark, the only light coming from the occasional headlights from cars in the oncoming lane. Even those faded to nothing after half an hour of driving.

My life was ticking by.

"Do we take her all the way home?" Meg asked. "I don't like that Han guy. I don't think—"

There was the sound of a sharp, hard slap cutting her words off. "You aren't supposed to be thinking." Dick growled.

I laughed. "That's ironic, coming from the guy who doesn't have two brain cells left to rub together."

I knew I shouldn't have said anything. Should have

kept my mouth shut and just let Meg take her just desserts. Fingers tangled in my hair and dragged me up to my knees. I stared into Richard's eyes, saw the numbness there. He lifted his free hand, curling it into a fist.

Tell him the truth. You have power in you, little wolf. Use it.

The voice inside my head I didn't recognize, but it woke me up.

A shiver of my alpha power rippled through me, something I'd never dared use. My own strength there, buried under all that golden fur.

The truth. The truth was a bitter pill.

"You could have led the pack, Richard," I said, sensing that tiny slice of what could have been right there under the surface. "You had the strength and the smarts, you could have done it. Could have stopped Juniper. And she knew it. It's why she hooked you on the ogre beer. You could still stop her, Richard."

My power slid over him. And for the first time I could see the black, oily sludge that clung to the very essence of him.

Juniper's control.

It was filth and terror and pain, trapping him.

Through it, I saw his eyes.

Save me.

I blinked, the image gone, and I saw only his corporeal face. In his eyes there was a glimmer of something

—pain, regret…maybe hope? And then it was gone. As if that black sludge covered him up once more.

He let his fist fly into my face, the blow flipping me backward onto the metal floor.

"Keep your mouth shut, you dirty bitch." He slurred the words, worse than usual. "Or I'll break your jaw and make sure you keep it shut!"

"She's just trying to save her skin," Shipley said from the front passenger seat. "She's been doing it for years. Pitting us against one another. Trying to start a war. She knows we are stronger than her together."

His words were so far from the truth I was surprised that lightning didn't strike him down where he sat.

I closed my eyes, reaching for my siblings with my own power.

They were all coated in the black oiled sludge. Shipley, Meghan and Richard looked…desperate within it. As if reaching for a hand to pull them free.

You could be that hand.

I turned my mind to Kieran. He…the oily black was different on him. He was not buried in it, He had become it. Kieran as I knew him, was gone.

But the other three…maybe I could convince them to let me go. Maybe.

Lying there in the back of the van, I could feel Death breathing down the back of my neck, just waiting to take me. What a coup though, for Death at least. I died and the world died with me. A whole slew of souls all at once.

Another half an hour and the van began to slow. I was dragged out of the back, along with Bebe in her cardboard box. A house was before us, surrounded by old buildings that had been boarded up, and a dark street, absent of even a single light.

A second van pulled up next to us. Men I didn't recognize spilled out of the van, wearing tactical vests and carrying AR-15s along with what looked like a solid army-sized arsenal.

The bright hair of Soleil drew my eyes. "Soleil? How did they find you?"

Shipley backhanded me, casually, but it still made my eyes water and stars dance across my vision. My lip started to swell immediately.

"They found us too," Soleil sobbed. "I thought...I thought giving you the bracelets would do the trick. Sven told me that was the only way to escape the curse. I thought...I thought I'd be safe!"

"Well, I'm guessing Han hasn't figured it out yet," Bebe snapped from inside her box. "Or he would have left you alone."

Even as we stood there, Han rolled up in a very nice sports car of some kind. It seemed silly, really, but he was flexing his power even now—trying to show off. He stepped out of the car dragging an axe reminiscent of Havoc's.

Only Han's weapon had a single edge, rather than the double blade. The handle was solid black, poker straight, and the blade itself was a dark silver, like tarnished steel. My eyes locked onto the runes etched into the blade. They glowed with a low blue light as he tightened his hand on the shaft.

A hand tangled into my hair and yanked my head, so I had to look up into Kieran's face. "She's going to die quick and painless. I won't say the same for you, Cinny."

There was no moment of hesitation in him, no pity or sorrow. Han walked up to Soleil, standing between two soldiers, and swung the axe straight at her.

She didn't have time to scream, flinch, or even try to get away. The thunk of the axe through bone and flesh was so fast, so incredibly terrible that I couldn't look away.

Her bright blue eyes were wide, and she stared at me as the light faded from them, her neck collapsing and her head sliding off the stump. Her body fell to the ground, her head rolling and coming to a stop, still staring at me. Her mouth moved once, like a last gasp, a last reflex.

"What happened?" Bebe shouted. "I can smell blood!"

"I'm here," I said quietly. "Be still."

Han turned slowly to see me on my knees. "It seems I chose correctly in taking you from the shelter after all. Your actions brought me to my Soleil, as I'd hoped. Now, I am off to claim my reward. Enjoy your time with your family, mate. I won't be coming back for you. Do as you wish with her."

He bent as if to kiss me.

"Try it and I'll bite your fucking face off," I growled.

He paused and laughed. "So be it. I thought you'd like a last goodbye from me."

I didn't want him close.

Sven had been able to see that I carried the sun now, as had Havoc.

For whatever reason, Han had not made the connection. Maybe because he wasn't looking for it. Maybe because it was dark. I had no idea.

He turned his back on me, and it didn't hurt that he was leaving me behind. I could still feel his connection to me as his mate. But he was a horrible person, and I could only be grateful that he'd forsaken me.

What was more problematic was that if I didn't get fucked by a prince, the world would end. What few friends I had needed me to be better than just pissing him off. They needed me to get laid. And Han was still a prince, just as his brother had been.

I felt a part of me shrivel up, but I would do what—and who—I had to do, to make this happen. To save those worth saving.

"Your brother has a bigger dick than you," I said. "And at least he knows how to use it."

Fighting words, I know, but really, what did I have to lose? He would either turn away, or he'd try to prove that he was better at fucking me than his brother. It was a long shot, but I had to try. I had to.

Han slowed and leaned on his axe. "A crass insult."

I shrugged as best I could. "Doesn't make it any less true. Just thought you'd like to know. Seeing as you're about to rule the world, or whatever it is you're going to do. You could add it to your list of things you need to work on."

His face tightened ever so slightly. Ah, yes, that *was* a sore spot. I took a literal stab in the dark. "Always been a problem, hasn't it? The ladies like Havoc better. Not surprising."

He moved like lightning. I was on my knees one second, flat on my back the next, staring up into the night sky, wondering how I'd gotten there.

"She's ours to kill!" Kieran snarled. "You swore it!"

I rolled onto my belly, literally shoving my ass up toward his face, forcing a laugh from my lips. "Yeah, knocking me flat only proves that my words struck a chord. A *tiny* one."

Han wrapped his fingers around my throat and dragged me up until I dangled, my feet well above the ground. He pulled me close, putting his nose to my ear. "You are my mate, until the moment of your death, which is coming soon. I would know if you'd fucked my brother. If you'd fucked anyone."

Shit.

Well, so much for that idea. He was close enough that I did the only thing I could—if he wasn't going to fuck me, I could at least wound the bastard.

I turned my head and bit his ear, tearing it off as he reared backward, dropping me to the ground. I gasped and scooted away from him as he stood there, hand cupped over where his ear had been. His eyes were dark as night, as if all the color had been leached from them. "Make her suffer. Do not kill her right away."

He crouched and smiled at me, blood running down his cheek. "I want to feel her pain through the bond for hours. Days."

"That we can do." Kieran chuckled.

I made myself smile back at Han, knowing my words were just bravado at that point, but I said them anyway. "You crossed the wrong woman, Han. You'll regret this moment. I swear to you that you'll look back on this moment right here and realize you were too stupid to live."

He stood and laughed. "I doubt that I'll even remember you three seconds after you're dead and I no longer have to feel the connection to you that my foolish grandfather put into place." With that, he tossed his axe into the back of his fancy car, got in and spun a lazy, drifting circle, spitting gravel and dust at everyone before he shot off.

The men who'd shown up with the weapons

spread out around the house. Humans, hired killers. Masked and faceless.

Which left me with just my fantastic siblings, who'd been given the green light to make me suffer.

I let out a slow breath. This day was seriously fucked.

3

TORTURE IS NOT AS FUN AS IT SOUNDS

The next few hours I was literally at the mercy of my siblings, which is to say there was no mercy from any of them.

Well...maybe some mercy.

Kieran and Meg took their turns and their time, beating the shit and piss out of me. More than once my bladder let go, so I was kneeling or face down in my own urine. They'd just laugh and keep beating me. That included Meg, though I felt her pull her punches.

Richard didn't lift a hand to hit me. Which would have surprised me if I hadn't felt him reaching for me.

As if he were fighting through the bonds that Juniper had on him.

Shipley struck me, but even more than Meg, he pulled his punches. A glimpse of his face, his eyes said it all. He was terrified.

"Hit her harder," Kieran snapped and backhanded Ship, sending him flying across the room and into Richard.

They went down in a tangle.

Richard pushed to his feet. His eyes met mine. Fighting, he was fighting whatever was going on inside his head. He helped Shipley up. "Knock it off, Kier. We have all the time in the world. I'm tired as fuck. So's Ship and Meg."

Kieran snarled. "You going soft?"

Richard laughed. "Take a break. She'll be here in the morning."

The standoff was...interesting. Had my words to Richard done something?

It was Kieran who broke first. "I'm hungry, what's upstairs?" He clapped his hands together as if it was his idea to take a break.

Meg, who'd been standing between me and the boys, watching the standoff, spoke quietly. "There are three pans of lasagna, fresh rolls, and two chocolate cakes. I also made sure there's plenty of drink to go with the food. If you want more, I can go get it right now."

Kieran smiled at her. "See, that's a good girl. Well trained!"

Then he glanced at Richard as he went up the stairs. "You're going to have a go at her on the next round. I want to see you do some damage."

Richard gave a nod but didn't say anything. I didn't think he wanted to beat me. Maybe it had to do with what I'd said to him in the van. Didn't matter though, not really. I could feel Kieran getting bored with the pain he was inflicting. He wanted to kill me. Even if Richard didn't. Even if Shipley didn't.

Hell, at that point, I wanted them to kill me too I hurt so badly.

Through one eye—the other was mostly swollen shut—I watched my three brothers head up the stairs. Meg watched them go too.

When they were gone, she approached me slowly. "You know...I did what you said. What you taught me to do."

I would have arched an eyebrow, but my face hurt too much for me to move anything. I could hear Bebe crying in the cardboard box, alternately swearing and sobbing, the sounds quieter and quieter as she passed out from exhaustion no doubt. Of course, she'd heard every blow, heard me scream when they'd broken fingers, skinned parts of my back, set deliberately dislocated joints only so they could pull them apart a second and third time.

"What is that?" I managed to ask.

"You told me when I was little that I was to survive, no matter the cost. No matter what I had to do. No matter who I had to hurt." She took a bottle of water off a side table, from next to Bebe's box and tipped it up to my mouth.

I didn't drink. I just let the water fall off my lips and land on the floor, despite how dry my mouth was from screaming.

She frowned and tears gathered in her eyes. I wasn't sure I believed her tears though. "You've chosen to survive at the cost of another's death." I struggled to speak around the broken parts of my mouth, the missing teeth. Given time to heal, I'd be okay. But I doubted I'd be given any time at all. "At the death of the one person who would have died for you."

Her eyes closed. "Don't."

"You started it," I said. "Go be with the ones you chose, Meg."

"I had no choice!" Her eyes flew open, and she threw the water at me. It stung the cuts on my face, but I refused to stick my tongue out and gather the few droplets. I would take nothing from her.

I stared at her, looking past her to the same oily sludge that coated the boys, coating her bonds to Juniper. But she wasn't as deep in it as the other three. "You could have chosen not to shoot me. We would have made it out. I would have fought with everything I had to save you."

Her eyes were wide, fully dilated in the dim room, and she reeked of fear. "No."

"Yes," I said. "Yes, is the answer. But you made a

choice. It stands now, always and forever, you will be the coward of the family, below even Dick who had it in him to change our fate if he could only have found his courage. At least he didn't take part tonight. At least he had the courage to hold himself back from sinking further into what she made him."

She turned and fled the room, her feet pounding up the stairs.

And I hung there, waiting to die.

TORTURE IS something you need to be really good at to keep someone alive for a long time and still make them suffer. To be fair, that is not a strength Kieran had. He had to keep stopping his beatings, letting my body heal itself enough that he could break me down again. He was too eager to cut into me, to make me hurt, that he had no choice but to take breaks. It was on one of those breaks that the clattering from above started.

THE PAIN just ebbed and flowed, and there was nothing I could do to slow or speed up my very imminent death. Or so I thought until I found myself looking up into Havoc's eyes.

4

A RIGHT ROYAL FUCKING

Havoc wasn't dragging his axe, but held it loosely at his side, the edge of it catching the light and glittering. Double-headed, wickedly sharp, and coated in blood.

Bebe shot out from behind me, puffed up and screeching. "You bastard! I'll kill you myself! Oh shit."

Havoc locked eyes with me. "I doubt that."

"Chicken!" she screeched.

He didn't even glance at her. "Pussy."

Shock rippled through me. "You were killed. Kieran said he did it."

Chopped up. Those were his words. Maybe I was hallucinating. That was possible with the silver in my bloodstream. With the injuries I'd sustained. Maybe I was seeing Havoc, but it was really Han.

No, my nose didn't lie. It was Havoc in front of me. Alive when I was so sure he'd been dead.

"It happened," he said. "But I don't die easy. You on the other hand, will die very easy."

I should have been terrified. Should have been freaking out. But if he ended this now, then at least I wouldn't hurt anymore.

"Going to finish this?" I slurred. "Get it over with? Might as well, I'm halfway dead already."

"You are far more than half-way dead, Goldie."

With a flick of his wrist, he had the axe up and swinging toward me, swinging his axe at the chains holding my hands above my head. They clattered as they fell, and he caught me in one arm. Both legs had been broken, so I wasn't about to do any standing.

"You aren't dead?"

His eyebrows shot up. "I'm surprised *you* aren't dead. Lucky for you, at least one of your brothers likes you."

"Go team!" Bebe yelled. "Now let's get us all out of here, yes?"

There were no screams left in me, but the groan that escaped was nearly as loud. One of my brothers had helped him find me.

Richard. It had to be Richard.

Maybe I'd reached a part of him after all.

Bebe bounced around at our feet. "Kieran beat her so badly, man, you gotta be careful."

"No time," Havoc and I said together.

He slung me over one forearm, as if he were carrying a sack of potatoes. Then he started up the stairs. I threw up twice before we reached the top.

On the main floor, chaos reigned as if Loki himself had been set loose here too. Then again, Havoc *was* related to him. There was screaming, the splintering of wood, the shouts of men, and the snarls of many were-wolves fighting. Havoc's pack was helping him get me out. The men with the guns were outside, the *pop-pop-pop* of their weapons going off.

Bebe ran ahead of us, her tiny claws seeking out the hamstrings of any members of the opposition who got too close. Twice I saw fighters go down, reaching for their legs.

"Good job, Bebe," I groaned as the pain dragged at me, taking me in and out of consciousness. Through the haze, I saw my brothers and Meg working together to keep Havoc's pack at bay. "Leave them," I said.

"Why?" Havoc all but snarled the word.

"Because I want to kill Kieran myself and maybe... maybe the others aren't as bad as I thought." I breathed out those words and then the pain was too much for me to keep consciousness. More than that, I knew I didn't have to. Havoc would get me out of there.

We still had time to stave off the end of the world.

I mean...the asshole who'd cursed me hadn't stipulated that I had to be conscious for the whole banging the prince thing to work. Right?

I floated in and out of awareness, dipping into a place of dreams and memories.

I saw Mars, his face was a mask of pain and sorrow even as he reached for me. "I can't save you, sweetheart. My girl, I am so sorry."

"I know." I held my hand out to him. "But I love that you want to. Love knowing that you still see me as your little girl."

He was swept away and replaced with a man I didn't know. Tall and broad-shouldered, he had a trim dark beard that matched the long locks that hung from his head. Portions of his hair were braided, beads and bones woven through it, and one side was shaved down to the scalp. He wore dark clothes with runes drawn on them. His eyes seemed to change color, shifting from brown to green and then blue before deepening to a darkness that I'd only seen in Han's eyes.

"Who are you?"

The man bowed at the waist. "Tyr. Of the Norse Pantheon. I see that you've been tangled up with Loki and the wolf brothers? Not much fun, those ones."

"I didn't have a choice." I winced, pain from my body making the vision, or dream, or whatever it was fade.

I blinked and found myself staring up at a blank

white ceiling. There was a crack running through it that reminded me of the roots of a tree. Tree. Tyr. Something was tugging at my battered head. Something I'd read about the Norse Pantheon. An important tree of some kind.

Tree of life.

"She's too injured," Sven growled. "She won't heal in time for...that."

I smiled, tasted blood. "You can't say fuck?"

"She's awake." Havoc came into view. "Get her onto the bed."

"You can't be serious." That was a woman's voice. Not Bebe, someone else. The woman from his pack.

"Means life or death for the world," I whispered. "It's only a little pain. I'll survive."

Havoc scooped me up, and the pain must have made me loopy, because I said, "Do me a favor, growl while you fuck me."

"What?"

"Growl, it will help me orgasm." My head lolled against his shoulder, and then I was being laid on a bed. I really hoped the sheets weren't white. I looked to the side, and the sheets were terribly white and clean. "That's not good. Going to stain."

Someone was taking my shorts off. The woman. Her hands were gentle. "Are you sure you have to?"

"We have an hour before dawn," Havoc said. "She

will revert to her dog form, and then what? I am not fucking her in dog form. We do this now."

I closed my eyes. Havoc put his hands on my thighs as he had before. Only this time I winced and my breath hitched. His fingers loosened their grip.

I opened my eyes, because I could feel him hesitating again. I reached down and put my hand over his —as if he needed the comfort. "Havoc. It's fine. Just do it."

His eyes raised to mine, the scar across his eye tightening. "It is *not* fine. You are broken to a level that I have not seen in many, many years. And yet I must break you further to save this god-forsaken world. It is *not* fine."

I didn't know where Bebe was, I didn't know where Denna was, or my roommates and Mars, but I knew their lives were all on the line. Everyone's lives were on the line. I could feel the pressure of the sun coming. I forced myself to sit up, wrapping an arm around my middle.

"Don't move," he growled.

I shook my head. "Don't boss me."

He put a hand to my chest, palm over my heart, fingers wrapping up and over my shoulder. "Why are you being so accepting of this bullshit? Why are you not screaming and telling me to get away from you? It's hardly better than rape." He spat those words, as if they tasted of rot and ruin.

"For both of us," I said. "It is not a choice either of us would make."

Havoc stared hard at me, his hand flexing. Once more I put my hand over his. "I'll be fine, Havoc. It's not like I haven't had to bear a moment like this before. I am, after all, a woman."

The words were out of my mouth, the truth coming easily because my body and soul were so battered. Maybe I didn't want to die with some things left unspoken.

I didn't know what I expected to see in him...no, that's not true. I thought it would ease him, so that we could get this over with.

He snatched his hand from my shoulder and turned away, his fists at his side, shaking. I didn't understand why he was reacting this way. We barely knew each other, and by all accounts he didn't much like me. I understood his hesitation—I was his brother's intended mate and thus tainted. That automatically put me on the wrong team, whether I liked Han or not.

But time was ticking, and him having a mental break down wasn't going to work. I had an alpha wolf in me too, and I dug down deep to find her, pushing past the golden retriever that had all but drowned me in fluffy long fur and whimpering yelps.

My wolf clawed her way to the surface, and I put every ounce of alpha into my words.

"Havoc, damn well get over here and fuck me so we can figure out a way to stop Han!"

His back snapped straight, and he turned to look at me over his shoulder. Me and my wolf, we locked eyes with him, holding him steady with my gaze. "You cannot shy from this now. It must be done."

And in answer? He strode from the damn room, flinging the door open so hard it banged off the wall and slammed shut on its own behind him.

"Moon goddess," I breathed past the pain in my body, and slowly let myself back down onto the bed. As carefully as I could, I peeled the rags that were left of my clothes off in chunks, so I was completely naked. I doubted I could entice Havoc right now, but the blood on my clothes surely wasn't helping.

My legs were healing slowly, but I didn't think I could get to the bathroom on my own to wash up.

How was I going to make this happen?

The door clicked open, and I looked up to see Sven step into the room, which was something of a surprise. Then again, Havoc had called him a king.

I didn't even care right then. I just wanted it all to be over so I could either lie quietly and heal or lie quietly and die with the world.

"Havoc has asked me—"

"Got it. I'll close my eyes. Might be best if you do the same." I turned my head to the side, eyes closed. Just breathe deep and think about other things. Think about all the things I had left to do with my life. About my friends, about my sweet cat, Martin. He was supposedly under one of Petunia's spells too, Petunia being the witch who'd cursed me to be a golden retriever.

"I am not going to have sex with you," Sven said as he put a hand to my bare belly, the brush of his skin like smooth sanded wood, only warmer. "I'm going to try and heal you enough that Havoc will not hurt you when he breaks the curse."

My eyes flew open as his wooden fingers pressed carefully into my middle, a tingle emanating from him, like a low-level electrical pulse. "It will be painful."

"Life is pain, Princess," I whispered.

His eyebrows raised, "Succinct, if incorrect on my title," and then that tingle from his fingers amped up to a buzz that rattled my back teeth. His magic slid through my bones. The first crack caught me off guard as a bone in my leg snapped into place. I gritted my teeth and stared straight at the ceiling as tears gathered.

"Strong woman," Sven said. "You are doing well."

I breathed through the healing, gasping and hissing but refusing to scream. I'd screamed enough for my family as they'd tortured me. Though it didn't feel any better—the reverse was happening now. Sven was knitting my body back together. Bone by bone, wound by wound.

It wasn't long before his hand slid way from my belly, but even so, I knew that the time had been precious. Sven wobbled as he stepped back, his frame thinner than before, frail looking. "It is all I can do. The worst has been mended."

Apparently, Havoc had been waiting just outside the door. "It will have to be enough," he grumbled.

All my bones had been knit back together, and my head was clearer than it had been since before my brothers had taken over my care. I was sore but not in pain.

Distantly, I heard Sven leaving, his feet scraping across the floor, fatigue making him drag no doubt.

"We have less than thirty minutes," Havoc said. "Are you well enough?"

I nodded. "Thank you. I would have been fine."

His jaw ticked, and he reached for the wall and flicked off the light. This caught me off guard.

"Seeing the bruises bother you?"

"Do you consent to this?" His voice was rough, the sound of his jeans hitting the floor in the dark making my heart speed up.

I could say no. And I had this strange feeling that if I *did* say no, he wouldn't force it on me. Even though fucking me would save the world—and him—he wouldn't do it if I said no.

"I...yes. I consent." I paused, thinking it had to go both ways. "Do *you* consent to this?"

His hands were on the edge of the bed, which sagged a little under his weight. The pause was long enough that I began to wonder if he would back out.

"Havoc?"

His growl rumbled out and around me, caressing my skin in a way that had me gasping and my body clenching in a very pleasant manner.

"Yes. I consent."

He'd kept his shirt on, that was the first thing I noticed as he slid his body up mine, the fabric brushing against my bare skin. He held himself up on his forearms, our faces close together but not touching, not kissing.

And he was hesitating. He didn't say anything, but I knew he was holding back. Maybe he still thought he'd hurt me. Maybe he believed I didn't truly consent. The man was a damn mystery, one that I didn't have time to crack.

Time. Time was against us.

"On your back," I said, hooking one of my legs through his and rolling him to the side.

He let out a grunt of surprise as I straddled him, positioning his cock so that it was right there at my entrance.

I could have just slid onto him, could have just been as mechanical as possible to get the job done. But someone took that moment to knock on the door, bless their heart.

And he snarled at them. "Fuck off." His snarl rolled into a low growl that reverberated through my bones, kissed along my skin, and shook my clit as if he'd pressed his mouth to it, humming it into pleasure town. Moaning, pushing down on the tip of his cock, I placed my hands on his chest to balance myself.

His cock flexed and he growled again, his hands sweeping up over my thighs to grab my backside. His hands were huge, and he was able to palm each cheek, squeezing them, his fingers traveling up and down the line of my ass. Stroking. Kneading. Pressing me tighter against him.

He was still wearing his shirt, and I wanted to feel every inch of him. So I grabbed the edges of the top and ripped it open, buttons flying across the room.

In the dark, I could only see a little. Edges of things, the dark shadow that made up his body.

But I could *feel* everything.

He tugged me closer to him, his big (large, immense, huge, I couldn't settle on a word) cock stretching me as it pushed into me, inch by inch. Gasping, I felt a low moan building in my chest, fighting it's way to my lips.

My breasts were heavy with the need to be touched, to feel every piece of him, against every inch of me.

I flexed my hips, rocking myself onto him even as I splayed my hands over his chest, fingers digging into his muscles. Teetering on the precipice of desire and anticipation.

We needed to hurry.

I wanted this to last.

So sue me, it had been a long dry spell.

I tipped my head back, grabbed one of his hands and swept it away from my ass and up to my breast that ached for something more. "Help me out here."

He groaned as I slid all the way down his shaft in one exquisite thrust that had me gasping and arching my back as he filled me up. Was it love? Nope, not a chance. Was it a royal fucking?

You betcha.

Havoc moaned and clutched at me as I began to move, riding him slowly, taking my time, savoring every inch of him. I angled myself a little more, taking him deeper.

His other hand slid from my ass to my front, dipping into the wetness, dragging it across the sensitive nub, starting slow. But I didn't need him to start slow—I was already nearly there, my body attuned to his and his damn orgasmic growls.

And he finally seemed to realize it, letting out a low rumble that had me whimpering and slamming myself harder onto his cock, as he pressed his thumb against my clit, taking the pressure up even further. I wasn't sure I was breathing anymore. Didn't care.

Maybe I'd die after all. But man, what a way to go.

All I wanted was to find that climax, my body all but writhing as I fought to get closer to him.

He slid his thumb in a steady circle, pulsing and pressing, driving the pleasure through me with each swipe.

"Come for me." He growled the words, and my body came apart at his command, the orgasm an explosion that had me fighting not to scream as I rode his cock, my body clutching at him, milking him as he began his own climb.

"Fuck me," he snarled as he grabbed hold of my hips and helped me ride him, harder and harder, the tip of his cock finding that elusive spot inside of me. The pressure was building again, different this time as I writhed there, at his mercy.

"Harder," I whimpered. "Please. Don't. Stop."

He all but howled as he drove into me, our bodies meshing as he fucked me senseless, his own climax rocketing through us both as my second orgasm clutched at his cock, dragging it from him.

The pull of it went on and on, the pleasure spilling through me, and for a few breathless moments I could forget everything.

I fell forward onto his chest, struggling to breathe, limp from two back-to-back big 'O's.

I didn't know whether to say thank you, or come again, please.

As it was, he made the decision for me.

He pushed me off and got out of the bed, gathered his clothes, and left the room without another word.

I lay there, not all that bothered. Hell, I'll admit it only to you. I was smiling like a damn cat who'd gotten the canary. Until it hit me.

Every time I had sex after this, I would be forever comparing it to this.

"That's a bummer," I whispered to myself. Because there was no way anything would compare to what could only be called a royal and complete fucking.

5

ACHIEVEMENT UNLOCKED: DRY SPELL OVER

Bebe shot in through the door as Havoc left. "Oh my God. How was it? World-saving sex has got to be earth shattering, right? I heard you scream, and I heard him howl...and I was like...oh man...that sounds amazing!"

I pulled a sheet over my still sensitive skin. There were some sore points from my siblings' beating, but they were overwhelmed by the lovely soreness that came from—

"Epic fucking are the words you want," I said.

"Jealous here, totally jelly." She curled up beside me. "I mean, not about the torture part. But Sven healed you, right? That's what I heard him muttering as he left the room."

"Mostly. I think it drained him. He looks...less than before. Smaller."

She was quiet for maybe a single breath. "Havoc didn't stick around though. That bother you?"

I shrugged. "Maybe if we'd been in some sort of relationship. This was just...fucking. That's it. Saved the world. Ended my curse. I hope."

"You did have an orgasm, right? Sven and Havoc were arguing about that, before the two of you got it on. That maybe it only had to be sex, but it would be better if you both orgasmed just to be sure."

"Twice." I grinned.

She rolled onto her back; her mouth wide open. "Oh, now I am jealous! I bet he could hit that G spot like a mo-fo."

I shifted onto my side, drowsy, not feeling like sharing that he had indeed hit that G spot like a mo-fo. "Let's see if it worked. It won't be long now."

We lay in the room, waiting for the sun to come up. Wondering if the world would end, or if I'd be turned back into a golden retriever. To be fair, the world ending wouldn't technically happen until tonight...but the golden retriever part, that would be the tell-all. That first curse I mentioned earlier? That one meant I would be forced back to four legs when the sun rose. Fingers and toes were crossed that I stayed on two legs.

The light shifted in the room, brightening, glittering and dancing across my skin as the sun rose.

The world didn't end, and I didn't shift. I scooted out of bed as the draw of the sun called to me. Pulling the curtain back on the single window, I could see the sun was fully up, and the world was still very much the world as I knew it.

"No more goldie for me," I said. A funny wave of sorrow rolled through me. The curse was broken, I wasn't going to die.

Was I actually sad about losing the golden part of me? Not really. The golden retriever body was part of the curse broken. Still...the dog I'd been had gotten me through the last few days. I was grateful for that.

"Shit, you got some serious glitter action going on." Bebe leapt up onto the windowsill, her eyes narrowing. "Your skin is glowing like you rolled around in the teen section at *Bath & Body Works*."

I looked down at my skin to see there was indeed a soft golden glow. Making my way to the bathroom, I flicked on the light and then the shower before I took a good look in the mirror.

My belly, breasts, legs, everything was indeed glittering as if I had coated myself in something. All except for the dark S of a snake that seemed to be etched into the side of my neck, under my ear. A mark from Loki that had come with the first curse, the one that had made me a golden. Why was it still here? I rubbed a hand over it, wondering if it meant anything that it was still there on my skin.

I got into the shower and let the hot water wash away some of the last twenty-four hours. What a complete and utter shit show it had been. My brothers and sister were still out there. Han was still out there.

And while not all of them wanted me dead, I was sure Kieran wanted my head on a pike.

Richard...I'd reached him, I was sure of it. But was that enough? I frowned as I washed, thinking of my siblings. Wondering if any of them were savable.

Then my mind dipped to Han. How long would it take Han to figure out that I was still alive and carrying the sun? I carefully reached for the bond between us.

Still there.

Banked and muted with every effort that I'd made to cut him off from me. I could sense him in a very distant way, far to the west and north of me. Good enough for now.

I stepped out of the shower and wrapped myself in a towel.

Worry for Denna cut through me as the events of the last twenty-four hours caught up with me. She'd been with Soleil, and yet I hadn't seen her anywhere. "Bebe, do you know if they found Denna? Has anyone here mentioned her?"

"No." Bebe placed herself on the sink counter and began to groom her front legs. "They took Soleil, of course, but I have no idea what happened to Denna."

I frowned. As a ghoul, she could survive a lot, but that didn't mean I had nothing to worry about. I needed to try and find her. Which would mean going to another graveyard and trying the Ghoul pipeline again. That would have to wait until nighttime when the ghouls came out to play.

I brushed a hand over my collarbone, staring at the way my skin still had a sheen of glitter to it. "You were right. My skin's shining. I don't remember that on Soleil, not to this degree." I did look as if I'd been dunked in a bath of glitter lotion.

"Maybe from banging Havoc?" Bebe offered.

"Soleil had that glow too. In the beginning. It wears off." A soft voice spoke behind me.

I turned to see the only other female werewolf that was in Havoc's pack.

"Claire, right?" I tipped my head to the side, and she nodded.

"Yes."

The wolves we each respectively carried took a moment to check each other out. It took less than three seconds, but it was done, and I was above her.

Her head bowed. "I'll leave if you wish."

"No, stay. Tell me about this place, about everyone—"

"I can't. That is for Havoc or Sven to fill you in. I just came to bring you clothes. Make sure you were okay." She set a pair of jeans, a shirt, underwear, bra, and socks on the counter. "Hopefully it fits. I figured we weren't far off in size."

"Thanks." I slipped the clothes on and quickly wove my hair into a simple braid.

"Food is happening in the mess hall too, if you're hungry." Claire bobbed her head in my direction again and then slipped out of the bathroom. She was gone before I could ask her any more questions.

Bebe tapped my arm with her paw, getting my attention. "Is it just me, or was that a bit weird? You know, awkward as fuck."

I shrugged. "Hard to say. Every pack treats respect and hierarchy differently. She looks like she's the only woman here. It must be odd for her to have me around. To know that I'm above her in the hierarchy when I've been here for all of three seconds."

I left the bathroom and headed for the door of the bedroom. I wasn't sure if we were in a house, a complex, or some kind of apartment building.

Turns out, it was none of those things. We were in an old, abandoned school that they'd converted at some point to their...I wanted to say hideout, but that seemed so childish.

I made my way down through the halls, lockers on either side of me, following my nose toward the cafeteria.

"Looks like someone was trying to renovate this into a home at some point?" Bebe poked her head into different rooms as we moved through the school, her tail straight up as she trotted ahead of me. "Some are bedrooms now, and that one over there looks like an office."

"It's not a bad idea, especially if this is designed for a pack," I said, keeping my voice low. My nerves were still a bit hotwired for danger after the last few days. This quiet, this brief moment of peace, was actually freaking my brain out a little. I was waiting for an attack around every corner. It made it hard to concentrate on anything else.

Like the weirdness that was this place.

"Why would that be good for a pack?" Bebe asked.

"Werewolves, like real wolves, bond. We feel safest when we're close to one another. And, in theory, we should be safest that way." I trailed a hand across the lockers to my right. "It wasn't like that with my home pack. I was safest when Grayling was far in the rearview mirror."

A whiff of male wolf caught at my nose and I slid to a stop. One of the other pack members was just ahead of me. He smelled of springtime and rich earth, growing things, and the thick musk of male wolf.

He was the older wolf, the one who seemed to be closest to Havoc. I would guess he was second in line. He was there just at the corner, leaning against the wall with one shoulder. "Grayling has a reputation for being difficult. You have my sympathy if you had to deal much with Juniper."

I forced my feet to move. "You have no idea. Most people only see the surface of her craziness."

He dipped his head toward me. "My name is Berek. I am Havoc's *Jarl*."

Jarl. That was a new one on me, but I was guessing based on his energy that I'd called his position correctly. He was the second in command. I dipped my head back toward him, matching his custom. "Cin. And that there is Bebe. She's trapped in that body, but she is a human soul."

"And I'm wicked fast at throwing it down." She bounced on her feet, puffing up. He couldn't hear her, as far as I could tell. But he grinned and bent down, running a single finger along her spine.

"She's spicy for a little thing. She took out some hamstrings back there like a pro."

"That she is, and her claws are rather sharp as you've seen, so watch yourself."

Mind you, she somewhat melted when he touched her. "Oh, I like him, he can pet me anytime." Her tail flicked up, wrapping around his wrist.

I did not pass that on to him.

Settling into a pace next to Berek, I let him lead the way through the school. "How long will we stay here?"

"That's up to Havoc. We are trying to nail down where Han went. See if we can gauge what he'll do next. He will know by now that you are the new carrier of the sun."

I gave him a nod. "He's way north, and to the west. A good distance away. And I doubt that he knows I'm the new carrier of the sun."

Berek shot me a look. "You do not know Han."

"Maybe not like you do, but you weren't there when he handed me off to my brothers. He doesn't know I carry the sun. Or at least he didn't know then." We paused outside of a set of metal doors, a bar across the middle of them.

If I were a betting kind of woman, I would have said we were headed into the gymnasium, and I would have made a good deal of money on that bet. Berek pushed a door open and tipped his head at me to precede him.

So much for going to get food.

The gymnasium was set up like a triage center. There were at least a dozen simple cots, six of them arranged on each side of the gym with lots of space in between. Crash carts waited near each cot. And there were several—I took a quick breath, tasting the air, getting a lungful of blood and viscera along with what I was looking for—humans working on the three people who lay on the cots.

Three werewolves on cots.

"The run in with Han did not go well for our pack. We didn't expect him to have picked up your family and the human fighters. They fight dirty." He let out a rumble of a growl. "They used silver in their weapons."

I winced. It wasn't my fault, and I held no love for my family, but it still sucked. "Survival was key in our pack. No matter the cost. For what it's worth, I am sorry. They've poisoned me more than once with silver."

Which made me wonder just what kind of magic Sven had to have healed me so completely, not only from broken bones but from silver poisoning.

Berek's eyes settled on me like a weight. "Havoc is there. He wants to speak with you."

My body tightened at the thought of being near Havoc so soon after the multiple orgasms I'd shared with him. I blew out a quick breath, steeled my shoulders, and headed in the direction that Berek had pointed. Not that I couldn't have scented for Havoc. But in a room where there was blood and other things heavy in the air, I didn't want to breathe in much deeper than I had to. Once was enough.

"I like that one." Bebe trotted along beside me. "He has magic hands."

She spun around once to glance back at Berek.

"He probably has a mate, Bebe."

"We could totally be Beberek. Mash our names together like celebrities." She was obviously ignoring me.

"His mate would eat you." I was near the far end of the gymnasium now and could see Havoc. He stood leaning over a table, three others from his pack with him, including Claire.

Who had her hand right next to his. Touching him.

My wolf, who'd been silent since the golden retriever had arrived, suddenly reared to the surface of my mind.

Because Havoc was *mine.*

6

JEALOUS MUCH?

The flare of jealousy was instant and so hot that I actually stopped moving and closed my eyes to block out the sight in front of me. Claire was touching Havoc, he was allowing it, and my wolf was coming unglued inside of me, demanding that I put a stop to what I was seeing.

Let's be clear here. Wolf brain is very different than human brain, and this moment highlighted that truth. I had to get control of my wolf before she sent me to tackle Claire to the ground and beat her senseless. Not exactly a good first—okay, second—impression.

Bebe rubbed herself against my legs. "Hey, you okay? I thought I heard you growl."

No, I was not okay. A single bedding did not mean I had any right to jealousy or claiming a man who was not my mate. Havoc most certainly didn't want anything to do with me. For all I knew, he and Claire were an item, fully mated. I grimaced, thinking about how I would feel if our roles were reversed.

I would not have been so kind had I been in her position, forced to watch my man fuck another woman —even if it was to save the world.

I was lucky she hadn't cut me open when she'd brought me clothes. That's the least of the damage I would have done to her.

Very carefully, I opened my eyes.

Havoc was looking at me, Claire kind of tucked in behind him, close enough that they were nearly touching. She was almost...hiding from me.

A low growl slipped out of me—the most I'd lost control in years. I was not doing this. Not here.

Guts rolling with anger that was misdirected, I turned on my heel and strode back between the cots. "I just need a minute," I called over my shoulder.

Bebe ran to keep up with me. "What is it? I mean I know it stinks in here, but—"

I all but blew through the double doors in my hurry to get away. Not because I was going to cry or throw myself at Havoc.

Nope.

My wolf wanted to kill Claire. I suspected I knew why. It had been a long time since I'd had any kind of intimacy, and my wolf was lonely. It took me another minute to find a set of stairs leading up to the second floor. I jogged partway up and sat down, putting my head in my hands, trying to calm my wolf.

Trying to find a way to make her see that Havoc was not ours. That our mate was northwest of us, and moving further away even as I sat there.

My wolf didn't give a shit.

Bebe wormed her way onto my lap. "Talk to me, girlfriend. What is it?"

"My wolf is angry," I said, giving her the simple version. "I need to calm her down."

"What about your goldie? Where did she go? Maybe that side of you would be better?"

I shook my head and started to say there was no more goldie in me, but even as I thought it, I felt the soft brush of long fluffy fur as if against my arm, like the ghost of the golden retriever I had been.

I kept my eyes closed and focused on my breathing and on drawing the two energies together—wolf and golden—until my wolf was calm.

"How do you do that?"

I stiffened at the sound of Claire's voice and fought a growl that wanted to ripple out of me. Instead, I cleared my throat. "Do what?"

"When you looked at us, I could see your wolf in your eyes. How did you calm her?"

One more slow breath out and I lifted my eyes to Claire's. She took a half step back, putting more distance between us. "Years of practice under threat of death and torture. Normally it wouldn't even get that far out of hand. My apologies."

I could have lied then and said it was a one-off, but I was guessing I would have to work with this woman. I shook my head. "It has been a long time since I've... had sex with anyone. My wolf was pissed off when I saw you touching Havoc." I held up a hand as she covered her mouth. "I am sorry. I don't want to step between the two of you, but my wolf doesn't understand. Just know that what happened was out of necessity, nothing more. And I will need to keep my distance as much as I can from the both of you. So I don't slip up."

Her eyes were so wide, she looked years younger. "Oh. I see."

That's it. That's all she said and then she turned away and headed back toward Havoc.

"Damn. She didn't even appreciate you being honest!" Bebe sneezed and shook her head. Her steady warmth against my middle and on my thighs helped me calm myself further and get my head on a bit straighter. I had pressing matters to attend to beyond my wolf's jealousy.

"Despite how badly this is going, I do need to talk to Havoc. I don't think he knows about Soleil. I have to tell him about my brothers, his brother, and I need to find Denna." I stood but kept Bebe tight in my arms. "You stick close. I don't want to lose you too."

"Done." She latched her claws into the shoulder of my shirt.

I passed through the doors and the wounded bodies on the cots quickly, focusing on what had to be done.

Survival, at any cost.

I would not think about how Havoc felt against my body, or how his touch sent me over the edge. Nope.

No dirty thoughts.

No thoughts of him with Claire.

To be fair, it was easier the second time I saw him because Claire had left the room. It was just Havoc, Sven, and Berek.

"Oh, see ya," Bebe whispered as she leapt from my shoulder and into Berek's arms.

"Traitor," I muttered.

"Opportunist," she said as she wrapped herself around Berek's neck. He reached up and stroked her back, I looked away. I wasn't going to tell her what to do, or how to do it. I had my own problems to deal with. Sven looked...thinner than before. I frowned at the sight.

"Apologies." I tipped my head in Havoc's direction. "I needed a minute."

"Claire said as much." Havoc tapped the table and a single sheet of paper, but he didn't elaborate on whether Claire had told him *exactly* what I'd said.

Sven next. I nodded toward him. "Thank you, Sven. You healed me, at a cost to yourself, didn't you?"

He grunted and flapped a hand at me. "It was necessary. Don't make me do it again."

I huffed a laugh. "Sure thing. You do remember that I have a whole bunch of people hunting for me? Wanting me dead?"

Havoc tapped the table. "On that note. Tell me about your family. There isn't much in any file about the Grayling pack other than that it's secretive and violent. I'm curious why you aren't listed."

I glanced at the paper, spinning it around so I could see it. There was an image of Juniper, plus one of Mars. Nothing else beyond their children's names. I was *not* listed, which wasn't terribly surprising. Hell, it didn't even hurt that much anymore. I shrugged. "That about sums it up—secretive and violent. Juniper had an affair and that produced me, which is likely why I'm not on this list as family. If you want other specifics, then you need to ask specific questions."

"What happened to Mars?" Berek asked. "I knew him when we were young."

That did surprise me. "You knew him?"

Berek nodded. "He was a good mate. It's hard to believe that this rap sheet could be about his pack. Murder. Missing werewolves. Torture. Rape."

I shook my head and pointed to the image of

Juniper. "My mother runs the pack, has for over thirty years. Mars has been gone that whole time."

Berek's eyebrows shot up. "Every missive that comes from the Grayling pack has been signed with Mars's signature. It is impossible to forge the signature of an alpha." He didn't say it, but I could see his lips forming the word *liar*.

How did I explain all of this to them without giving away too much of my own story? I rubbed my fingers across my forehead. "Look, there is a large difference between impossible and difficult. It is very *difficult* to forge the signature of an alpha, not *impossible*."

"Yeah, people do it all the time," Bebe added, and though I was sure Berek couldn't hear her, I knew that Havoc could. "They sign Michael Jackson's name on some memorabilia and try to pass it off as the real thing. Sometimes it works. Makes for a good payday."

I shot her a look. "That's very specific, Bebe."

She grinned at me, flashing her canines. "I might know a thing or two about forgery."

When I looked back up, Havoc and Berek were staring hard at me. Sven was sitting in a chair, his eyes closed with his head tipped back. Sleeping.

I didn't squirm under their gazes; I was no child.

Havoc took the paper back from me. "The *how* of it does not matter right now. Tell us of your pack, any details that could help us deal with your siblings."

My jaw ticked. "Kieran is a master manipulator.

Mars trained all of them before he left, so they're all extremely good fighters—with the exception of Meghan, who I haven't seen in years. I don't know where she's at in her skill set. Mars was gone before she was born. After Mars left, Juniper changed how things were done." I paused, images from my past trying to push forward.

"Stay with us," Havoc said, as if he knew I'd slid into my memories. "What are their skill sets?"

"That's a list," I said. "You ready?"

Berek handed Bebe back to me. "I'll take notes."

I took a breath and rattled off everything that I knew my brothers had been trained in. "Hand-to-hand combat in multiple disciplines; usage of firearms, knives, bow and arrow, and explosives; evasive driving; tracking; torture; code breaking; guerilla warfare..." I paused, thinking. "Basic spell craft, poisons, trapping, negotiations..." I looked up because the sound of the pen moving had stopped.

Berek was staring at me. "Are you serious?"

I stared back. "You still think I'm lying? I didn't say they were excellent at all of this, just that they've been trained in it. They have a basic understanding of these things, and they're each really good at a few of them."

Berek let out a string of curse words that rhymed heavily with duck. I looked at Havoc, who had not taken his eyes from me.

"And you? Are you trained in all these things?"

I shook my head. "No."

"But forgery was on your list, wasn't it?" He didn't speak as if it was a question. I grimaced.

"It was."

We spent the next fifteen minutes going over my siblings' weaknesses and strengths. When it came to which of my brothers was the most dangerous...that gave me pause.

It was on my lips to say Kieran. Because of my history with him, it was easy to think he was the most dangerous. Then I thought back to what I'd told Richard in the van.

"If they were all sober, it would be Richard you'd want to watch out for." I frowned. "I wonder if that's why Kieran hasn't tried to get him to stop drinking the ogre beer. To keep Dick from challenging him. He's smart and strong, and his wolf is the best of the three by far."

It made me wonder if it was the reason why Juniper never stopped Richard from drinking. Because maybe sober he'd be willing to stand up to her?

Sven slowly stood. "You don't think your mother is the most dangerous? She's had more years and time to hone her skills."

I shook my head. "No. I've never seen her fight. She always has someone else step in for her. And Meg is an unknown. I don't think she's going to be an issue, though, not when it comes down to it. She's just trying to survive."

I still wanted to believe that, to believe her. Even if I had seen the glimmer in her eyes that said otherwise. That maybe a part of her enjoyed watching me get hurt. Maybe she was more like Juniper than I wanted to believe.

Berek stared at the papers he'd taken notes on, the smell rolling off him already speaking of defeat. "There is nothing good about any of this, boss man. Especially if they're working with Han. He will only supplement their strengths. We should have killed them back there."

His eyes cut to me, speaking volumes. It was my fault that my siblings were still alive. Anyone that was hurt by them from here on out, was on me.

I didn't drop my eyes. "I stand by it. I will kill Kieran when the time comes."

"But not the others?" Berek said. "Why not them?"

Hope. I didn't want to say it out loud, but I hoped that what I saw in Richard, that the reluctance I felt in Shipley meant something.

Havoc motioned at the table, tapping the list of their skills. "We will deal with them. They don't know that we know about them, it gives us an edge now. Go get some rest. We will have to move soon. Even if Han is at a distance."

I nodded. "And still moving further away."

I had so many questions. Like what was this place, located just where we'd needed it, with doctors and everything? How were we going to stop Han? But there was a more pressing question in my mind.

Havoc and Berek turned away, and I was dismissed just like that.

I frowned and snapped a hand on the table, stopping them from leaving. "Are you not worried about Soleil? And I want to know what happened to my friend who was with her. I've answered your questions. It's only fair that you answer mine."

"Soleil is missing," Havoc said.

"She's not missing, she's dead," I insisted. "Han took her head right in front of me."

Havoc's eyes shuttered, hiding whatever emotion went through him. From the way his muscles tensed and flexed, there was some emotion there—but was it guilt, grief or, worse, relief?

"Why would he do that?" Berek asked. "You carry the sun now, not her."

This was where I suspected we had a small—very small—leg up on Han. "Like I said earlier, I don't think he realized there had been an exchange. He...he has a mate bond to me."

Shit, that meant he knew I'd been bedded. But did he know it was Havoc? Probably not. I shook off the wayward thought and put myself fully in the present. Both Havoc and Berek were staring hard at me.

"What about the mate bond?" Havoc's words were sharp, but it didn't seem he was overly bothered.

"He already had a connection to me. I think he believes that what he is feeling, is just the mate bond. Not whatever connection you two thugs have to the carrier of the sun. I think it drowned out whatever he would have sensed about me swallowing the sun. I don't think he realized there was a difference. Not yet, at least. That's my guess."

Berek shot a look at Havoc. "That could buy us some time. He won't realize that Ragnarök isn't happening until the night of the dead moon. If we're lucky. Could be why he's headed north."

Bebe snorted. "Not ominous at all. When is that exactly?"

Havoc answered her. "About ten days from now. It's why he was going so hard for Soleil."

I frowned. "You knew there was a time limit he had to follow for cutting her down?"

"Every year there is a dead moon." He leaned against the table; his palms flat. "There is a window just before the night of the dead moon when the elimination of the sun would have the most impact on the outcome of Ragnarök."

"I love how we're just talking about the end of the world like it's a sure thing," Bebe muttered.

I tightened my hold on the edge of the table. "So, if

I can stay out of Han's way until after this window, he'll leave me alone for a year?"

Havoc shook his head. "No. He'll hunt you still, but he'll wait to kill you if he captures you."

Ten days. I just had to survive ten days, and then there would be a slight reprieve.

"Okay, so what about my friend who was with Soleil? Has anyone seen her?" I had a hard time believing that Denna had just taken off.

Berek grunted. "The ghoul that was with Soleil? Ghouls are not friends; they are pests at best."

"Yes, the ghoul. And yes, she is my friend." I turned my eyes on him, hardening myself up to match his gaze. "Where is she?"

Berek didn't break away from our staring contest, though his left eye was twitching like mad as he fought to hold my gaze. "She tried to tangle with one of your brothers, the short one. He threw her into the river last I saw."

I spun on my heel and was running before either of them could say another word. Ghouls didn't do well in the sun, and water was almost as bad. Running water was even worse. Denna didn't deserve that. I had to find her.

"Fuck. Bebe, we have to find her!" I bolted through the main doors, knowing there were feet behind me. A hand brushed against my arm and then clamped down.

Havoc stopped me dead in my tracks, spinning me around to face him. "You can't run off. You have a duty to stay safe, the world depends on—"

"The world can kiss my ass. I won't turn my back on a friend in need." I jerked my arm out of his hand. Tried to, anyway. He didn't so much as flinch as I pulled against him. "Let me go!"

"No."

"You let Soleil live her life, let me go!" I kicked out, catching him in the shin, but it seemed to have little effect on him and just made my foot hurt like hell.

In a split second he had me wrapped up, face against the wall, his chest pressed hard against my back before I could so much as go for a more sensitive spot.

I wish I could say that I kicked him in the balls and sent him to his knees like I'd done to Han. But with his head bowed to mine and the feel of his body pressed along the length of my spine, his thighs hard against the back of my legs, it was hard to think of anything but going for round two right there in the hall.

"You are not Soleil. You draw trouble to you like a bee to honey. I will not be letting you out of my sight." His growling voice was way too close for me not to react. I bit my inner cheek and tried to be as still as I possibly could.

"Get off me." I spit the words out as I fought to get a hold of my body's reaction to him.

He stepped back but didn't let me go. With his hand clamped on my arm, he all but dragged me back through the halls.

I didn't know where Bebe had gone off to, but she caught up to us as we reached the door to the bedroom where we'd...moon goddess, maybe he did plan to go for round two.

But no, that was not my luck. He just tossed me into the room. "You stay in here until we're ready to leave."

I glared at him from my spot on the bed and waited till the door was shut, the sound of the lock sliding into place before I spoke. "I've escaped you once, I can do it again."

7

HOW TO ESCAPE IN THREE EASY STEPS

O kay, so it took me more than three easy steps.

It took about ten.

And some serious reconsideration of my life choices.

The only place that I was going to be able to wriggle out was the ceiling. All the vents were too small for me to maneuver—even if I was in golden form—but the ceiling was the drop kind with panels.

It was just a matter of getting enough height to reach them and balancing my weight on the cross beams to avoid crashing through.

I shoved the bed across the room to the wall, looking for the section that would hold my weight.

"I can't believe he just threw you in here!" Bebe said for about the twentieth time. "I mean, I get that he wants to keep you safe, but this is stupid. Like he mansplained that he knew best!"

"*I* can believe it." I muttered as I pulled a ceiling panel down, dust and gods only knew what else sprinkling down around me, getting me in the face and making me sneeze. "He does what he wants. Alphas can be that way."

She shook her head, throwing off bits of dust and insulation. "Yeah, but we escaped him once already. What makes him think he's keeping us down now?"

I grinned and laughed quietly as I pulled myself into the ceiling, then reached down for Bebe. She leapt up and I placed her on the beam I was balanced on. "Stay on the studs for the walls. They're our best bet to keep from falling through the ceiling tiles."

I crawled along them, careful to keep myself from brushing against the drop ceiling inches below me. I needed to find my way out, which was not as easy as it sounds considering we were in a gigantic school.

Light filtered in from below us, giving me something to work with. We had to hurry to find Denna. I could only hope that she'd found some place to hole up.

"What do you think this place really is?" Bebe asked. "I mean, how could they have had a place like this ready so close to where your brothers had us locked up?"

"I was wondering the same thing," I breathed out. "Ask later. Quiet now."

"Oh, right! Werewolf ears!"

Not that they all could hear her, but Havoc could. Who knew if someone else could too?

We crept along until we reached a section that dropped away from us on a steep angle.

"Stairs." I breathed out. At least I was pretty sure that's what it meant. I leaned down and grabbed the edge of the ceiling panel below me and pulled it up into the tight space with us.

There it was—below and to the right of me: a set of stairs, with a landing and everything. I scooted forward, gripping the edge of the wall, and lowered my body down so that I dangled over the landing.

Dropping lightly, I crouched and listened. Nothing. I held my arms out for Bebe and she leapt into them.

Down the second half of the stairs we went, which led right to the main doors of the school.

I paused at the bottom of the stairs, listening. The only thing I could hear was two sets of heartbeats—mine and Bebe's. We were alone in this portion of the school.

Moving slow and steady, keeping my steps silent, I made my way across the open foyer to the doors. Pressing the bar that opened the door, I winced as the metal creaked.

I paused, listening. No one came running for us. I

breathed a sigh of relief and pushed the door open just enough for us to slip through. Once we were out, I held the exterior handle so that there was no loud clicking as I eased the door shut.

"You are really good at this," Bebe said, bouncing along beside me. "All those things you said your brothers are trained in, you learned them too, didn't you?"

I shook my head as I jogged away from the big building, scenting the air around me. I knew Denna wouldn't be here, but I had to keep an eye out for anything else—my siblings included. "Not all of them, no. Mars taught me as much as he could in secret. Juniper didn't want me trained. She wanted me to be weak and easy to control."

"But you know enough that you and I could survive on our own, don't you?"

I paused. "Yes. If we can find Denna, I think we should make for Europe. Like I'd planned before. Meet up with Taini and Copper." Get my damn cat back. I missed Martin. I'd like to find out who he'd been before Petunia put that spell on him.

"Seriously?" She raced ahead of me. "What about Havoc?"

I flinched. "What about him?"

"Wait, why did you flinch? Do you...have feelings for him?"

I waited until we were three streets from the

schoolhouse before I tucked myself against the side of an abandoned building. "Not feelings exactly. Not like what you mean. My wolf wants him. She thinks he's pretty fucking good in the sack and after a long dry spell...her interest would make it difficult for me to travel with his pack. He has a mate in Claire. I am above her in strength, so she'd be always slinking away from me. That's not fair to her."

Bebe slowed next to me. "Oh, right. I saw how she was hanging onto him. I didn't think about that. But how are we going to do all this? We need money. Travel papers..." Bebe's tail violently lashed side to side. "I wish I still had my forgery kit. I could have us a passport in no time."

I nodded and then paused, my mind ticking over the possibilities. "I don't even know where we are, which makes this harder yet. I mean, I have a rough idea, we couldn't have gone that far. Probably still on the west side of the country, but that doesn't narrow things down much."

And there was not much traffic in this area of town, despite it being the middle of the day. We'd been near Portland when I was snagged by my brothers...I squinted, thinking of the hours that I'd been stuck in the back of the van with my siblings. At least four. Four hours from Portland.

"They talked about picking up something in Boise at one point," Bebe said. "Would that help?"

Boise. I smacked my hand against the wall of the building. "Yes, that's amazing. Means we probably aren't far from Highway 84. Boise is where Richard gets the best ogre beer from. And Kieran picks up news from a pack he's friendly with there too."

The Snake River pack.

A pack that I most certainly was not friendly with, but I could avoid them. "We'll head west. Back toward Portland. Toward the river Shipley tossed Denna into. We'll get close, then work our way west, following the current until we find her."

If we found her.

I started to strip out of my clothes, rolling them up into a bundle. More than once I'd had to carry my clothes with me this way. It wasn't a new trick for any werewolf worth their salt.

A howl cut through the air, and I dropped to my knees, the wind knocked out of me as my body reacted. Havoc's power rolled over me, sinking into my bones and reminding me that he'd been *inside* of me, tasted my skin and made me writhe under his hands.

I whimpered, fighting the urge to just lay there and wait for him.

Because if I let him, that power would hold me to him, caging me. Making me depend on him instead of myself for survival. I was not going back to that, to a place where one single wolf controlled my life.

Never again.

"Fuck you," I gritted my teeth as I growled the words out and forced my body to shift to my wolf form.

I blinked and blew out a breath, the howl easing off in the distance. I wasn't surprised that he was hunting me—he wanted to keep me safe and away from Han. But it had nothing to do with caring for me. He just wanted to keep the world from exploding into flames.

Another sigh slid out of me. "You ready to run?" I looked at Bebe, who was staring at me, her eyes so dilated there was only a sliver of the usual yellow-green color.

"What?" I woofed the question. Woofed. My eyes shot to my legs and the glittering golden hair floating around me. "Jesus, what the fuck?" I barked and danced around as if I could shake off the form that I'd shifted into.

This could not be. I'd broken the curse. I wasn't supposed to be golden anymore.

I wanted to howl at the unfairness of it. But I didn't have time to wallow in self-pity and I doubted I could howl all that well. I settled for another woof. "We gotta go."

I grabbed my bundle of clothes in my mouth and turned east—yes, dogs and werewolves have the ability to tell directions—but mostly it was the sign that said "Highway 84" with an arrow on it that clued me in.

I took off running, Bebe pacing me. "If I get tired," she said, "I'm jumping on your back."

I bobbed my head but couldn't answer her with my mouth full of clothes. I'd left my boots, there was no way I'd be carrying those. I could find more shoes somewhere else.

Finding new shoes was not a problem in comparison to my big one: I still couldn't shift into my wolf form. Somehow, I was still a golden retriever.

The neck tattoo was still there, the one from Loki. Was that why?

Did it mean the stupid curse had only partially broken? Sure, I wasn't dead, so yes, that was a win. I knew it, but...a part of me wasn't sure *this* was the better deal. The horror of being a golden retriever flooded over me again, as it had just a few days before. I couldn't wrap my head around how and why this had happened.

That bit of grief I'd felt at losing the golden form was gone as I tried to figure out what happened.

Had the curse been more complicated than I'd realized? Had we skated too close to the deadline, and this was the result?

I tried to reach for my wolf, and while she'd been happy to be at the surface while we were doing the tango with Havoc and being pissed at Claire, she was silent now. Silent and not all that worried. For lack of a better sensation, she was sleeping. Relaxed and content with how things were.

I thought back to the moment that I'd brought the golden forward to help calm my wolf.

The sensation of the two of them blending.

Fuck, had I done this to myself?

Terror suffused me, driving me to run even harder, as if I could outrun all of this. I struggled not to gag on the fear that was choking me.

What if there was no way back from this? What if... what if I was always a golden retriever?

While my thoughts raced and tangled with one another, chasing each other the way my stupid golden self wanted to chase my fluffy tail, we made our way through the small town and to the highway.

"Do you plan to just run along the highway?" Bebe asked as the first car zipped by.

I spat out my clothes and stared at the oncoming traffic, focusing on one problem at a time. Denna first. Golden issue later. It took all I had to push my fear away.

Later. I would deal with this later. Lives were on the line, and not just my own.

I was going to have to shift. And that meant I needed calories—a lot of them—if I didn't want to end up a bag of bones—or dead if I wasn't careful. I had to be smart.

"No. The river runs alongside it. I'll stop traffic, then we'll slip into a vehicle and make our way back to Portland."

"How are you going to stop traffic?" Bebe tipped her head up at me.

I grinned, tongue lolling out of my mouth. "Easy. Show some boobs."

She laughed, then stopped. "Wait, are you serious? That's brilliant!"

I backed down the bank and coaxed my form to shift back to two legs. The transition was easy, no pain and almost no time—very different from the first time I'd shifted into a golden form, as if it was getting easier each shift. I couldn't help but reach up and touch the tattoo on my neck.

Fucking Loki and his games. I drew a slow breath. "Bebe, see if you can sneak some food out of a car. A chocolate bar. Bag of chips, whatever you can grab."

"Got it." She bobbed her head. "Consider me your cat burglar."

Naked as the day I'd been born, I climbed back up the embankment and pretended to stumble to the edge of the highway. I waved my arms, and it took about three seconds for the oncoming cars to all slam on their brakes. The air filled with the screech of tires, smell of burning rubber and brake pads, and then the shouting as people got out of their vehicles.

"Are you okay?"

"What are you doing?"

"Sweet Jaysus, girl, the whole world can see you!"

I got lucky, the cars closest to me were being driven

by men, including the one in the slow lane, who was driving a semi-trailer attached to an open-backed, covered flat deck.

"Help, please!" I yelled, "I need help!" I slid back down the slope. Before they came over the edge, I quickly shifted back into my golden form and started barking.

The men and one woman came down the slope, looking for the naked woman they'd seen just a moment before. I loped up the hill, grabbed my clothes in three quick bites, and headed straight for the open, covered flat deck.

I waited at the back until Bebe appeared, a bag in her mouth. I took it from her, squeezing it next to my clothes, and leapt up into the back of the truck.

Bebe joined me as I curled up tight against the back of the sleeper cab. "That was some seriously sneaky shit. I think you'd make a good cat. It's almost like you've done it before."

I spit the clothing and bag of food out. "I'd like to make a good wolf instead of a damn dog. And yes, I have used that trick before. Boobs for the win, any time." I grumbled as I opened the bag with my nose. A couple of chicken burgers, fries, and an apple hand pie. Good enough. I wolfed them down. "Thanks, Bebe."

"No problem. I remember how it was for you." She butted her head against mine. "I got your back, girl."

I curled tighter around myself. Bebe shoved herself in between my legs and body, making herself a little nest out of all my fucking fur.

"How do you know this will take us all the way to Portland?"

"I don't. But it will get us far away from here, won't leave a trace of our scent now, and we're going in the right direction. I'll keep scenting for Denna." Though I doubted she'd gone upriver. She would have just floated along with the current. Assuming she didn't manage to get to the shore.

I watched the humans through hooded eyes as they searched along the side of the highway. They found no sign of the woman, of course, and it wasn't long before the truck driver hitched up his sagging pants and headed back to his truck. He was on a tight schedule, no doubt.

The truck rumbled to life, and I braced against the back of the sleeper cab as the driver lurched through the gears. "He's not very good, is he?" Bebe yelped as we were nearly thrown out from our little tucked-in spot, hidden from view.

"No, he's not. But he's what we've got. Try to rest. We'll be on foot soon enough."

As the semi rumbled along the highway, I wondered how pissed Havoc was going to be. My lips curled a little. The grumpy ass deserved a few more gray hairs. Not that I'd seen any, but surely after so many years he'd have a few.

I'd add to his collection.

Besides, I was going where my brothers and Han wouldn't think I'd be dumb enough to go.

My brothers knew I was aware of their connections to the pack in Boise. If I were them, I'd be looking south for me. Then again, they might send one sibling in each direction. That was what I would do.

It's what Richard would do if he were in charge. But he wasn't. So I was betting on them heading south.

Han, I wasn't sure what to do with that connection to him. I knew that there were ways to close the bond down, to make it quiet. I'd done that as best as I could. Would it be enough though?

A voice whispered in my mind, paired with the image of that man I'd seen—the one who'd called himself Tyr. *Try to cut the ties to him. That will slow him down. All the ties. You already know how.*

Good advice, even if it was a little creepy to have it from some stranger who'd just happened to find his way inside my head.

These Norse gods were a right pain in my ass.

"Go away," I mumbled. Bebe started and I shook my head. "Not you. Errant thoughts."

Even so, I dug around in my head until I found the bond to Han. I could see it clearly now that I was look-ing. He wasn't trying to connect with me. At the moment, he was fucking someone way up north. And enjoying it immensely.

As long as he was banging that woman, he wasn't looking to me.

I grimaced and began to work at blocking the connection. Could it be cut? I wasn't sure. But I was damn sure going to try. I'd cut other ties, the ones that had bound me to my family. But that was blood, this was…fate. Magic.

Stupid. It was stupid that's what it was.

The bond looked like a thick, silver rope twisting between us. Of course it was silver—it was poison. I snorted and imagined myself pulling the threads of the rope apart. Like a cable being unwound a thread at a time. They pinged away from me, cutting me loose a piece at a time.

He just kept on fucking the poor woman he'd convinced he was a good guy.

He'd rejected me—obviously. I'd rejected him. Surely the bond was going to be easy to get rid of.

It took me a good couple hours to get only half of the threads pulled apart. Doing that much had exhausted me, and I fell into a proper doze. And I feared that the bonds would snap back into place.

If I ever ran into Loki again, I was going to make him release me from Han.

"Havoc will know where we're going," Bebe said, cutting through my drifting thoughts.

"Yup. But he's not trying to kill me," I said, my words muffled by the wind and the rumble of the truck. Havoc would figure it out. But hopefully not before we found our friend. I couldn't leave Denna behind. That's not how it worked for me.

"We're coming, Denna," I whispered.

8

MAGIC SNAKE? SOUNDS LIKE A STRIPPER NAME TO ME

The semi took us almost all the way back to Portland before we disembarked. The driver stopped at a brake check as we were seeing signs for a city called Troutdale.

"That's a funny town name," Bebe yawned and stretched as we jumped off from our spot on the covered flat deck. I trotted away from the semi, mouth full of my clothes, scenting the air.

Humans. Shit. Piss. Vomit. Nothing supernatural here in the brake check parking lot.

"Hey, doggo!" a man yelled. "Come here, beauty!"

I ignored him and kept on trotting away from his and other voices that tried to convince me to come with them, making my way around several trucks and continuing to the edge of the road where I could look down and see the river. I dropped my bundle of clothes and stared at the frothing, rolling water. Here and there rocks peeked out from the waves. Denna could cling to one of those. But now that the sun was up... how long would she last? Not long. I had to believe she'd found a way out of the water and was hidden away somewhere along the shoreline.

"You think we're close enough to start looking for her?" Bebe asked.

I frowned, feeling a pull to the water that I didn't understand. Was it because I was a golden retriever? The water beckoned, begging me to leap into the waves. I let out a low whine. "I don't know. I'm hoping to find a little help at the river."

Yes, there was something in the water, and it called to me. Now that we were closer, I could tell it was a supernatural pull for sure. Could be good.

"What kind of help?" Bebe asked. "Like a fisherman in a boat who wants to take a dog and a cat on a trip down the river?"

"Like some river creatures who might be able to help us find Denna. Maybe a river maid, or a water nymph. I'm not sure." I picked up my bundle of clothes and hopped over the guardrail, sliding down the rocky and bush-strewn slope on my butt and hind end.

Was it smart to follow a magic I didn't understand? At this point, I didn't know what I was doing. I only knew I had to keep moving.

Bebe followed, and we slid to the edge of the river,

where I considered whether or not being on two legs would be helpful.

A scent crossed my nose, and I drew it in, identifying it faster than I ever would have as a wolf. Yes, I was trying to convince myself this—being a golden—was better. At least for now.

"Serpent," I muttered around the edge of my bundle of clothing. I dropped it so I could taste the scent along the edges of my tongue.

"Like a snake kind of serpent? How is a snake going to help us?" Bebe peered over the edge of the river into the water. "I don't really like snakes. Is it like a little garden snake? I hope."

I sniffed the air and half closed my eyes, images flickering through my head from the smell. "Serpent is kind of a broad term for what I'm picking up on, because this serpent carries the scent of magic."

That wasn't exactly the right way to put it—it was as much a feeling as a scent—but I couldn't think of a better way to describe it.

"Um. Magic snake? That sounds dirty. Or like a bad stripper name." Bebe backed away from the water. "And while usually I'm all for the kinks, I don't like the sound of this one."

I drew the smell in through my nose and followed it downriver. The serpent had passed by here less than an hour before. I didn't catch the scent of any other magical creatures, so the serpent it was.

"Come on, let's see if we can catch him. He might help." Unless of course he wanted to eat us. Maybe he was using the magic to lure other creatures in, but I kept that possibility to myself.

"Him? The snake is a him?"

"Yes. He smells musky, male." I picked up my pace, leaving behind my clothes. It was fine, I'd run around naked before, I was sure to do it again before someone finally killed me. The smell of the serpent pulled me forward, making me want to run after him, which was a solid argument for the magical lure possibility.

"You sure this is a good idea? Is it a big snake? A mean snake? A talking snake like you and me are talking animals?" Bebe yelled as we hurried along.

"Big snake. Talking. Probably not a happy snake." I glanced at the river, keeping an eye on the waves, watching for an undulating body.

"How did you know there would be something supernatural in the water?" Bebe yelped as a wave splashed up and over the edge, washing across our feet. I slowed and nudged her to my left side, tight to the bank.

"I...don't know." I frowned, going back to the moment I'd seen the river. "Something called to me."

"Please tell me it isn't the grumpy magical snake calling to you?"

Another wave sloshed up over our feet and I saw what I'd been watching for. The scales of a serpent making its way through the water with the ease of a fish, barely visible even though I was looking for him.

"Unfortunately, it probably is." I pushed away from the edge of the river while the serpent slid in a tight circle in front of me, as if it couldn't feel the waves and current of the water. Long, that was my first impression of him other than the color of his scales. Blues in so many shades that he blended into the water.

Iridescent, his scales reflected the light, glittering as the sun hit him.

His head was a perfect diamond shape, but when it rose up from the water and he opened his mouth, I saw not just two fangs but a multitude of tiny sharp teeth that rimmed the gaping hole.

"Sunshine, I wondered if you would sense me."

I tipped my head sideways. "Why do you call me that?"

"You hold the sun within you. If you're killed, I will be set free on the world. Of course, I can't kill you, *that's* against the rules." His voice was smooth, cultured. Made me think of a European aristocrat. Educated and charming, all bundled up in a big, slithering snake body.

"Right. Rules." I bobbed my head as if I knew what was going on. I chose to ignore the whole *him being set free if I died* bit of news he'd so casually mentioned. "I'm looking for a friend, she fell in the river. I don't suppose you would help me find her? Or maybe you've seen her?"

His mouth gaped open and eyes that had been mere slits popped wide. Blue, very bright blue eyes. "Are you shitting me?" So much for cultured aristocrat.

"You made the big snake swear. I don't like this." Bebe cowered behind me. I didn't blame her. He was rising up out of the water like a cobra.

"Sorry, I didn't mean to offend!" I dropped to my belly, smooshing Bebe under me. "I'm just looking for my friend. I followed your scent because it called to me!" I was babbling, which wasn't like me. Not at all. But his magical signature, combined with my golden retriever need to roll to my back and beg for mercy, was lethal to my ability to do anything else.

His face came right up to mine, so I was looking down the length of his head to his eyes. "You have no idea who I am, do you?"

If I answered this wrong, we were dead. I could feel it in my bones. "I'm sorry. I could tell you had great magic. That was all I could sense."

His eyes narrowed. "Great magic? What did it smell like to you? Describe it."

I licked my lips, and a low whine slid from me before I could catch it. "It smelled of all the colors of the rainbow, of the sound of musical notes floating through the air. Your magic smelled like nothing in this world, and everything in this world, all wrapped into a single droplet hanging in the air, waiting to be breathed in and it called to me. I...I couldn't help but follow it."

A sigh rippled through his body. "I like you. You make some pretty words."

"Jesus," Bebe breathed from under me.

The serpent shook his head. "No. He and I did not get along when I met him. Come, we will find your friend, Sunshine. You and that cat of yours that is not a cat. She is interesting."

I swallowed hard and slowly stood. "You aren't going to kill us?"

"Don't be stupid. I already told you I can't." His head swiveled back to me, one eye narrowing. "Unless you wish to die? That might be a loophole."

I shook my head. "No. I'm good. Even if I'm stuck looking like a giant stuffed animal."

The serpent slid back into the water. "Run beside me, we will discuss the scent of my magic. I like how you described it."

Bebe glanced at me, fear written clearly in her eyes. "He's like a dragon, isn't he?"

I shook myself to unhook my frozen legs from the ground. I had a suspicion of who he was, but I didn't want to say it out loud. "I...don't know. But he's going to help us find Denna."

"You may call me Jor, it is a shortening of my much longer, far more difficult-to-say name." The serpent called from the river ahead of us. In the Norse mythology I'd read, there was one serpent who stood out—the Midgard serpent. One destined to destroy the world once Ragnarök was set loose.

Jörmungandr. He can be a bit of a dick, do be wary. It was Tyr's voice again, accompanied by a flash of his face.

And I'd just happened to find him in the river? Somehow, I didn't think it was a co-inky-dink. I suspected he had either followed me or followed Han and Havoc.

"Which of the brothers are you friends with? Han or Havoc?" I asked as we made our way downriver. I had to keep my eyes on the ground ahead of me to keep from tripping on my face.

"Ha! Neither. I am neutral."

"Doubt it," Bebe shot back, and then she squeaked. "Sorry! Please don't eat me!"

His laughter rolled the waves around him. "I *am* neutral. I must be. But I also follow those two because my future is tied to them completing their destinies. And so where they go, I am never far away. Of course, I am somewhat confined to water. I suppose if I was invited I could come on land, but no one has ever done that."

Well I'll be damned. Did I have someone right here ready to fill me in on the whole situation?

"Han's destiny is to kill me, right?"

"Actually, no. Havoc's is. But he has been shrugging off his duties, and so Han has been filling in." Jor rolled so he could look up at me. "You think only Han is trying to kill you? Let me guess, Havoc said you must be killed just before the night of the dead moon if Ragnarök is to swing in Han's favor."

"Were you listening in through the pipes?" Bebe snorted. "How do you know that?"

"Because it is the truth. Or at least, half of the truth." Jor slithered along, swimming effortlessly through the rough water.

I kept scenting the air. Now that the serpent was to my side, I could smell other things. The other animals that had passed by, none of them supernatural. "What is the other half of the truth?"

"If Havoc kills you before the Solar eclipse, then Ragnarök will be placed on an indefinite hiatus. Your death assures the life or death of the world. Especially since the moon was already killed in all nine realms. To be fair, when Han killed the woman who carried the first moon, it broke Havoc. Since then, Havoc has tried to stop his brother. But fate is working against him. And the rumor mill has it, that Havoc is tired. He is ready to do what he must to stop Ragnarok from happening."

He said it all so casually.

"That lying son of a bitch!" Bebe shrieked. "I knew that he was too good to be true!"

Especially since the moon was killed. My heart was racing. I felt a truth coming to a head, like the pressure of a geyser against the ground. "Who carried the first moon?"

"Havoc's true love. She embodied the moon. He was supposed to kill her, but instead he kept her alive. Protecting her while Han tried to kill her. An old feud between them, I think. Once he killed Havoc's love, he kept going, killing all those who carried the moon, then he started in on the suns, chasing the soul through the nine realms. He has basically done both jobs. You seem to be giving him a bit of the slip, as they say."

A wave splashed up over the bank, soaking my legs, but I barely felt it. His words didn't make sense. "Explain what you're saying about the nine realms? I don't understand."

"Right, education on Norse pantheon and legends incoming." He slowed, and I was able to also slow to a walk. "There are nine realms. Asgard, home of the gods. Jotunheim, home of the ice giants. Muspelheim, realm of fire. Vanaheim, home of the vanir. Niflheim, the ice realm. Niðavellir, home of the dwarves. Alfhei, home of the elves. Helheim, land of the dead. And of course, Midgard. Earth. Home of humans and the final battleground before Ragnarök. Each of those realms holds a connection to the tree of life, Yggdrasil."

Tree. Like I'd seen in my mind?

"Say that ten times fast," Bebe muttered. Jor ignored her.

"When all this—" He flicked his tail in a swift circle, as if to encompass the world, "—was set into motion, the whole Ragnarök business, it was determined that each realm would hold a sun and a moon. But that there would only be one true soul for the sun, one true soul for the moon." He flipped his tail up as if making a point. "So within each realm, the sun and the moon had to be killed. Once killed there, the soul of each would flee to the next realm, and the next, and the next. Thereby giving champions many chances to save the worlds and forever stop Ragnarök or...set me loose." He grinned, flashing all those teeth. There was no long tongue in his mouth, just teeth.

I asked my question with fear in my heart that I already knew the answer. "How many of the realms are left? How many...suns and moons left to be killed?"

"Oh, there are no moons left, Sunshine. Not a single one survived once Han realized that Havoc loved the soul of the first who carried the moon within her soul. The sun has been destroyed in every realm but this one. Earth's realm. You are the last, Sunshine." He'd stopped, and so had I, staring at him.

Bebe suddenly put herself between me and the Midgard serpent. "What the fuck are you saying? Spit it out!"

His eyes were on mine, considering. Weighing me.

"You are the last to carry the sun inside of you. Your death will secure the outcome of all nine realms. For the light. Or for the dark. Depending on which of those boys spills your blood. And when they kill you. Tricky business. Havoc could try to keep you alive, but he couldn't even keep his true love alive. And if he fails, then Ragnarök starts. I imagine...it is a hard decision for him. Perhaps the loss of one life is better than losing the world. Yes?"

The smell of the serpent flooded my senses as he drew close to the edge of the embankment, and I turned to stare at him as he spoke. "What will you do with this knowledge, little Sunshine? Will you run and hide like all the others? Find a semblance of a life for a short period of time? Find someone to transfer the curse of the sun to, so you don't have to carry it?"

"No." I shook my head. "No, that's not me." I was a survivor first, but...I was a fighter too.

"Then what will you do?"

I stared at him, smelling him, and caught a whiff of something I did recognize. I narrowed my eyes and bared my teeth, a bit of my wolf coming to the surface as my anger flared. "Why do you smell like Loki?"

He grunted. "Gods. Don't tell me I smell like that lush. He is my father. Why? Wait, have you met him?"

"He stuffed me into this body! Marked me with his damn symbol!" Well, Petunia had, but Loki could have helped unstuff me and had chosen not to. "You are an agent of chaos then. Like him."

Not a question.

He grinned. "Perhaps from time to time. But in this instance, with you, I have spoken truly. You can sense and smell lies, can you not?"

I could.

Fuck.

Double fuck. I did not want him to be right about Havoc. Because that meant I was indeed running from both brothers.

A howl behind me spun me around. Speaking of brothers.

One of mine had just found me.

Son of a bitch. Literally.

9

FAMILY REUNIONS SUCK ASS

"Run, Bebe!" I yelped.

Jor thrashed in the water. "What are you running from? That isn't Han or Havoc. I know them well and neither sound like that."

"Have you ever had family members try to kill you?" I huffed as I ran.

"Ha! All of them at one point or another." He swam alongside us. "That howl, that was a family member of yours?"

"Yes." I didn't dare look over my shoulder. Bebe ran just ahead of me, her tail straight up and fluffed like a toilet brush.

"Faster," I breathed out. Ducking my head, I flipped Bebe onto my back. "We have to go faster."

Another howl ripped through the air. One voice. It

was just Shipley as far as I could tell, but he was calling the others to him.

"How did he find you so fast?" Bebe clung to me.

"Don't know. We don't have ties any longer," I breathed out as I ran for all I was worth. I'd done everything right, gotten my feet off the ground, gone a direction they shouldn't have anticipated I'd go...not even Havoc had found me yet and he *knew* I'd be going this way, looking for Denna.

"It has to be magic," Bebe said. "I mean, how else would they know where to find you?"

I didn't want to agree with her, because that would mean I was in deeper shit than ever. If my siblings had a new way to find me...how was I ever going to lose them?

Right then, I had one choice. The water was my best bet, I knew it, but color me nervous about jumping into a raging river with the Midgard serpent who had already pointed out that my death would benefit him.

I didn't want to have him 'accidentally' drown me. Maybe that was a loophole for all I knew.

"If you rode on my back, I could speed you away from them," Jor said, all casual like. As if he would do it for free.

"What is the cost?" I barked at him.

He rolled in the water. "Perhaps a favor at a later date. Nothing big of course."

Another howl ripped through the air behind me. "No killing anyone. I don't want to kill anyone for you."

Jor flipped his tail. "That is the only thing you would ask not to be held to?"

I thought it through. "Pretty much." I'd done so much in order to stay alive in the Grayling pack, it didn't make sense to pretend I had many morals left. No killing. No hurting my friends. I would stay loyal to my people.

And survive. Above all else, survive.

"Excellent. Yes, hop on, and I will make it so they cannot see you, smell you, or realize where you've gone."

Hop on, as if it were that easy. "Hang tight, Bebe." I said as I took a running leap into the river and straight for the back of the Midgard serpent in the middle of the river.

I was insane.

This whole situation was nuttier than a bag of squirrels snorting peanut butter.

My hair kind of floated around me as I flew through the air, Bebe clinging to my back, and then I was knee deep in water, paws sliding on Jor's scales.

"My magic will cover you," he said in that oh-so-smooth voice once more. "Good timing too."

He swam lazily down river as two wolves came into view, racing down to the edge with their noses to the wind.

I stayed silent, balancing myself, feeling Bebe tense on my back. What a circus, I could just imagine what we looked like.

Snake. Dog. Cat. Stacked like a freakshow.

The two wolves were as familiar to me as my own face. Shipley was the dark gray one. The other was larger than when I'd seen her last. Meghan was a deep russet, the color of her hair. She was lean and not the chubby cub I remembered her wolf to be.

They shot on past us, down the riverbank.

"There," rumbled Jor. "You see? They didn't even know you were right in front of them." He picked up speed. "Let's follow them, shall we? See what becomes of them."

"No." I shook my head, but he didn't slow and I didn't want to swim for the far shore and lose the cover of his magic.

"Don't be silly, they can't see you! They can't even see me for that matter." He turned, his face coming dangerously close to mine. "You are truly afraid of them."

"They will kill me, but not until they have taken me back to my pack to be tortured. Again." I shuddered, thinking of horrors I'd already endured. "If I am lucky, they will kill me quickly, though that's unlikely to happen. Then you would be free to destroy the world. You might like that."

His body undulated in what felt like a shrug. "Life

is what it is. If you are killed by someone other than Han or Havoc, what would happen then? It may be that there is a third option to Ragnarök that I am unaware of. Interesting. I shall have to divine that."

I crouched low, putting my belly against his back, sinking partway into the waves. I had better balance that way, but Bebe didn't much like it. "I don't want to go swimming."

"I'm trying to keep you from getting any wetter. I don't slide as much this way," I ducked my jaw into the water and lapped it up. I hadn't even realized how thirsty I was until I could finally breathe.

The cold water sluiced down my throat, easing my thirst and filling my empty belly. Just thinking of how empty it was made it growl. But not like before when my body had basically been eating itself alive because of the shifting.

This was...better. The shifts weren't costing me as much.

"Oh, it looks like they've found some friends!" Jor chortled. "Fun. Who is that with them?"

I lifted my head and my body tensed. Shipley and Meghan had caught up with Richard and Kieran. Not a surprise there.

Han, he was the surprise. I was sure I'd felt him so far north. How had he gotten here this fast?

He stood on the edge of the water, looking straight at us. "He knows I'm here."

"Ah, no, my magic coats the bond too. You are unfindable right now." He tipped his head and winked at me.

"Winking snakes. Bad idea," Bebe whispered.

Jor slid toward the shore as Han beckoned him with an easy smile. "Old friend. Have you seen a golden retriever on the riverbank?"

Jor shook his head. "And if I did? What would it matter to you? What do you want with a dog?"

"Well, it would be worth something I'm quite sure. If I find and kill her, you'd be released."

Shit.

Apparently he knew I carried the sun now.

I looked from Han to my four siblings, who had cringed away from Jor. Yeah, they'd never seen anything like him, but did they understand that he was a legendary monster? Probably not. Kieran recovered first, his fur rising along his spine. He and Richard were both dark brown wolves. They could have been twins except for the fact that Dick was a good four inches taller and significantly heavier.

Han put his hands on his hips. "What do you want, old friend? A woman? A sacrifice?"

Jor turned his head slightly, zeroing in on Meghan, who tried to stay behind Shipley. "Hmm. Maybe. That one there, the girl. Maybe I'll take her."

I dug my claws into his back, trying to telegraph that he was not to take Meghan.

She tried to slink backward, a whine rippling out of her mouth.

Jor raised himself up. "I could eat her up I think, she is lovely. And then once I've taken my pleasure, I could eat her for real. Yes?"

Bebe let out a squeak. "Don't."

I didn't know if she meant that don't for me or for Jor. Either way, I stood up. Jor's back rippled under me.

Han started to nod. I had to move before he made the agreement, before his mouth said the words that would take away Meghan's choices, giving control of her body away to someone other than her. I couldn't...I couldn't do that, not even to her.

"Hang on," I said to Bebe. Her claws dug in.

"Jesus on a donkey, I don't want to get wet!" she screeched. But she didn't tell me not to.

I leapt off Jor's back, his magic sliding off me, and we hit the river, going under and then bobbing back up as I swam hard with the current.

I looked over my shoulder and saw Han's mouth hanging open. There might have been howling, there might have been words, I couldn't tell.

Bebe clung to my upper neck. "I hate this! It's not warm like the ocean was!"

"Just hang on!" I yelled back as I paddled hard, not heading for either shore. The current was strong, and I worked with it, letting it rip me downstream faster than I could run on either bank.

Something bumped against my back hip. "Why did you do that?" Jor demanded, swimming beside me.

"That's my sister," I growled.

"Your sister who wants to kill you," Bebe howled from my back.

I kept on swimming. "Death is one thing. Rape is another. Death is just death. Rape is a form of torture, and I won't be a part of that, not even for her."

"Hmm. I never thought of it that way." Jor rolled under the waves, so he was looking up at me as he swam backward.

"Is that really why you jumped?" Bebe asked.

"Yes." I bit the word out. I wasn't going there. It had happened years ago, and I was past it, but the trigger was still close to the skin at strange times. Like seeing Meghan cower. Knowing she would beg for mercy and find none.

I wasn't about to let myself go back to that place, but I also wasn't about to let it happen to another woman if I could help it. Even one who wouldn't offer the same protection to me.

"I'm an idiot."

"I think your heart is bigger than even you knew." Jor slid to the surface to swim beside me. "It happens sometimes, when someone is becoming a hero. They do things they otherwise would not. Save people they should let die. It's the way of myth and legend. It is the way of growth."

I glared at him. "If you'd just wanted to kill her—"

He grinned, his lips pulling back over all of those many, many teeth. "You still would have jumped."

"Fuck you," I growled. Hating that he was right. Feeling it in my belly that I would still try to save Meghan.

He lifted his head and looked back down the river. "I think you have a few miles on them now. You are so much more interesting than the others who have carried the sun. I really hate to say this, but I rather like you, Sunshine. I hope you live a very long time."

I started toward the far shoreline. Of course, that would have been all well and good if not for the pull of the water and the fatigue of keeping my head above it. "Shit. Bebe. If I get close to the shore, jump for it."

"Wait, why?"

I tried to lift my head further, but a sudden flash of fatigue cut through me, sharp as a knife. What the fuck was this nonsense?

My mate bond flared, even though I'd cut through so much of it, and I *felt* Han on the other end, draining my reserves, fighting to hold me in place. "Mother-fucking limp dick!" I fought against the urge to just give up, putting everything into my swimming.

"You could help her!" Bebe shrieked as Jor circled us.

"I helped her once. That's enough of a good deed for the day for me, even if I do rather like her." Jor rolled in the water, his body creating a wave that took me toward the wrong shore. As his tail went by, I lurched forward and grabbed the tip of it, biting down with everything I had.

He bellowed and flicked it, throwing me toward the shoreline that I wanted.

"Oh, you tricky little bitch!" He laughed. "That was clever. Don't make me like you!"

I struggled up the edge of the riverbank, across the rocks, and stood there panting. My mind raced. If Han could steal my energy, then I was screwed.

I had to break free of him.

Forcing my feet into a jog, I started down the shoreline and immediately caught a whiff of someone familiar. Fate was being kind about something, at least.

"Denna!" I barked her name, and a surge of energy flooded me.

"You got her?" Bebe shrieked. "Wait, I think I see her! Over there!"

Ahead of us was a cluster of bushes, thick with dense foliage. A thin arm stuck out and waved in our direction, then jerked back within the cover she'd found.

I ran straight for her and stuffed myself into the bushes where I'd seen her arm. Denna was alive, or as much as a ghoul could be.

"Cin." She reached for me, and I threw myself into

her arms. "That brother of yours tossed me into the river."

"I know, I know! I'm sorry, we came for you as quick as we could!"

She pushed me back and got a good look at me. "Why are you still a golden retriever?"

I sighed and sat down, my stupid tail thumping the ground and making a soggy, wet sound. "I don't know. But I'm stuck with shifting to this for now. Saved the world, got stuck as a dog."

Bebe shook herself, and her hair stuck up all over her body. "We can't stay here long. Cin's family is looking hard for her on the other side, there's a giant snake in the river with a sadistic streak, and...Havoc might be trying to kill her too."

Denna shuddered. "Where is Soleil?"

I shook my head. "Dead. Han killed her, thinking she was still carrying the sun."

Which led into a quick explanation of what we knew so far. I was now cursed to carry the sun. Han was trying to kill me before the dead moon. Havoc would probably try to kill me before the solar eclipse. We also talked about Jor and his understanding of the situation. And then my family, of course.

"That's a lot." Denna said softly, touching her glasses as she did when she was worried. "Are you okay?"

I frowned and my tail slowed its thumping. "I don't

know. I don't know what to do. Where to start to get myself out of this mess."

Bebe pressed herself against my front legs but said nothing. At least not at first.

"You know, you have a lot of skills," she said softly. "What if you turned it around on them all? Soleil never had a chance, not really. She wasn't trained. But you are. What if...what if *we* hunted *them*?"

My tail picked up speed. "That's not a bad idea, Bebe. But I need to get somewhere I could find weapons, gear. All that."

Bebe tipped her head up at me. "You thinking what I'm thinking?"

I had no idea, but I knew a place. The same place that I was sure my siblings had been headed to. The warehouse in Boise.

It was stocked with everything you could need for an ambush. Of course, it belonged to the Snake River pack, but it wouldn't be the first time I'd stolen from them. Grinning, my tongue lolling out, I bobbed my head. "Okay. Mission Kick Some Ass. You both in?"

Bebe stood on her back legs and shadow-boxed at my face. "Ready to claw their eyes out."

Denna nodded much slower, and with far less enthusiasm. "As soon as it's dark."

Right.

Sleep would be good anyway. We had a few hours until dark. "Rest then, and we'll go as soon as we can."

"We going to use the highway again?" Bebe asked. "That means we'll need to cross the river."

I opened my mouth to answer. But someone grabbed me from behind and dragged me out of the bush. I tried to spin around and bite the hand that had me, but the fingers had dug into my scruff, holding me up high so I could look into his face.

His scar tightened over his eye. "I should kill you right now for that stunt."

10

NUDE BOOBS FOR THE WIN

I shifted in Havoc's hand, letting my body slide back to two legs for two reasons. One, I wanted to have the satisfaction of slapping his hand away from me. Two, because he was a man, and a good set of boobs was an astounding weapon against the male brain.

My feet touched the rough, sharp rocks and I winced. "Let me go!"

His eyes dipped to my chest. Just the slightest movement, but I saw it. I knocked his hand away from me. "I am not your slave, Havoc. I told you that I was going to find my friend."

The growl that rumbled through his chest suggested he wanted to do bad things to me, but I was too pissed to care.

Too pissed at myself to be honest. I'd let my guard down for like five minutes and I'd been caught again.

He said nothing. Grabbed me around the waist and threw me over his shoulder.

I jerked to the side so I could jam my elbow into his neck. He let me go for a split second, and then he was on me again, grappling with me. But I was naked and still damp from the river which made me slippery as fuck.

His fingers slid off my arm as I yanked away from him, stumbled over a rock, and fell backward into the river. The water rushed over my head, but I pushed off the bottom, swimming to the surface. I was already being swept downriver with the strength of the current.

The familiar body of Jor slid around me. "What is this? An offering of a pretty piece of ass?"

"Knock it off!" I slapped water at his face as I struck out for the edge of the river.

"Oh! You were the dog? Perhaps I know what my favor will be after all!" he chortled at me.

I reached over, as if I were going to stroke his face, but instead I hooked my fingers into the slits of his nostrils and yanked him close to me. "I would let Han kill me before I ever let you touch me like that, you perv."

I closed my fist, driving my fingers deep into the

flesh of his nose. Once more he thrashed, throwing me across the river.

Only this time, it was to the wrong side.

I hit hard, my head striking a protruding rock. The blow sent my senses reeling, and I went under the waves. I remembered to hold my breath, but I was struggling to do much else as the undertow dragged me in.

Stupid fucking serpent.

Stupid me for falling back in the river.

Stupid damn Havoc for finding me.

I broke the surface, gasping for air, but couldn't seem to make my limbs work.

The water seeped into every part of me, my nose, eyes, ears, mouth. My lungs burned with it.

I floated along, bumping into things, thinking that I should be dead already.

Hands slid around my waist, and I was dragged out of the water. A mouth on my mouth, pushing air into my lungs, forcing the water out. Hands on my chest, doing compressions.

I wretched to the side, throwing up far more water than it felt like I'd gotten in.

"What the actual fuck are you thinking?" Havoc roared before my eyes even began to unblur from the near-death drowning.

My words were straight from the heart. "I hate you."

"Mutual," he growled as he grabbed me once more and threw me over his back. I didn't have the energy to fight him. So, he packed me along, up the embankment.

I wondered where Han and my brothers were in all this. As if my thoughts had conjured them, they raced into view on the far side of the bank.

"Han is there," I said, still choking on the water.

"I know," Havoc snarled.

"He knows I carry the sun."

"I know."

I waved a single finger at Han and my siblings. It was all I had left in me before I blacked out.

When I slid into darkness, the same strange man was waiting for me. "Well, you've been making quite the spectacle. Even after all the help I've been giving you."

I frowned at the bearded man with the partially shaved head. "I'm just trying to live."

"As we all are. Your life is tied to the world's. So you will have many, many people trying to make themselves a part of your life, for good and for ill. Be wary."

I jerked upright, wrapped up in a blanket. There was a plate of pasta on the table next to me. Chunks of sausage littered the top and I grabbed at it, shoving at the fork, shoving food into my mouth as fast as I could.

My head throbbed. My stomach was angry. I

paused mid bite and looked around the room. "Bebe?" I called.

"Your two friends are being held separately," a woman's voice answered me. "He seems to think that together you are more trouble."

I blinked to see Claire sitting in a dark corner of the room. "They aren't hurt?"

She shook her head. "No. Havoc is incredibly angry with you all, but he didn't hurt them."

That was enough for me for the moment. I dug back into the huge bowl. I wanted more protein, but this would do for now.

"Why did you run away?" Claire asked. "You were safe with us."

"Denna. She wasn't safe," I said around a mouthful. I wasn't about to tell her that I'd learned Havoc wasn't safe for me either.

Claire sighed. "I feel like we've been here before. I need to go tell Havoc you're awake."

She stood and left the room. The sound of the locks opening and closing was not lost on me. There were three. Most likely a combination of different types of locks. I sighed and kept working on the pasta. I glanced at the ceiling. This one was solid.

My friends were safe—locked up, sure, but safe. I was alive.

I touched my fingers to the side of my head and winced. Yup, still sore. I finished my bowl as Havoc approached the door. I smelled him first, the ice and cold coming with him so distinct that I knew I would never mistake him for Han. Not now.

The door opened and he stepped in, ducking his head to fit through the doorway.

I waited for him to say something.

It appeared he was waiting for me to say something.

I lifted my bowl and licked it clean, then set it down on the table and looked up at him.

His eyes were dilated, following my every move. My skin prickled as he stared at me, the sound of his heartbeat kicking up a notch.

The scent rolling off him shifted, ever so slightly.

Desire. Need. Lust.

Fuck. Me.

"I hate you," I whispered.

"Mutual," he growled as he strode across the room, jerking his top off first.

I reached for him and then he was on me, his mouth against my neck as he flipped me onto my belly.

His lips and teeth grazed along the length of my neck and down to my shoulder as I gripped the sheets and struggled to keep my senses—and remember that he was probably going to kill me at some point.

But not for the next ten days. That was my naughty voice, the one that wanted nothing more than to ride this pleasure until I blacked out, screaming my climaxes until I could feel nothing else.

He slid off me and the sense of loss was profound. For a split second, I thought he'd changed his mind.

The sound of his belt coming loose, the clink of the metal buckle as it hit the floor filled me with a sense of relief that I didn't want to think too much about. I stayed put but looked over my shoulder.

Goddess of the moon and stars, she had finally given me a man worth looking at—even if he was to be my end. His upper body seemed to be etched in stone, but I knew from the feel of it he ran hot, not cold. His dark hair fell forward, half covering his face and softening the scar, and the cut of his jaw was rugged, demanding that I reach out and touch it.

Havoc's eyes swept from my feet, along my calves, over my thighs, ass, and back to finally meet my eyes.

"Before this is done, you will obey me."

I arched a brow, ignoring the bit of fear that sliced through me at his words. "Don't think you can keep me caged, wolf. I will do as I please. I am no one's bitch."

His hands locked onto my ankles, and he slowly pulled me toward him, spreading my legs as he drew me close. "There is more than one way to keep you captive, Goldie."

I laughed and lifted my ass in the air, an invitation if I was ever going to give one. "You think fucking me will bind me to you?"

He leaned forward and bit my ass, sucking the flesh into his mouth until it made a popping sound. I dug my fingers into the bedsheets, letting the urges of my body lead me, and rocked back and forth, pushing myself closer to him.

Wanting what his body did to mine so badly it was an ache through my bones, a need like the breath in my lungs.

Havoc gripped my hips and dragged me all the way back to him, where he stood at the edge of the bed, hard in every sense of the word.

I'd never stopped looking at him over my shoulder. Never stopped taking it all in.

He slid his hands over my hips, along the inner curve of my ass, all the way around to my center, cupping my wet heat. I tried flexing my body to get him closer to my clit and that fickle bundle of nerves that wanted his touch.

He slapped my ass with his free hand, just hard enough to sting, not hard enough to make me think he was serious. Fuck me, he walked a fine line.

I loved every fucking second of it, even if I hated him.

"Hold still," he growled as he worked his fingers through my slit, gathering moisture on the tips, then working his way to my center and that damn nub that ached for him.

I closed my eyes as he made a single circular pass over it.

"Look at me."

"No," I whispered. "I'll think of whoever I want while you fuck me."

Fighting words, and I knew it.

His snarl filled the air, and I scrunched my eyes tightly shut. I wanted this, every piece of it.

But I didn't *want* to want him, and I was telling myself the need I felt was just about breaking the ole dry spell.

It was a conundrum, and I knew it.

His fingers were suddenly gone from my clit. I did open my eyes then, looking back at him, more than a little concerned he was going to stop.

"Eyes on me," he growled, infusing the words with the power of an alpha. "Or I stop."

"Blackmail," I snarled.

His smirk slid over his face as he ran his hand up my inner thighs, fingers digging in just before he flipped me onto my back. "This will make it easier." He paused. "To swallow."

Fuck me.

He yanked me to him, and I gotta admit it was a damn turn on to be man-handled some. Because he wasn't hurting me, just showing off his strength and letting me know he could do damage if he really wanted.

But Havoc was focused on a different kind of damage.

He lifted my lower half up, so he didn't have to so much as put a bend in his back and buried his face between my legs, his eyes locked on mine.

I couldn't look away, balanced on my shoulders, he'd taken every bit of my weight, holding me close to him as he mouth-fucked me, deep and thorough.

As his tongue swiped over me, *in* me, he let out a low, deep-chested rumble that slid out of his mouth and over my already tightwire sensitive parts. I bit my lower lip as I fought to hang on.

Not because I didn't want to orgasm.

But I wanted it to be on my terms.

Havoc...wasn't going to let me have that.

Fucker.

Balanced as I was, I was well within reach of what I wanted.

"Two can play," I whispered through gasps as his tongue circled me, pressing and flicking, demanding my attention.

It took all I had to reach up and grab his cock, sliding the silken shaft through my hand.

He grunted and his eyelids fluttered shut. I couldn't resist throwing his words back at him.

"Eyes on me, Havoc."

His eyes flew open, and gods and goddess be fucked, neither of us looked away.

I wanted to tell him that I hated him again, mostly for making me want this—with him. A Norse lordling who was going to try and kill me. I say try, because there were enough others out there who wanted me dead, it would be a real competition.

I squeezed harder, drawing a groan from him, twisting my hand slowly, pushing all the way to the base and back again as his tongue dipped low into me.

"Fuck," I whispered.

"Done." He dropped my hips and climbed on top of me, his mouth going once more to my throat, demanding I give into him.

I didn't care. Not right then. The world could have ended, and I wouldn't have cared as long as this didn't stop.

Havoc slid his arms around me, holding me up again as he slid into me. "No more running."

"I will do as I please," I gasped out.

"No. It's my job to keep you safe."

His pace was slow and deadly, sliding in and out of me, pressing on every part of my body.

He dipped his head and sucked a nipple into his mouth, drawing another low moan out of me.

"I will survive on my own!" I arched into him, wrapping my legs around his waist and angling my body so that each thrust of his cock slid over my clit, sending ripples of need through me.

He grunted and picked up his pace. "No. You won't."

Grabbing my hands, he slowly pressed them above my head, his face in front of mine. He could have kissed me.

But he didn't.

There was no brushing of our lips, not a single dip of his head in my direction. Because it wasn't like that between us. There was no love. There was nothing but raw need.

My body was screaming for release, demanding for me to finish this with Havoc or take care of things myself.

I tightened my legs around him and rolled my hips, getting the perfect thrust, the tip of his cock rubbing against my clit, driving the sensations deeper.

That big fucker seemed to know exactly when I was close, as he let out a growl that filled my mind, body, and the whole damn room, sending me crashing over the edge as he drove himself hard into me, holding me tightly beneath him.

Filling me up in a way I didn't want to think about. Because I hated him. He was going to try and kill me.

But fuck me upside down and inside out, he was a rockstar in the sack. I wouldn't deny it.

His thrusting grew erratic as he climbed his own peak and then a second orgasm caught me unaware, throwing me back into the abyss of pleasure that he'd opened up in me.

I might have screamed, might have howled along with him for all I knew. A very distant part of my mind hoped that Han could sense me fucking his brother.

I slid down from the precipice, holding onto awareness by a thread.

Panting and unable to move, I lay there pinned beneath him. The only solace I had was that he seemed equally unable to move, the weight of his body pinning me to the mattress.

A delicious fatigue stole over me, and I closed my eyes. I might have fallen asleep.

All I know was that he was suddenly pulling off and out of me, and there was a voice in the room that made me cringe with shame.

"Sven needs to speak with you," Claire said.

Claire. Havoc's mate, and she'd just walked in on us in bed.

11

SHAME ON ME

"Fuck. I'm sorry, Claire." I struggled to get to the side of the bed and find some clothes. Something. She turned and fled the room, her eyes sparkling with unshed tears.

Goddess, I was lower than dirt.

I was just like my mother, fucking other people's mates. I hadn't thought of Claire once in the whole time that Havoc had been with me. Shame fell over me like a heavy, wet woolen blanket and I wanted to gag on it.

I managed to get a sheet wrapped around me, but there were no clothes.

"She's not my mate," Havoc said as he pulled on his clothes. He turned, dressed in just jeans. "You will have an escort every minute of the day and night from here on out. Or I will chain you to a wall."

I realized he was waiting for me. My brain was still firing on the 'she's not my mate' business. "Are you sure? She seems...attached to you. I am not interested in—"

"Being like your mother? I have no mate, Goldie. Get dressed, Sven is waiting."

I looked around the room. "Sorry, do you see clothes?"

He did a quick sweep and frowned, then grabbed something off the floor and tossed it to me. "Here."

I caught it. A soft cotton shirt that smelled of Havoc. "This isn't going to fit me."

"It'll cover your ass. Let's go."

I realized he wasn't kidding. I sighed and stood up, pulling the shirt over my head, the ice and snow smell sinking into me. The hem of it fell to mid-thigh and I looked up to see Havoc staring hard at me. "What?"

He shook his head and started out the door, leaving me to follow his broad, bare back. My feet were silent as I padded after him, keeping my nose and ears alert for any signs of Bebe and Denna.

"Denna is safe?" I asked as we reached a set of stairs that led up. "She won't do well in sunlight."

"She has the basement," Havoc said.

"And Bebe?"

He snorted. "She's taken to Berek. He can't hear her, but I can."

I laughed, I couldn't help it. "She's detailing what she'd like to do to him?"

He glanced over his shoulder. I thought I saw another smirk, but I couldn't be sure. "It's an extensive list."

"Well, maybe you can pick up some pointers."

He paused halfway up the stairs. "You are not satisfied?"

"Are you?" I asked and saw that dark glitter in his eyes. He turned and was down to my step in a flash, his body pressing mine to the wall. I took a deep breath, which pressed my body to his.

The tension between us was a highwire pulled taut, ready to snap. His hand slid from my thigh, around to my ass, pulling me tight against him, against his already hard cock.

"You two. Knock it off," Sven snapped from the upper level. "We have a problem."

Havoc pushed away from me, but not before I felt a very definite urge on his part to show me just how satisfied he could make me. Again.

"Bebe's not the only one with detailed pointers," I said under my breath when he was at the top of the stairs.

He didn't pause, but I knew that there was no way he hadn't heard me. I smiled to myself.

Shit, I had no reason for smiling after everything that had happened.

I frowned.

Was this a side effect of the golden retriever I carried in me now? Rolling with the good and the bad?

"Well shit, maybe that wouldn't be all bad," I said under my breath, following Havoc to the room at the end of the hall.

A corner room with lots of light, full of living plants and growing things.

"How can this all be here?" I asked as I stepped into the room. "I mean...I just happened to be kidnapped within an hour or two of one of your safe houses? A safehouse that's the size of a school? And now here, again? Once I could believe, twice, it doesn't make sense."

Sven lifted his hand and the roof above us peeled away, showing the sky as it dipped toward night. "I am what I am, and because I am what I am, I can do things that seem impossible to you."

I frowned. "That's a non-answer if you ask me."

"He has the magic to turn any place into a safe-house and hide it from Han for a period of time," Havoc said.

"Why didn't you do that for Han?"

"Because Han does not fully understand my capabilities," Sven said.

"What have you found?" Havoc made his way over to a window and peered out. "Are they on us already?"

"No, we are still hidden. I am not fully sure if Han even knows she carries the sun."

"He does." I said. "He told Jor that if he killed me, that Jor would be free."

"Fuck." Havoc growled. "That was the one edge we had." He paused. "And the mate bond between them?"

"Is intact but damaged. There are very few ways to break a mate bond, you know this. Very few cases of it happening." He raised his woody-looking eyebrows.

And suddenly the vigorous second round made more sense—sheer strategy on his part, and I couldn't blame him for that. There was an old tale, one where two brothers—Daven and Rook, legendary werewolves —fought over a mate bonded to the younger brother, Rook. The older apparently stole her away and managed to get the bond to switch. "Right. So, if you fuck me enough, the mate bond would shift to you? Is that what you're hoping for?"

"I don't want your mate bond, but it is worse that Han has it," Havoc said. "We think he is using it, to allow your brothers to find you for him."

Lazy, Han was lazy. Just like looking for a dog to do the tracking of Soleil, he would use my brother's hatred of me to do the dirty work. I held up a hand. "That is an old wolves' tale. There's only one way to separate a mate bond." Not true, but I wasn't sure I wanted them to know.

Sven looked at me. "And what is that?"

"One of the mates must die. That will shatter the bond. It does not go beyond death." Just like a marriage, till death do we part. I lifted a hand and ran my fingers over the fronds of a large fern that had seemingly sprung up out of the floorboards. Nothing here was in pots, just growing, twisting around the room and hiding the walls. "And seeing as you want me alive, and Han can't be killed...we're stuck. I've buried the mate bond as deeply as I can to block him out." And I'd keep worrying at the threads too.

"And you say that what I suggest is impossible." Sven snorted. "You can't block a mate bond."

I smiled, though I doubted it reached my eyes. "You can when you've been rejected. He rejected me—not once, but twice. The bond will not hold tightly to him, and it allows me space to effectively live my life. I can —and always will—be able to sense him and vice versa, but the rejection on his part dulls it. The rejection on my part dulls it further."

Just like being rejected from Grayling had allowed me space to figure out how to cut through those bonds. If I could do it once, I could do it again. I just needed time and space to work at it.

"He could just accept you now," Havoc said.

I shook my head, running my fingers along the thin tendrils of the plant, marveling at how soft they were. "No. Because I rejected him, too. It was a mutual thing. It would take both of us agreeing to get back together

—not that we were ever together—to make it work properly again."

Havoc and Sven stared at me, but it was Sven who spoke. "You know a great deal about mate bonds, something that most find mysterious."

I scrunched up my face, thinking of Claire and my fear that I'd hurt her. Maybe she wasn't Havoc's mate, but she obviously wanted to be. "My mother is a power-hungry sex addict. She...she studied how best to get away from things like mate bonds, how to remove them, how to circumvent them. She had me help her with her research."

Havoc hadn't moved from his spot in the window. "I thought my family was bad."

My lips quirked up. "Yeah well, we can't all win the family lottery and end up in the Norse pantheon."

"Regardless of all that, I asked you to come here because there has been a shift. Han is up to something. Something new." Sven said.

"When is he not?" Havoc grumbled.

"This is...different. Her brothers are involved now, and they're actively hunting her on his behalf. Han slipped away from the river after you stole her out from under his nose, and I have no markers on him. The mate bond would normally allow him to find her. If what she is saying is true, then right now he can't. But he's given them—her brothers—the ability to track her, using the bond somehow. Shared it with at least one of them."

My fingers clenched around the fern and Sven winced. I made myself let go and instead grabbed the edge of my shirt. My mate bond shared with one of my brothers. I'd bet it was Kieran.

I tried very hard not to think of that brother, of the fact that he'd been willing to force me to be his mate at Juniper's request.

"Anything else?" I asked.

"Nothing that I'm aware of. I spoke with Odin, in Asgard." He threw the names out like he was talking about catching up on gossip with Bob at the Post Office. I stared at him in disbelief.

"What, so like over coffee this morning?"

Sven dipped his head in my direction. "Yes, but he prefers cappuccinos now. He said that Han has made some new alliances. Loki is still mucking about, and Jor...well Jor is always an issue on the horizon. He said to look to Hel."

"Fuck." Havoc dropped his head.

"Hell?"

"No," Sven held his hand out, and a hundred or more little fireflies raced in through the open roof, wreathing his arms. The light had shifted to darkness outside. "Hel, one L. She is the queen of the dead, undead, and many dark realms."

I scrunched up my face. "Okay, so that's not great." What had Jor said? Helheim? Realm of the dead.

"Not great?" Havoc turned around finally. "She could turn the tables in Han's favor."

I realized then that Havoc didn't like being an underdog.

Yet I'd been one my entire life. I shrugged. "It'll be fine. What's the worst she could do?"

Sven held his hand out to me, and I took it, the fireflies racing around my body, fluttering around my legs and then back up. They danced along my arm as they returned to Sven, shining brighter, as if they'd taken in some of the sun that I carried.

Sven nodded as they swept around him, lighting up the crags and crevices of his face.

"The worst she could do," Havoc said quietly, "is increase Han's strength. She could twist your death out of you. She could unleash a great deal on this world."

"Meh," I shrugged. "I've dealt with worse." Bluffing of course, I was bluffing. But until Hel actually took a step in our direction, I wasn't about to freak out.

Havoc narrowed his eyes at me.

Sven put his hands together and bowed over them. "The glittering one has spoken. It shall be fine."

"You know, for someone who really didn't like me, you're warming up to me." I gave him a wink.

Sven laughed. "You are not like any of the others who have carried the sun. You don't seem overly bothered about being hunted. About the constant threat to your life."

His words gave me pause, so I took a moment to answer.

"My whole life I have fought to survive. This is just more of the same. But why is Han hunting me now, by using my brothers and not doing it himself?"

"That is simpler," Sven said slowly. "You escaped him—something not many do, and you ran to his brother, whom he hates. It is a matter of possession and ownership in his mind. You belong to him. He would rather see you dead than on the arm of his brother. But he is also on the lazy side."

"He thinks they will catch me, and bring me to him."

Sven smiled widely; his teeth made of highly polished wood chunks. "Yes. It is all about posturing. He doesn't even have to do the work, because he is the mighty Han, bringer of Ragnarök."

Someone cleared his voice in the hall. "If I may add to the discussion?"

I spun. Loki stood in the hall, dressed in dark brown pants and boots, a deep blue cloak, his dark hair and eyes shining.

I took it all in a split second before I leapt at the motherfucker who had caused me all this grief. The one who could have freed me from my first curse, but didn't. The one who could have kept me away from the second curse, and didn't.

I tackled him to the floor before he so much as stepped into the room. Maybe my wolf was still with me after all.

I pinned him to the floor by his throat, wrapping my fingers as tight as I could. "You got some balls showing up."

He grinned from his place on the floor. "Yes I do, would you like to see them?" And then he grabbed my ass with both hands and jerked me to him.

As suddenly as he'd grabbed me, I was caught around the waist and tossed into the air, yanked away from him.

Havoc stood in front of me and snatched Loki to his feet by his throat, his fingers replacing mine. "She is mine."

"Ah, well, Grandson, *actually*, if we are being technical, she belongs to Han. Besides, you know we all have excellent taste in women." He smiled and knocked Havoc's hand away from him as if it were nothing. Even though I could see the marks from his fingers on his flesh. Or maybe my fingers, hard to say. "I came to offer my help."

There was a screech of a caterwauling cat from down the hall, like the oncoming siren of a firetruck drawing closer. Bebe shot toward me, right past Havoc and Loki.

"Loki is here! Loki is here! I smelled him!"

She leapt and I caught her. "I know."

"Sorry, I came as soon as I realized! I caught a whiff of him!" She was breathing hard, her pink tongue hanging out of her face. "Oh, Havoc caught him, that's good!"

Loki chuckled. "Good? I let him ca-gggth." He choked on the last word as Havoc's hand shot out and grabbed his throat again.

"What are you doing here? You favor Han, so do not lie about your intentions," Havoc said, his voice soft and low, a wolf crouched in the shadows waiting to take his prey down.

For a second time, Loki brushed his hand off and put some space between them.

"Fairly said. In the past, yes, I favored Han. I had some...realizations recently. You see, I think that she —" here he pointed at me, "—is causing enough chaos on her own without me adding to it. Chaos is also about balance. There needs to be chaos and peace to make the world work."

He smiled. No one smiled with him. A sigh slid out of him. "I can admit that I made a mistake. I thought that sending her to Han as a mate would soften him and help him see the world was worth saving. I never expected her to end up carrying the sun. That was... not in the plans."

Havoc's eyebrows shot up. "And since when did you

care about the world other than what you can take from it?"

"Love," Bebe whispered. "You fell in love for the first time, didn't you?"

Loki shot a look at her and then glanced away. "I realize that I could change things, make this world last longer. So I am here to give you what help I can. First, a warning, Grandson. Han has figured out that she carries the sun."

"We know," I said.

"Good." He smiled and winked at me. I gave him my best resting bitch face. Thinking of him fucking my mom, and all that came after, helped.

He cleared his throat, clasping his hands behind his back. "And he has employed another pack. He hasn't done this for years."

"Again, old news," I pointed out. "We know my family is working with him. Unless you are going to give me the answer to breaking my curse fully—because, motherfucker, I still shift into a golden retriever—"

"Ah, that's because you didn't break the curse with your mate." He made a sheepish face, then promptly took his index finger and put it through the "O" he'd made with his other hand.

Havoc snarled and took a step toward Loki, who dodged his grandson's hands. "Look, I didn't make the rules. Petunia—"

"Do not throw me under the bus, you bastard."

She stepped into the room from the shadows of the hallway. Her face harsh as before, her eyes slid over the T-shirt barely covering my thighs.

Loki dipped his head in her direction. "Lovely to have you here, Petunia, my heart. As always."

Somehow, I didn't think it was Petunia that he'd realized he was in love with.

Watching her walk into the room, it occurred to me that she was almost certainly more than a witch.

"Are you a Norse goddess then?"

Her eyes glittered. "I am. But that is all you need to know. I see you survived. Shocking."

"That's my job. Shock and awe." I shrugged, feeling the edge of my T-shirt slide up further.

Petunia's eyes narrowed.

I fought to hold still. To not give her reason to throw another curse at me.

Havoc moved between me and Petunia in a step that said it all. He was literally and figuratively putting himself between us.

No one had protected me since I'd lost Mars. Not like this.

I didn't want to say it affected me, but it did. I had been on my own for so long, even before I left Grayling. To have this man who barely knew me put himself between me and danger was...surprising. I wasn't sure I liked how it felt, the emotion I couldn't quite name, wrapping around me.

"Speak your piece," Havoc said. "And speak it quickly before I lose my patience with you, Loki, father of my father."

I noticed he didn't add Petunia in there. I wasn't the only one who noticed.

"Broken family much?" Bebe whispered.

Petunia's eyes shot to the cat in my arms, and Bebe ducked her head, hiding her face.

Loki held up both hands. "I was wrong to help Han. I can see that now. I would prefer to keep the world intact. Which is why I am going to tell you what I can."

"Thirty seconds," Havoc growled.

Petunia stepped toward him, her hand raised, covered in green magic. "Do not threaten my husband, Welp!"

I moved without truly thinking, stepping up beside Havoc, presenting a solid front. "Don't."

Just that one word. Petunia's eyes slid to me. "Just like your mother. Fucking anything that moves."

That same shame I'd felt earlier slid back around me.

Havoc rumbled a warning, putting his arm out and slowly pushing me back so that again he was in front of me.

"Enough!" Loki said. "Han has drawn on the

powers of a new bed partner. I don't know who he is fucking, but he's using her powers to supplement his own. He thinks it will help him once Ragnarök erupts. Which of course is not happening because she—" he pointed at me, "—is still alive. For now."

"And?" I asked. "What else, because you are just repeating what I already know. I felt him banging the shit out of someone. Somewhere way up north."

Sven looked at me. "Hel. Hel is in the north."

Havoc grunted. "He would do it, her, if it got him more power. Shit."

"Wish you'd thought of it first?" I offered sweetly. "Instead, all you got was a golden retriever."

Havoc tightened his hold on me. "This is not in our favor. If it's true."

Loki nodded. "Good, you understand. I don't like not being able to just say things."

I snorted. Right, as if anyone believed that.

"Your fate is tied to your mother's," Petunia stepped up, pushing Loki to the side. "You need her to side with you against your enemies if you wish to survive Han."

Nothing could have shocked me more.

Which is why I burst out laughing. "No fucking way is that happening. Hell will freeze over before she sides with me."

"Hel," Petunia said quietly, "is exactly your problem."

12

JOKE'S ON ME

"You gotta be fucking kidding me!" I was laughing, struggling to speak, but from the looks on their faces, Petunia and Loki weren't joking. "What possible reason could there be for her to want to side with me? Let me answer that for you, none."

"You must convince her," Loki said. "If Juniper sides with you, it will turn the tide against Han and open the way to...end this. That is what you want, isn't it? I cannot see all the why of this, but that does not make it less true."

"Wait..." Havoc took a step toward Loki. "What do you mean by end this? You mean Goldie here dies still?"

"No, I mean that the threat of losing the sun and the moon will end. Ragnarök could still come about by another means, I suppose, but the games between you and your brother would end. Done. Kaput. Finito." Loki clapped his hands together just once and a burst of smoke and light burst up around us.

Petunia and Loki disappeared with that burst of light and noise. *Of course* they'd left before we could get more information. Then again, Havoc had given them thirty seconds. They'd taken those seconds and not one more.

"Fuck." Havoc shook his head.

"If it's true," Sven said, "it could mean the difference to everything. If we could end this, simply by aligning with a werewolf queen...is it not worth it?"

"But why would Juniper be a key in any of this?" I turned around to look at Sven. "She's no Norse goddess or queen. She's *just* a werewolf. A strong one, a wicked one, but just a werewolf."

"It's a game," Bebe said from her place in my arms. "A game that Loki understands but we don't. I'd lay money down that even Petunia doesn't even know all the ins and outs."

Havoc grunted. "The cat is right."

"The cat has a name," I said. "Use it."

I walked toward Sven, feeling like I was floating along in a world that I just didn't recognize anymore.

"Han *was* fucking someone. When he was in the north. And you think that would be Hel?" I squinted at the sky above us, through the roof that Sven had opened with a wave of his hand.

"That would seem most likely," Sven said. "If he is taking some of her power, then we need to be better prepared. If we knew exactly where he was, that would help too."

Sven gave me a look.

"I'd have to tap into the bond, which means it would open things both ways." I frowned, because doing so would leave me more open to Han too. Like how he'd sucked down some of my energy.

"No," Havoc said with a finality that I felt in my bones.

"You aren't the boss of me." I pointed out again, even though both my wolf and my golden wanted to roll to their backs and let him stroke our belly. Stupid animalistic reactions.

Yeah, okay, so I'd have let him stroke my belly in any form.

"If you open the connection to him, he'll be able to find you, as you said. We don't need that. There are other ways to find him," Havoc said.

I scrunched my face up. There had to be a way around this.

"We need a loophole." Bebe leapt from my arms. "Or someone who understands mate bonds incredibly well. Better than you."

"It's not urgent for us to find out where he is right

now," Havoc said. "Sven. What are the chances that Loki spoke truth? That bringing Juniper to our side would help?"

Sven strode to a table in the middle of the room. "She'd be able to help us stop this one's siblings. That would slow Han down."

"This one has a name," Bebe said. "It's Cin."

Sven glanced at me. "Sin?"

"Cinniúint," I said. "It's Irish and a mouthful."

His eyebrows raised. "Cin for short. Pleased to meet you properly."

I dipped my head in his direction. "Sven. May I say something? I'd like to add a rather important piece of information that you two don't have."

"Yes?"

I took a slow breath and then bellowed, "MY MOTHER IS A FUCKING PSYCHOPATH!"

Sven jumped backward and even Havoc took a half step back.

"She will destroy this world before ever helping me. She hates me with a passion that should be reserved for an enemy that has betrayed you over and over." I shook my head. "The only thing she loves is power. Going to her is the worst idea I have *ever* heard, and I've heard some exceptionally dumb ones. You said yourself that Loki has always favored Han. How do you trust him now to give good advice?"

Havoc gave a slow nod. "Then I should go to her. Not you."

Here's the thing. I knew my mother. She'd see Havoc as a damn smorgasbord of power and fucking, and she'd smell me on him.

"Nope." I shook my head, my wolf fighting to get to the surface to make herself known. Because my wolf knew as well as I did that Juniper would want Havoc, and that did not sit well with me. Not one bit. If I had to see him with someone else, I'd much rather see him with Claire.

"Loki may just be sending us in that direction," Sven said. "Perhaps the journey to your old pack will turn up something we need. That is how it works at times. We may never even reach your mother."

"Again," I breathed out. "You are not even looking at the past! You said Loki worked with Han!"

"He didn't lie," Havoc said. "Not today, he didn't."

"How do you know that?"

"Because Petunia won't lie, and if he lies in front of her, she beats him," Havoc said.

That didn't make me feel any better. So, regardless of whether that was true, I knew going to my mother was a terrible idea. The absolute worst.

A knock on the door turned us all around. Berek stood in the entryway. "Dinner is ready."

Food.

Fuck, I was starving. My stomach growled loud

enough for the entire room to hear even if they didn't have wolf ears.

Sven tapped his long fingers on the table. "I think this needs to be decided. If we are to leave, then we should leave as soon as possible. There is only one other option, one other player we might reach out to—"

"No," Havoc said. "We will not involve her. She's as fickle as Petunia and far more deadly."

Sven sighed. "And Juniper may try to kill Cin. While the prophecy suggests Han must be the one who wields the axe, it isn't impossible that another could kill her. Incapacitate her long enough for Han to find her. Or perhaps even act as his champion. In all the years we have gone back and forth, I do not think there has been a more complicated time."

I wanted to hug him. He was taking my side, trying to turn Havoc away from this path.

"Petunia does not want the world to end," Havoc said. "If Loki had said something untruthful or deliberately misleading, she would have intervened. It may even be that she foresaw this path and told him to send us down it."

Sven grimaced and did not look at me as he spoke. "On that I can agree."

Fuck, was this really happening? "It's a terrible idea. The worst. Literally the worst."

"And if it saves the world?" Havoc asked. "What are

you willing to do, to keep those you love alive? This is happening. We leave for Grayling as soon as we eat and get the pack ready to move."

I closed my eyes as the memories of my time in Grayling rushed up and over me. I couldn't go back a second time. I'd tried to return to save Meghan, and look at how that had turned out. It would be madness to try again. Madness to think that Juniper would give a single shit about me.

No, I wouldn't be setting foot in Grayling territory. But they didn't need to know that.

I'd escaped Havoc twice already, what was a third time? Easy peasy.

Still, I was sweating, fear making me hot and nauseous at the same time. Because what if I couldn't get away? Havoc didn't understand the depth of depravity that waited in Grayling. How bad it would be if he was taken.

The only reason I'd found the strength to go back was because I'd thought I was saving Meghan's life. That had seemed like a worthy cause.

Going back to try and make nice with my mother? Fucking no.

Bebe squirmed in my arms. "You okay, girlfriend?"

"No," I whispered as I turned and followed my nose to where the food waited. I walked the halls until I reached the dining area, moving like a zombie, as if there was no connection between my body and brain.

I sat at a place in the dining hall, far away from everyone else, and put food in my belly.

Thick steaks, mashed potatoes with gravy, barbecue chicken, and a bright salad covered in a dressing that tasted of avocado.

I barely tasted a single bite of it. Stuffed myself until there was no room for anything else.

Had to fight not to throw it all up. They wanted me to go back to the pack that had tried to kill me on multiple occasions. That had tortured me. The place I'd fought so damn hard to escape.

A body slid onto the bench next to me, her scent giving me a sense of calm. At least I had my friends.

"Cin?"

I wrapped an arm around Denna and side-hugged her. "Are you okay?" I asked.

"They are giving me a very comfortable place to sleep, food, and books. Are you okay? You look like you've seen a ghost. Well, you know what I mean."

I shook my head. I wouldn't lie to my friends. "No. I am not okay."

Denna sat with me while I shoveled food in my mouth. There were few constants in my life, but needing lots of calories was one of them. And it gave me another distraction from what Havoc was planning.

But it didn't last long, because before I finished, his voice filled the room.

"We'll be headed to the Grayling pack in one hour. Get your shit together. We go fast and light."

No one countered him. No one said it was a bad idea. I stood up, leaning on the table.

"She'll try to kill you or take your pack. That's what she does," I said. "I don't care what your...family member said. He's wrong. It's a terrible idea."

Everyone swung around to look at me, more than one with wide eyes. Of course, I was breaking rules.

Defying an alpha.

I clenched my hands into fists and drew on every bit of strength I had as I stared Havoc down. "I won't go."

The gasp that went up around the room was like the sound of the north wind rushing through the trees.

Havoc grunted. "You don't have a choice."

And he turned away from me. Not dropping his eyes—dismissing me as if I was not worthy of the challenge.

Motherfucker.

I turned away from the table, Denna and Bebe with me.

"Separate them. She will lean on her friends to escape," Havoc said casually, as if it was nothing to me. A couple of the other werewolves in his pack stood. Berek, and a young male I didn't know.

Not even for the pleasure that Havoc gave would I go willingly back to Grayling. My blood pounded through my veins, heart beating hard as the fear slid through me. The thought of seeing Juniper, of being at her mercy in any way left me struggling to swallow my food. Left me knowing that despite Havoc standing between me and Loki, he didn't see Juniper as the threat she was. And so he didn't understand that she would kill me faster perhaps than even Han.

I didn't trust Loki.

"Denna," I said softly. "Upstairs. Go, there is a way out."

Denna took off without another word, her galloping gait taking her out of the room in a flash.

Bebe danced at my feet as the pack started to draw around me. I'd fought my way out of tighter spots than this one, though, and they wouldn't want to kill me.

Maybe Claire would. Her eyes glittered a little darker than the others. I smiled at her. "If I'm gone, you have a shot with him."

She did a double blink. "You'd leave him?"

"He's going to kill me. Eventually. That's what this comes down to."

The gasp that went up through the pack was immediate. I didn't know if they'd believe me, but I had to try and make them see.

"Maybe not today, maybe not tomorrow, but he will kill me," I said.

Havoc growled. "Jor told you this, didn't he?"

I was backing up, but the pack wasn't advancing. I

looked at Berek. "Ask him yourself. There is no way out of this for me. Either he kills me when the time is right or Han does."

"Then why didn't he kill Soleil?" Claire asked.

I laughed. "Maybe he liked her. He hates me. It's a mutual thing."

A snarl ripped through the room as Havoc shifted to his wolf form, and the sound tore what was left of the tension apart. I spun and bolted, still wearing his shirt. Still smelling him on me. That scent left something like regret to slide through me, but I didn't have a choice other than to leave. If I didn't leave now, I knew he'd drag me to my mother's feet.

And she would win the day. There was no way she'd actually help us. Loki had no idea what he was talking about.

All this flashed through my head as I hit the doors to the main room and rattled my way through the building.

There were no feet after me, no wolves scrambling to pull me back.

The howl of Havoc caught me, trying to pin me in place, but it didn't dig in like it had before. Was I growing immune to him?

A hand shot out and clamped down on my arms, jerking me to a stop. I spun and found myself looking up at Sven.

"I do not trust Loki either, but I cannot defy Havoc

like you can," he said as he slipped a set of keys into my hand and slung a bag over my shoulder. "Go. And I will do what I can to stave him off from going to Grayling. I have sealed the doors behind you and have bought you minutes."

He let me go as a thunderous bellow erupted behind us.

"Thank you."

"I don't want to like you, little sunshine. But you are changing the game, and so I see in you hope, that we might yet survive what the gods put into play so many years ago. If you can find Freya, she might help you."

Freya. Another of the Norse Pantheon. Did I dare? It seemed I might not have a choice since Han had gotten extra help from Hel.

I didn't have time to question his advice.

"Go."

I took him at his word. "Bebe!"

"I'm here, keep running!"

I spun, hoping Denna had found the ceiling opening. "Denna!"

"I'm here!" She loped toward us from the other direction.

I hit the key fob, and one of the SUVs parked at the front of the building blipped to life—the lights and horn going off at the same time. I reached the door of the SUV as the doors of the building behind me burst open.

The black wolf that I'd first seen in Edmonton stood on the steps, ice blue eyes locked with mine. I jerked the door of the SUV open and hopped in, Bebe right behind me, Denna crawling in from the other side.

I couldn't look back as I peeled away from Havoc. I couldn't.

Because even though I hated him—and truly, I did, okay, pretty sure I did, mostly hated him—I couldn't help but want to believe that if he had a choice in this, that if my life wasn't tied to the life of the world, that he *would* keep me safe.

"Damn it," I whispered as I powered through two sets of stop lights, weaving around the traffic that had come to a halt as if I were a normal citizen.

I should not want to turn around. And yet I felt a pull on my body, as if there were strings connecting me to Havoc.

I blinked, my vision going fuzzy for a second, an image of both brothers floating across my eyes.

Both brothers attached to me.

One by fate. One by fucking.

I gripped the steering wheel, sweat rolling down my back. "Sweet moon goddess, I'm in trouble."

13

ON THE ROAD AGAIN, TAKE THREE

Bebe was quiet as I drove at high speed, avoiding cars and slipping through stop lights, putting as much space between me and Havoc as I could.

Denna was restless, answering questions as I checked in with her. "Are you sure you're okay?" I asked for the third time. Knowing that she was not.

She shrunk in on herself. "I...I'm scared, Cin. I am not alive like I once was, and some days I barely remember what I was before being a ghoul, but I can still feel fear. It...it's my curse, I guess."

I reached over to take her hand and she recoiled from me. "Denna?"

"When you stop...I think I should go. I think I could be used against you. I'm not strong enough for this." She ran her hands over her head, as if washing her face.

Go?

I blew out a slow breath, because I couldn't be mad, I couldn't blame her for wanting to leave. "I understand, Denna. I am not safe to be around. And you're right, they might hurt you to get to me."

She started to cry, covering her face with her hands. "I'm sorry, I'm a bad friend."

"You aren't. You're scared, and you have every right to be. My life is a shit show. You didn't really know what you were getting into when you said you wanted to come with me. I didn't know it would be like this. I figured we'd be in Europe with Taini and Copper. With Martin." I wanted to give Denna comfort, but she was curled as far from me as possible, stuffed against the far wall of the car.

I rolled a window down, letting the fresh air sweep in and around us. With it came the smell of the dead, making the timing impeccable. I slowed the car, pulling off to the side. "There is a graveyard not far from here."

Denna fumbled with the door, finally getting it open, pausing in the door edge. "I want you to be okay, Cin. I want you to be happy."

I smiled at her. "And I want you to be safe, Denna. You're my friend, always. When this is over, we'll get our own bookstore, okay?"

Her lower lips trembled, and she stepped back. "I'm not a good friend. I'm sorry."

She shut the door and I waited, watching as she did her funny loping run up a slight slope and then disappeared out of sight.

I pulled back onto the road and kept driving. Wondering if Bebe would abandon me too. If she decided to leave, I wouldn't blame her. I mean, let's be honest, I had a bunch of people hunting for me, I was dealing with Norse gods, and I was destined to die, one way or another. So yeah, not exactly a fun road trip.

Bebe and I drove until I found a large box store parking lot a good hour from where we'd started. There were plenty of light stands and cars spread throughout the space, even in the back. Perfect. I needed to swap vehicles, and here I could take my pick.

"That was unexpected." Bebe said quietly. "Did you see it coming?"

I shook my head. "No. But I'm not surprised either. She's not a bad friend. She's afraid. There is a big difference."

I wondered if Bebe would want to leave too.

It wasn't until we stopped that Bebe started asking questions. "What are we doing here?"

"Swapping vehicles," I said as I dug into the pack Sven had given me. Clothing, a pair of runners, and a stack of cash that had to be at least a couple thousand dollars. That was good.

I paused, hating what I would say next, for fear she would take me up on it. "You can go too, if you want. I wouldn't blame you."

Bebe was sitting on the middle console of the SUV. "Girlfriend. Thelma and Louise. We are in it to the end, my bitch."

I laughed and the laugh caught on a sob that I stuffed down as quickly as it tried to escape my mouth. Her tiny paw patted my forearm.

"I'm with you, Cin. Remember? Ice cream and strippers, you promised me and I'm not going anywhere till I get them both. In bucket loads."

I nodded, my throat tight. "Let's get out of here."

I slid into the clothes from the pack and tucked Havoc's shirt into the bag, not wanting to think about what it meant that I was keeping it instead of leaving it in the SUV.

Nope, I was not going to think about those ice blue eyes, or the hurt that had flashed through him as he'd watched me run from him. Again.

"He hates me too," I said, more to myself than to Bebe.

Bebe snorted. "Oh please."

I glanced at her. "You don't think he hates me?"

"I don't think *you* hate *him*. I think you scare each other." Bebe shrugged. "I got some of the story out of Berek. I mean, he heard it from that Claire chick, but still, I got the goods. It goes along with what Jor said.

Havoc loved the first girl, and he couldn't keep her from dying. There's more to it than that, but you get the gist."

My eyebrows shot up. I wanted more details, but I figured there would be time for that later. That was the surprising thing about being on the run—there was plenty of time for stories.

I held my hands out to her once I'd stepped out of the SUV. She leapt to me, butting her head against my chin. "Not every friend can stick out the hard stuff, girl-friend. Doesn't make her a bad friend, just not the friend you need right now."

Her words struck right to the core of what I was feeling. "I know it. Thanks for being the friend to stick through the hard stuff."

She gave me a wink and then jumped out of my arms. "Just to be clear, I'm totally taking the best friend spot in your life. Bestest of the best friends."

I laughed softly. "Done. Escaper of boxes, sasser of sea serpents, seducer of werewolves. Who wouldn't want you for a bestie?"

She flicked her tail. "Right? Exactly. Now, let's go find us a nice car."

Nice was a relative term. And I wasn't going to do a straightforward swap like she thought. Because my brothers, Han, and even Havoc would be looking for a car or a truck. My brothers knew most of my talents, and they were well aware that I could hotwire a car.

"They can smell where we go," I said. "So we need to make our way through the parking lot, and I'm going to touch a lot of cars."

"Oh, throw them off the scent?"

"Literally." I headed for the cars closest to the SUV and let my fingers brush over the handles, trying them, and then the trunks.

More than one was unlocked, and each time Bebe would gasp. "This one?"

"Nope."

We took about fifteen minutes to walk the parking lot. I even pulled a few of my hairs out and looped them around a couple of door handles.

But it wasn't until I saw the two young men wobble out of the main doors of the big box store that I knew I had my marks.

"Hey boys, wanna give me a ride? I'll pay." I held up a hundred-dollar bill.

Two minutes later, I was in the back seat of their car, their eyes glazed with the beer they'd so obviously been drinking. Bebe shot me a look.

"It seems like a terrible idea to ride with two drunk teenagers?"

"I just want you boys to drive me around the parking lot. Let's do some donuts, how about that? Can you drift?"

"Hell to the yeah, you're crazy! Love it!" The driver slurred his words only a little less than his buddy, who was already snoring lightly on the passenger side. I reached over and patted him on the belly, my hand slipping around to his pockets, looking for...there it was. I tugged my treasure away from him while he grinned at me like a fool.

We spun around the parking lot doing sloppy donuts, Bebe shooting me weird looks, but it was important to cover a lot of ground so those tracking me would be less likely to figure out just what I'd done.

"Over there," I pointed to a docking bay. "You can drop me off over there."

"Really?" He squinted at me. "I thought you were coming home with us."

"I'm going to give you another hundred to go and sleep it off in the corner of this parking lot, okay? Without me."

Or for as long as he could stay awake. Not that I told him that part.

He pulled up to the shipping dock I'd indicated, and his car lurched to a stop as he threw on the parking brake. "You sure?"

"Yes. Thanks, kid. And when they find you, don't lie."

His eyes fuzzed further. "When what finds who do I lie to?"

"Just stick to the truth." Which I suspected would be muddied with alcohol even if it was tomorrow morning.

This was where it was going to get tricky. I opened the door. "Bebe, jump up onto that truck over there."

"The semi?" She looked at me and then grinned. "Fuck yeah, girl, you can drive a semi!"

"That I can," I murmured. "Go. Don't touch the ground."

She bounded over me and up onto the foot railing of the semi, waiting for me. I leaned out of the car, grabbed the bottom of the mirror and pulled myself over.

My unintentional getaway driver backed away, not even looking at me. He'd taken my money and was going straight back to the store to buy more booze no doubt. It wasn't great to send him off, but I'd told him to stay in the parking lot. Hopefully he listened and just parked to the side somewhere. It was the best I could do.

I grabbed the handle of the door, and it opened right up.

"How did you know it would be unlocked?" Bebe scrambled up into the truck, taking the passenger seat.

"I didn't know for sure, but I could have broken the window if needed." I set myself into the driver's seat and pulled down the visor. The keys dropped into my hands.

"Luck is turning our way!" Bebe said. "Now, how do we find this Freya chick? That's who Sven said to look for. Is she someone magic too?"

"Norse goddess, so yes, I'd guess so." If my memory served me right, she was married to Odin. Who Sven had coffee with just this morning. Maybe he'd spoken to her there?

I really didn't have a clue where to start looking, though. I knew I had ten days—nine now—where Han would be truly hunting for me—now that he'd realized that my significance to him went beyond being his fated mate.

Starting the engine of the big rig, I let it idle, warming. I had a few minutes before we took off.

I pulled out the phone that I'd taken from the kid. Not even locked. I swiped it open, went straight to the internet, and typed in 'Freya.'

A series of hits came up, mostly about the mythology attached to her. A few famous actresses had played her, but even if their security let me within fifty feet of them, I doubted they had any intel. From what I could see, there were no temples or shrines I could visit. The third page in, there wasn't a single listing that looked like it held even a slim glimmer of potential.

I didn't even tap on the shittiest of the links that came up, just kept on scrolling.

Only, it opened on its own.

Blue and white, it had a cartoon version of what had to be Freya, her breasts all but spilling out of a metal corset, her head encased in a classic Viking helmet, her long braids flung out around her.

I blinked and the image beckoned to me. Literally crooked her finger. "Did you see that?"

"See what?"

I held the phone still, hoping the image would move again. But it had only done so once. Seeing as I hadn't taken any hallucinogens, that could only mean one thing. "She knows we're coming. Maybe Sven tipped her off."

Maybe they'd already discussed this over coffee.

Yes, that felt right.

I skimmed the front page of the website. "There's a group devoted to following Freya. They hold meetings every Tuesday night. They call themselves the New Asgardians."

"Seriously? Where are they?" Bebe looked over my shoulder and snorted as I tipped the phone for her to see. "She won't look like that, will she?"

I shrugged. "Unlikely, I'm guessing, but you never know. Says they meet just outside of Coutts, Alberta. Just across the border."

I put the phone down and looked up and out the front window. A black SUV matching the one I'd driven out of the compound had pulled into the lot. I wasn't surprised. I fully expected that Havoc would have some sort of tracking device on all the vehicles. The SUV slid to a stop next to the one we'd abandoned. Berek, Claire, Havoc and one other man I didn't know stepped out of the vehicle. I cracked the window of the semi and strained my ears to hear what Havoc was saying.

"...won't be here, pick up her scent...not far ahead."

"Havoc found us," I whispered under my breath.

"Oh shit!" Bebe ducked and then peeked up over the dash. "What are we going to do?"

I looked at the phone again and the address on it. Was it a coincidence that this weird little cult of Freya was on the Canadian border of Montana, home state of the Grayling pack? No, I didn't think so either.

Something was driving me back toward my old stomping grounds, whether I wanted to go or not. At least we were headed toward the Canadian border and not directly to Grayling.

"We're going to go, nice and slow, not in a rush." I slid the truck into gear and rolled it forward, smooth as butter. I reached over to the passenger seat and grabbed the grubby hat that the previous driver had left and slid it on. As we exited the parking lot, I leaned as far back in my seat as I could, feeling Havoc's eyes swing toward me.

Working through the gears as quickly but smoothly as I could, I had the truck out and on the main road in under a minute.

"You think he suspects?" Bebe whispered as if Havoc could hear her.

I looked in the rear-view mirror. How strong were those ties between us? I didn't dare check.

Havoc was still watching the truck, eyes narrowed. Cold anger that I could feel even here, this far away from him. Because of that fucking tie between us.

I couldn't look away from him, even it was just the reflection of his dark eyes, the silver fleck catching the light.

Did he know I was in here? Despite what I'd felt earlier—what I'd seen in my head—I couldn't *feel* a bond to him. Besides, I couldn't be mate bound to both brothers, could I?

Movement drew my eye in time for me to see Havoc running for the SUV, motioning toward us.

Son of a bitch.

14

ROAD RAGE REALLY IS CATHARTIC

"He's chasing us, isn't he?" Bebe climbed over my lap to peer into the rear-view mirror. "Shit, how does he know it's you?"

I grimaced. "I...I think maybe, somehow, possibly, there's the slightest chance it's because—"

"Oh my God. Because you had two epic fucks?" Bebe turned and stared at me, her eyes narrowing. "Is that how it works?"

Of course, she hadn't been there for Sven and Havoc's discussion of trying to get the mate bond to shift. Neither of them had thought I'd be able to develop *two* mate bonds.

"I think...Sven said they were trying to make the mate bond switch from Han to Havoc. And listen, you would have banged him too—"

"Well duh. Of course I would have! But I don't have anyone trying to tie their mojo to mine."

I was working my way onto the on ramp that would take me onto Highway 84, East, sliding through the gears.

East, back toward Montana and then further north. Leave it to some crazy Canadians to start a cult following an old Norse goddess. Leave it to a Norse goddess to let them worship her once more.

"Aren't you worried that they are going to catch up to us?" Bebe leapt up to sit in the front window.

"I don't have to be worried. Havoc will catch up, I have no doubt. But this thing has two full tanks of diesel," I tapped the screen, pointing out the fuel levels, "and they'll have to stop before us to fuel up. We'll just keep going. Once we lose them, we'll switch vehicles again."

It wouldn't be as easy as I was making it out to be. I knew that. But I could swap this truck for another one at a truck stop and then ride it out. Not that switching vehicles had worked this last time. I mean, everyone seemed to have some sort of mental tracking device on me at this point. Havoc. Han. My asshole family.

I'd forgotten (not really, but it had taken a back seat for a hot minute) about my asshole family.

I should never have let it slip that I was running from them too. Because whatever abilities Han had given them, they were using them to the fullest.

Particularly the ability to track me.

"Oh shit," I breathed out the words as I looked in my rear-view again. Two large trucks were on our ass now, but not really our ass.

No, the SUV was on our ass—and the trucks were working the SUV over, slamming into it on either side and trying to flip it over.

It was closing in on midnight, and blessedly the road was mostly empty of other vehicles. A small mercy at this point.

The SUV wobbled on its tires, almost tipping over.

My wolf roared to the surface, and even my goldie got her hackles up. I could feel fear running through a bond so tenuous it was like thin filaments of spiderweb woven through and around my soul. As thin as they were, they *were* there, and they'd begun building the minute that Havoc had rescued me from my brothers. Tying me to him, and to *his* pack.

I might not like it, but that was my pack now.

We were in a good straight stretch, grass and light bush to either side of the highway. I wouldn't get another chance at this.

"Mother fuckers, don't be messing with my pack!" I snarled.

I didn't just gear down to try and catch them off guard. I pulled more to the right, so I was directly in front of one of the big trucks.

Then hit the brakes so hard I stood up in my seat, as the semi skidded and jumped along the pavement.

I split the space between the trucks and the SUV, they veered to either side of me, and I caught a glimpse of Meg's eyes.

As fast as I'd hit the brakes, I started gearing back up. My family probably thought I was in the SUV. I was close enough on the highway that it made sense if they were indeed tracking me, which at this point I had no reason to doubt.

They didn't know I could drive a semi either.

"Bebe. Hang on. We're clearing the board."

"Did you freaking think I wasn't? I got my claws so deep into this fake leather you're going to have to pry me out!" she yelled, clinging to the dashboard.

I was picking up speed, no longer going for smooth, just fast.

The trucks and the SUV were well ahead of us now, the trucks hard on either side of the SUV.

"We're going to take out the truck on the right first, Bebe. You ready?" The truck was humming under my hands as I bore down on my first target.

So stupid. I should have just pulled off at the next exit, leaving Havoc and Berek and Claire to fight off my family on their own.

But my wolf had claimed them all by claiming Havoc. What a fucking mess.

With gritted teeth and a twisted snarl on my face, I

hit the truck on the right at full speed, catching the back bumper on my front end. Cranking my wheel to the right, I drove it off the road. The truck hit the guardrail and bounced back in front of me, broadside.

I didn't slow down, not for a second.

The impact of the semi on the back quarter panel of the truck was minimal to me, even if the screech of metal ripping through the air was anything but. Listening to the chorus of crunching steel, I pushed down harder on the gas pedal.

The truck was stuck to the front of the semi long enough that I was able to see everyone in it.

Shipley was driving. He looked up, and I smiled and waved at him. "Hey motherfucker!"

He lost color. I let my wolf rise within so he could see her through my eyes. So he would know how serious I was about protecting those in the SUV.

Shipley wasn't family, not anymore. He was just a wolf trying to hurt those I would protect with my life.

I jerked the wheel to the right, and then sharply back to the left, flinging Shipley and the truck away from me, across the middle of the highway, so that the truck spun out, facing the wrong direction.

The second truck was still molesting the SUV, seemingly oblivious to its partner's fate. Or maybe the other driver didn't care about Shipley and the others. That was more likely.

"Yes!" Bebe shrieked. "Let's get 'em!"

The semi responded beautifully, picking up speed quickly as I moved into position behind the second truck.

Apparently, they *had* been paying attention though, because they shot forward and got ahead of the SUV, avoiding being rammed from behind.

"Cowards," I snarled. I blew my horn at the SUV. I needed Havoc out of my way.

Except he wasn't moving. Not one inch.

Just like putting himself between me and Loki. I tried very hard not to feel warmed by the action.

"What are we going to do?" Bebe yelled.

There was a sudden and steady *pop pop pop* of gunfire. The windshield of the SUV shattered, and glass shards flew back toward us.

Shit fuck damn. I knew from experience that those bullets would be loaded with silver. The SUV wobbled —whoever was driving had been hit.

My heart clenched as pain burst through the spiderweb bonds. Havoc had been hit. So had another pack member that I didn't know.

The SUV slowed down until it was right next to us, on my left. "Bebe. We are going to jump."

"What the fuck are you saying?" she shrieked.

I couldn't look away from the road. "Those are silver bullets. They've hit the driver. They're in trouble, and I know that if I jump onto the SUV...my family will see me."

"And how in the shit balls will that help us?" Bebe was still in shriek mode.

I couldn't blame her. "They'll come for me, then, Bebe. I can slide off the SUV and they'll come for me."

"May I remind you that they caught you last time? And tortured you and stuffed me in a box?" I hadn't thought she could go an octave higher, but I'd been wrong.

"I know. But it will save the others." I didn't have time to remind her that I'd been about to bang Havoc in that car. We'd been distracted for obvious reasons. Same as Meg had been used as a distraction to get me to Grayling.

My brothers knew me, just like I knew them. They knew the best way to pull me in was to threaten someone I cared about. Something was wrong with me for taking the bait. But I couldn't just leave Havoc and the others to face my family alone, any more than I could have left Bebe behind in that basement, or Denna to fend for herself. I might not stand up for myself, but I'd damn well do it for someone under my protection.

I maneuvered the rig up to the right side of the SUV. "Bebe, hang onto me!"

"Holy shit, holy shit, holy shit, holy shit!" she was screaming as she leapt up onto my left shoulder and dug in with front and back feet. Her claws burrowed in and under my skin, but I barely felt it as I flung the door open, balancing so I could have one hand still on the steering wheel.

This was going to take good timing. Another quick glance at the empty highway. At least no one else would get smashed when I did this.

A breath.

I pushed off in a leap as I shoved the steering wheel to the right, steering the semi away from the SUV, toward the grassy side of this stretch of the highway.

There was a moment I thought I wasn't going to make it. The SUV kind of slid under me. Front end, middle of the roof, and then I was landing on the very back portion. I flattened myself onto the metal.

There was a thump underneath, and it only took me a split second to understand they were shooting at *me*.

"Idiots!" I yelled.

The skylight opened and Berek peered out. "Jesus!"

"Just Cin will do!" I yelled back. They had guns. That changed my plan immediately. "Give me a gun, preferably something with a scope!"

He stared up, and I glared back at him.

The second truck holding my other siblings, which had been conveniently absent, took that moment to show back up, slamming into the side of the SUV. My body went careening along the roof.

"Get into the SUV, Bebe!" I yelled as I grabbed the edge of the sunroof to stop myself from sliding. My legs dangled off the right side. Bebe scrambled up and across the roof before diving into the SUV.

"Havoc's bleeding!" she yelled up at me.

Nothing I could do about it right then, and I'd already known he'd taken a hit. He was still driving, so he couldn't be bleeding too badly. I hoped.

Richard was driving the truck to the left side of us, his eyes flicking from the road to the SUV. Kieran sat in the passenger seat. He gave me a dead-eyed stare and took a finger and made a slashing motion across his throat.

"Oh please," I muttered. "Grow the fuck up. Like I don't know you want to kill me."

I adjusted my hold and pulled myself up into a crouch on the roof. "Gun, Berek!"

A gun was slid up onto the roof, a nice 30-06 bolt action Winchester with a solid scope. That would do.

I stood up in a single smooth motion. "Hold my ankles, Berek!"

"Jesus," he muttered again. But he did as I said and grabbed hold of my ankles, steadying me as I stared down the scope.

I took out the gun in Kieran's hand first. The weapon exploding all over the place. It didn't slow them down.

Richard was driving, so he was the one who was going to get it. I had to do it.

"Right through the eye," I whispered. Staring down

the scope, I could see every detail of his face. The tension around his eye, the tight lines around his mouth.

I blinked, and his face smoothed to that of the brother who'd lifted me on his shoulders as a child. The brother who'd carried me safe on his back while sledding down the steepest of hills. The brother who had been ready to defy Juniper to keep me and Shipley safe, hiding us when her rage got out of hand when our dad wasn't there to protect us.

How had it all changed?

When had it all changed?

Juniper had done it to him, filling him with Ogre beer and putting Kieran in charge in his place the minute she'd gotten Mars out of the picture. The minute that she had the pack under her thumb.

A tiny, miniscule piece of me wondered if he could be dragged back, away from my mother. Saved from Grayling.

He'd contacted Havoc, to come and get me away from Kieran back at that farmhouse.

"Fuck," I whispered. I adjusted my aim and shot out the front tire, then the back in quick succession, sending the truck spinning out of control. I turned to see the second truck with Shipley in it had miraculously survived, but it was limping down the highway, in no shape to catch up to us.

I stood there for a moment longer, the wind tearing at my clothes and hair, Berek holding me tight.

I closed my eyes as memories I'd thought were long forgotten surged through me.

Richard teaching me to swim.

Protecting me from Shipley's teasing.

Helping me shoot for the first time.

Richard laughing with Mars.

Then something soured and changed, the memories taking a tumble into darkness.

Richard beating me unconscious.

Threatening me.

Belittling me.

Shooting me at the river—

"Get in." Berek tugged on my ankles, snapping me out of the memories that were drowning me as surely as the river would have. Dropping into to a crouch, I flicked the safety on the gun and then handed it in to him. Then I slipped into the SUV through the sunroof. I wanted to look to Havoc first, but forced myself not to.

Claire sat in the far back, her eyes wide and her face chalky.

"You hit?" I asked.

She shook her head. "No, Havoc and JJ were hit."

"I'll survive," Havoc said. "It's a scratch."

His voice, the timber of it soothed my fear for him. Stupid bonds. I looked to the other werewolf, the one I didn't know.

JJ was flat out on the back seat, a hand to his right shoulder, blood seeping out past his fingers. He was the other one I'd felt through the bonds. "It burns," he moaned.

I slid into the back seat, jammed between the driver's seat and JJ's head. "They use silver bullets."

Claire clapped her hands to her mouth. Because silver poisoning was not something werewolves typically survived from. Me, I'd done it twice now, but that was unusual.

"Let me see it." I pried his fingers away from the wound, and before he could protest, jammed one finger into it, feeling for the bullet. Hoping it wasn't in shards.

He arched up, thrashing. I held his arm with one hand and Claire held his legs.

"We have to get it out, JJ," I said. "So stop being a pussy and hold still."

"Hey, I'd be tougher than that," Bebe leapt back from the front seat and landed on JJ's belly. "I wouldn't scream and cry."

A tight smile slid over my face. "I can feel the tip of the bullet. It didn't shatter at least. Berek, you got a knife?"

JJ let out a low moan. "Please don't."

Bebe walked up his belly to his chest and swatted his face. No claws, I noticed, but she still drew his attention. "I didn't leap from a moving semi to listen to you cry about how scary this is. Grow some balls, boy."

"He can't hear you, Bebe," I said as I took the pocketknife Berek handed back from the front seat.

Sirens in the distance, JJ's shaking breaths, and the little gasps from Claire as I made my first cuts. My world narrowed to getting the bullet out. It wouldn't save him, but it would buy us the time we needed to give him a chance.

And time was everything when it came to life and death.

I made my next cut, opening the wound up a little further so I'd be able to dig around. JJ about leapt out of his skin. I crawled up so I sat on his chest, pinning him to the seat of the SUV, my left hand on the side of his head and my right hand free to do road trip surgery.

My wolf was at the forefront. I let out a low growl, pushing some of my strength into him to help him through this. He calmed, his breathing evening out.

"Three more cuts." I made them quickly, dragging the blade through the meat of his shoulder. "Be glad it didn't go into your belly."

Pinned as he was, given a boost from my reserves, he finally lay still enough for me to get business done. But no one could lie still and quiet while a bullet was being pulled out of them.

I jammed my finger into the wound, hooking the

edge of the bullet with my fingernail as I struggled to drag it out.

JJ screamed.

I felt the car slow. "Keep driving! We need to get him to Roosevelt General Hospital. It's in Bozeman, Montana. They pulled silver out of me, and I survived. They'll help him."

Hopefully the same doctor was there. I'd been so sick from the silver that I honestly couldn't remember his name, and when I came to, clear-headed after a few days, I'd run.

Claire gasped. "You survived?"

"Yes." I didn't look at her as the car sped up. Instead, I went back to my surgery on JJ. The bullet was stuck good, which left me only one option. I let go of his head. "Stay," I growled, pushing my own alpha power into the words. He went stock still.

I let go of his head and picked up the knife with my left hand. Using the tip and my fingernail, I finally managed to grab the bullet—like using chopsticks to pick up a fucking marble—and dragged it out of him.

I glanced at JJ, glad he'd managed to stay still. Nope, that wasn't quite right, he'd passed out.

"He's out. Berek, you need to drive so I can take the bullet out of Havoc."

"I won't die from silver poisoning," Havoc said, the sound of his deep voice soothing me. It was the first time he'd spoken, and I realized that I'd been afraid he was worse off than JJ.

"Oh, so you'd like to keep the bullet as a souvenir?" Bebe bounded up between the front seats. "That is the epitome of stupid. You *are* a werewolf, aren't you?"

Havoc grunted. "I am also immortal. There is nothing in this world that can kill me."

Bebe sat down and wrapped her tail around her legs, prim as could be. "Even Achilles had his heel, big boy."

I grinned. "She has a point. They are working with Han. How do you know he didn't lace the bullets with something that *would* hurt you? Maybe something Hel gave him."

Claire gasped again. "Is that possible?"

I moved to the middle of the car so I could look Havoc in the eye. "Pull over, let Berek drive. We can stuff JJ into the third-row seat with Claire."

I gotta be honest, I thought he was going to argue.

But he pulled over to the side of the highway as a couple of police cars raced past us, going the other direction.

Berek slid over to the driver's seat, I helped Claire get JJ into the back of the SUV, and Havoc let himself into the back seat.

I should have realized he'd agreed too easily.

His hands snaked out and grabbed me, twisting me

around so my back was to his chest, jerking me against his body as he slid into the seat. "Drive. Berek."

The smell of blood was on him, but he wasn't kidding when he'd said it was just a scratch. The shot had skimmed his bicep, and cut through the first layers of skin, but that was it.

"Yes, boss," Berek said. "To the hospital she said?"

"For now."

My arms were wrapped around my body, my back pinned to his chest. It was like my very own straight jacket. Once I was immobilized, Havoc adjusted himself, so he leaned against the door.

I looked back at Claire. She wasn't making eye contact with me. But she didn't hold back her thoughts now that I was all wrapped up, unable to move.

"It'll be your fault if JJ dies." She wiped sweat from his brow.

I snorted. "Really? Not the person who shot him? You want to take cheap shots, but I know that you signed up to help this one," I thumped my head backward into Havoc's chest. "And with that comes danger and possible death. Am I right?" I snorted again. "Never mind, I know I'm right. And to be clear, your JJ would be dead in an hour if I hadn't pulled that bullet out of him. Something you weren't about to do."

Claire ducked her head, unable to refute that. Because, as hard as my words were, they were the stone-cold truth.

Bebe hopped back to me. "You want me to claw his eyes out to make him let you go?"

Havoc growled and the sound vibrated through me in a most pleasant way. I blew out a careful breath, controlling the sensations his fucking growl unleashed in me.

"No, I'm going to take a nap while Berek drives." I gave a big fake yawn. "Let me know when the poison makes Havoc pass out."

And I closed my eyes.

I'd fully intended to pretend to sleep. I mean, shit, the adrenaline of flight and fight should have been enough to keep me awake for hours.

But the warmth from Havoc was too much, and the feeling of his arms around me resonated with both my halves.

In my mind's eye, the goldie fucking wagged her tail, tongue lolling out, reveling in his touch and the safety he offered.

And my wolf? She lied down next to the goldie and closed her eyes. But not before she wagged her fucking tail.

I was well and truly screwed.

15

NIGHTMARES SUCK ASS—
ESPECIALLY WHEN YOU'RE AWAKE

Sleep crashed over me, dragging me under. Everything had eaten away at my reserves— the memories of Richard, the shifting, the running, the pain of realizing I'd tied myself to a new pack. "Look at you go, little wolf."

I blinked at the man with the dark hair, braids, and the side of his head shaved. "Tyr, right?"

He tipped his head at me. "Yes. You are fighting many fronts. And now you head for Freya?"

I frowned at him. "Bad idea?"

His smile was fleeting as he shrugged. "It will depend on her mood. When you go before her, remember that she loves a love story—the harder the better."

He was gone before I could ask another question, my sleep settling into normal dreams of the past and the present. Of my fears catching up to me, glittering scales wrapping around my body, Kieran laughing at me as Juniper shot Havoc with a silver-loaded gun.

I jerked awake when we stopped for fuel a few hours later, sweat and fear chasing me from my dreams.

Bebe was laughing as I woke up. "What?"

"You drooled in your sleep. And talked too."

I wanted to laugh with her, but my mind was stuck in the darkness of the dreams. Seeing Havoc slump in my dreams, blood spilling from wounds I couldn't heal...

I didn't want to think about why it had bothered me so much. I mean...we were on the run from Han and my family. The injuries were going to add up. Even if I could see that his wound was already healed.

"No silver poisoning for you?" I asked.

Claire answered. "Silver doesn't bother him. And because we are tied to him, it bothers us less than if we were not."

A gift from him to his pack. One of safety. Unlike what Han had given at least Kieran. The ability to track me.

Havoc's arms tightened around me, and I let out a breath that pushed some of the darkness back. He was alive—and so was I. That would have to be enough for now.

I forced a smile to my lips. "As for the drooling, I

mean, come on, I'm apparently part golden retriever now. What do you want?"

She rolled her eyes. "Havoc, are you going to let her go?"

"No." he didn't so much as budge. "Every time I loosen my hold on her, she runs."

I tipped my head back so I could look up into his face—sort of. "I have to pee."

He stared down at me, his eyes looking deep into mine, trying to see if I was lying, the scar across his one eye tightening.

I was not lying, my bladder was right full.

"Let's go."

He released my straight jacket hold and slid himself out the door first. I followed him, and he immediately took hold of my hand.

I couldn't have this. Because he wasn't wrong. I would run again. I had to.

"Oh, that's sweet. You're into PDA." I wiggled my fingers, lacing them through his, fully expecting him to pull away.

"I don't know what a PDA is, and this is not sweet. You are slippery as any eel."

I had the urge to tell him I was no eel, but I never had the chance. Bebe stepped in, saying the thing that only he and I could hear.

"I'd think you'd say as slippery as a wet pussy,

seeing as you've indulged yourself in her twice now." She strutted ahead of us as Havoc actually stumbled. "By the stink of it, the bathroom is this way. I'm going around back, no way I'm going in there."

His hand tightened further on mine, but I heard the hitch in his breathing and knew that I wasn't the only one thinking about those two encounters that Bebe's words had dredged up.

Wet. Hot. Frantic with need and want.

I blew out a slow breath, doing my best not to imagine him naked. "Not working," I muttered.

"What is not working?" He tugged me in the direction of the bathrooms that were set around the side of the building.

"Not thinking of you naked. It's difficult." I let out another slow breath as I worked to replace sexy images with decidedly unsexy images.

Mud. Trees. Bears. Squirrels. Car exhaust. Lamp shades.

We reached the woman's bathroom and I moved to go in. "No."

He dragged me toward the men's bathroom. "With me. I'm not letting you go."

"Seriously?" I spluttered. Damn him. I'd actually not been planning to duck out. "There is no way out of the bathroom. One door. No windows that I can see."

"I don't trust you," he snarled as he pushed the

men's room door open with his shoulder and dragged me in behind him.

Awesome.

The smell was intense and immediate. I was shocked that I hadn't smelled it outside.

Piss.

All the piss in the world had to be in here, pooled at my feet to make sure I didn't miss it. I gagged, which only made me drag the smell in deeper.

Havoc's face was an instant mask of irritation, his nose crinkling.

"Girl's bathroom." I gagged again as I dragged him backward and across to the other door. It was a mark in his favor that he didn't fight me on it.

Then again, I had no doubt his nose was almost as sensitive.

The women's bathroom held no smell of piss, not even a whisper. There was a faint scent of lilac, maybe from someone's perfume. The smell of toothpaste and hair spray.

But no piss, thanks all that was holy.

Of course, there were women inside.

Two of them gave little gasps as Havoc followed me into the handicap stall. The giggles that followed were no doubt because of what they thought was happening. Or was going to happen.

"Can I have my hand back while I pee at least?" I managed to untangle my fingers from him.

He didn't even turn around. Just stared at me while I peed.

At least I didn't have performance anxiety and could empty my bladder.

Finished, I cheekily offered my hand to him.

"Wash," he growled, following me out to the sinks.

All washed, freshly peed out, and with the promise of him wrapping me up tight in his arms again, in the SUV, I didn't mind him dragging me along.

Contentment was a funny thing to feel in this particular situation.

Oh crap, it was happening. I recognized a faint echo of what I'd felt with Han when I'd first met him. A desire to stay. A desire to be loved. A desire for a mate who would protect me from the monsters and keep me warm during the cold winter nights.

But Havoc was one of the monsters. I had to remember that part. He would benefit from my death. Maybe he didn't want to kill me today, but what happened after the dead moon rose and fell? What if there was no other way out of this but to see me dead when the time was right?

Just like Jor had said.

And *that* realization burst the little happy bubble that had started forming in my head, giving my hormones and wolf instincts a good shake.

Havoc was no more for me than I was for Han. I

was just a pawn in this game between the brothers, in this game of will the world end, or will it not.

"Into the car." He tugged me forward and I went, sliding onto the seat and moving to the far side.

Bebe shot in through the door just as he was shutting it. "Were you seriously going to try and leave me?"

I held out a hand to her, and she shimmied close to me. "No. I wouldn't have let them leave without you."

"What's wrong?" She turned her head sideways. "You were happy when you left the car. And now it's like a thundercloud is hanging over your head. What the fuck did you do?" She turned on Havoc for that last part.

He reached across and grabbed my hand, clamping down on it. He said nothing to Bebe.

Bebe looked at me. I just shook my head at first, but then I figured, what the hell? Did it matter if I said the words out loud? Probably not.

"Look, realizations hit at different points in our lives, right? Like that 'aha' moment that Oprah always talked about."

She bobbed her head in agreement. "Sure, my mom talked about her and her show. So yeah, okay, go on."

I blew a little raspberry. "I just realized I was feeling happy for reasons that weren't real—for something that's so far from good or safe, it's stupid it was even a possibility in my head. Okay? It's a bit deflating. Havoc isn't here to protect me, Bebe. You know that. I forgot for a moment."

I thought I felt Havoc's body tense at my words, but it was so subtle I couldn't be sure.

"Oh," Bebe slumped in my lap. "Yeah. It's easy to forget when we're all running from the same people."

I leaned back in my seat, not really caring that everyone in the car could hear me as I added, "I'm just a pawn, Bebe. That's it."

And before there could be any more discussion, we were back on the road with Berek driving, taking us well past the speed limit. Claire sat in the third row back seat with JJ.

JJ who was holding up well. Whatever strength he got from being in Havoc's pack was keeping him alive.

Me, I was stuck in the middle with Havoc. Bebe sliding to sit between us. Because she was that good of a friend.

My stomach growled and Claire handed me a medium-sized cooler over the seats. "Here. We brought food."

I opened the cooler, took out the chicken leg and thigh and started in on it, not bothering to tear the meat off the bone, but eating it whole.

Claire tsked at me. "That's not very lady like."

Bebe reached up and pulled some meat off the bone for herself. "You sure it's good to eat the bones?"

"If I'm careful." I said around a mouthful. "I need the calories."

I ate until my belly was full, then did something that shocked even me. I stripped out of my clothes, feeling Havoc's eyes on my bare skin.

"What are you doing?" Claire asked. "Oh, those scars...they're so ugly!"

Yup, she definitely wanted Havoc.

"Silver bullets," I said. "They leave a mark."

And before she could ask any other questions, I shifted into my golden form and curled up on the seat furthest from Havoc. I tucked my nose under my tail and closed my eyes.

Was it weird that I felt safer in my golden retriever body? Maybe a little. But I wasn't feeling all that good about being next to Havoc on two legs.

Bebe tucked herself into the center of my tightly curled body, her face near one of my ears.

"You realized what exactly? Because I don't think it was just that other bit you said. There's something more, isn't there?"

"Mate bond kicking in. Makes me want to stay with him. Makes me think he's safe." That was the last thing I needed to do.

I had to be strong enough to get away from him for a fourth and final time. Which meant I needed to sleep and eat—and then sleep some more to conserve my energy. I knew we were still hours away from the hospital that sat on the outskirts of the Grayling pack territory. Bozeman was a five- or six-hour drive from the Canadian border.

I didn't know how much of that I'd be on foot, so I had to be prepared to run hard and fast, especially since everyone who wanted to kill me had a bead on me. I checked in on those bonds.

Han was the farthest away, headed back north where I'd felt him before.

My brothers were behind us, struggling to catch up.

The bonds to Havoc's pack trembled as I ran my thoughts across them.

A low moan from JJ tore my thoughts from my own situation.

"He'll make it?" Claire asked Havoc.

"I don't know," Havoc said. "Unlikely."

I snorted. He was wrong. I wasn't going to try and correct him.

"But he's fierce," Claire whispered. "He...was willing to come after her. Take her down."

Havoc's low growl silenced her. "Then he came on the wrong hunt."

"He's new to the pack," Claire said. "He doesn't understand. Not yet."

JJ would make it; I was pretty certain anyway. His heartbeat sounded steady to my ears, his breathing slow and even. Sleeping was good for him too, helping him conserve his energy.

The fact that JJ had wanted me dead didn't matter, not really. I wasn't really a part of their pack—I'd just gotten in by fucking their alpha. Those new bonds were slender and could still be cut.

Something I'd done once before. The sensation of cutting yourself out of a pack was...terrible. But I would do it again.

Because if I could use those bonds to find them, they could do the same. And I'd have to sever whatever bond my siblings had resurrected between us too.

Berek's voice interrupted my thoughts, mostly because he hadn't said anything this whole time.

"Our ferocity is not measured by the size of our teeth or claws, Claire, but by the way we protect those we love. That is something we live by. You know this."

I lifted my head, staring at Berek's profile. Seeing a little of my stepfather in him. Mars had been a compassionate man with the heart to lead instead of the steel clawed grip of so many of the alphas.

Berek's words resonated deeply in me, if circumstances had been different, I knew he would have been an alpha worth following.

It *would* have been a pack worth being a part of.

Berek tapped his hand on the steering wheel. "That is what you told me, Boss, the first time we met. I believed you then, and I believe it now."

Chills swept through me.

Havoc had said *that*?

"Good," Havoc rumbled. "Because it's only going to get more dangerous from here on out. This golden retriever is, I'm quite sure, planning another escape."

16

FLIGHT 101, PERMISSION FOR TAKE-OFF

Bebe tucked in even closer to me. "Jesus, is he a mind reader now?"

I didn't answer her. I wished we could still speak mind to mind. That would have been super handy. I could have told her that I was indeed planning an escape.

To be fair, it was pretty clear that she already knew.

So did Havoc. Obviously.

The drive went on and on.

And the whole time I worked at cutting my ties to the pack. They weren't tight yet, so it was easier than cutting my ties to the Grayling pack had been.

The method for pulling it off is simple in theory. You have to seek within yourself the feelings that you have for each member you have made a connection to.

For me that was only a few. Havoc. Claire. Berek. JJ. Sven.

Yes, even Sven. He was their mage, I realized. Most packs had one. He helped with protective wards, healings, and other things that many wolves couldn't do.

I went with the easy ones first. Berek. Claire. JJ.

The gossamer threads were visible to me behind my eyes, and I whimpered as I cut myself loose. Because even though the ties were loose, destroying them hurt like a fiery brand being jammed into my side.

Mild compared to how I'd had to excise myself from Grayling all those years ago.

Bebe kept butting her head into mine. "Are you okay?"

"Yes," I'd whisper every time.

I didn't think Havoc would know what I was doing. At least not yet. He might feel me cut my ties to him, though. We'd find out soon enough.

I started on the ties to Sven and then paused. He'd tried to help me. He'd sent me to Freya. I slid away from the viridescent threads that bound us together, deciding to leave them for now.

Which meant I had to untie myself from Havoc next.

I'd done what I could to remove Han from me. I didn't think there was much more I could do short of actually killing him.

Because that's the truth of a pack bond. You had to have someone on the other side that wanted you in the pack for some reason. It was why JJ and Claire were the easiest to cut loose. They didn't want me in the pack.

They did, but only because they had to. It was an enforced loyalty of sorts.

Han did still want a connection to me in his own twisted way. Which was why the bond to him was still there. I took a few experimental stabs at loosening it. And while I could remove a few threads, I could see that whatever fate or magic had bound us together, I wasn't going to be able to cut it away. So I covered it back up, muffling the connection as best I could.

The threads tying me to Havoc were the thickest in my mind, thicker even than those between me and Han. They shimmered and glittered in different shades of blue and green, braided over and over one another to make a cable of a connection between us. This was no simple thread.

This looked like my connection to my pack in Grayling. A bond that had taken a lifetime to create, and yet it had grown in only a few short days.

Fuck.

I worried at the connection, as if I were biting through it. While I did it, I made myself think of all the reasons why it would never work. He was immortal. He was a Norse god. He wanted to kill me. His brother wanted to kill me.

I was a golden retriever, not a wolf.

I shook my head and struggled to breathe as I fought the bonds. As each strand fell away from the cable connection between us.

He didn't love me. Fuck, he didn't even like me.

He didn't care if I was hurt, as long as I didn't die until he wanted me to die.

Maybe some of those things were lies, but I needed to believe them to make this happen. To cut myself free.

I made my way through all the strands of blue and green, finally snapping the last one.

The pain was sharp, the relief that followed it a cooling balm.

So I thought. I readjusted myself, checking for any other unwanted bonds.

That connection between Havoc and me? Underneath the thick cable of blue and green was a straight bar of solid gold.

Like a pipe, or a river of gold flowing between us. And even as I watched, the other threads *regrew* to cover the gold, hiding it from me.

I didn't understand how that could be. There wasn't a single tie that I hadn't been able to break between myself and the Grayling pack. Even my connection to my mother had been removable.

Sure, Han's bond hadn't been extinguished either, but it hadn't regrown. I quickly checked in and found it as I'd left it: sickly, silver, and as small as I could make it. But still there.

Fuck it all! I snarled, eyes still closed, teeth bared. But of course, everyone thought I was growling in my sleep.

So be it.

I tried again. And again. But every time I cut through the bonds between Havoc and me, they came back.

I could not fathom why.

In the end, I had to settle for masking the bond between us, the way I'd masked the bond between Han and me, covering it with other things in my mind. I coated it as if I were painting it black, hiding all the colors. That, at least, seemed to hold.

The mental work exhausted me, and I finally fell into a deep sleep.

"Hey, wake up," Bebe whispered.

We'd arrived at the hospital.

I blinked and sat up, stretching in a solid downward dog.

I looked through the window at the shadowy stars. Still nighttime, but hard to say how close we were to dawn.

Berek was already out and around the back of the

SUV, gathering up JJ and carrying him toward the emergency room.

Claire slipped out after them, leaving me with just Havoc and Bebe.

It was time to dig into my bag of tricks and pray to whatever gods would listen that I'd be able to swing this one last—hopefully last—escape.

I slipped out of my four legs, and back to two, which of course left me naked.

"Hand me my clothes." I pointed to the bundle at his feet. I didn't want to touch him. It was likely that every touch between us would strengthen our connection.

Havoc glanced at the clothes. "Get them yourself."

Of course that would have me bending over his knee, bare ass pointed up at him. Heat flared through me, the desire to go for just one more round intense and demanding.

"Bebe, please grab my clothes for me," I said.

She scooted over his thigh closest to us, flashed him her butthole as she bent down and grabbed my clothes in her mouth and dragged them back to me.

"You're afraid to touch me suddenly?" he said. Calm as could be.

I shrugged. "Maybe I just know that if I bend my ass over your knee, Bebe's going to get a show she didn't pay for."

Bebe laughed as I grabbed my clothes.

Havoc didn't laugh. I avoided his gaze. It was bad enough that I could feel the weight of his eyes on me, roving across my exposed skin. It felt like he was doing it with his hands. Leave it to him to touch me without lifting a finger.

"Who shot you?" he asked.

"My brothers." It was no secret. "They tried to kill me about ten years ago. Shot me full of holes and dumped me in a river."

His growl was immediate, and he shifted toward me. I put up my hand. "No touching."

He stopped moving, but he didn't stop with the questions. "How did you survive?"

"Hunters found me," I said as I finished pulling on the clothes, hiding the scars away. "I helped them dig the bullets out, and then they dragged me to the hospital. Good men. Hard to find around here."

"Humans?"

"Yes." At least, I thought they were. At the time my senses had been muddled from the poisoning of the silver.

Shit, they could have been fairies for all I knew.

"This hospital has dealt with shifters for many years. Mars set it all up before he...died." There, I said it. He hadn't gone missing. Juniper had him killed, I was sure of it. "To make sure we had a place to go to when we were injured beyond what we could heal on our own."

"JJ won't make it," Havoc said.

I snorted and now fully dressed, pressed myself against the door on my side of the SUV. "Goes to show how little you know. His heartbeat was strong. He'll make it. I gave him some of my energy."

"Why would you want him to, now that you know he wanted you dead?"

I shrugged. "I have a lot of people who want me dead, Havoc. Haven't you noticed? I mean, hell, you're one of them. I just need to survive. I don't have time to go on the offensive. You know?"

The soft meow of a cat turned my head toward the open back of the SUV.

I blinked a few times because it could not be. It was..."Impossible."

Bebe leapt up and wove her way to the third row. "Hey. There's a great big gray cat out here."

"I have a name, thank you very much."

That was the other cat speaking.

"Martin!" I launched myself over the seats. Havoc didn't try to grab me, shockingly enough.

I all but fell onto the pavement outside as I bent to scoop up my cat—only...His voice, it was as familiar as if it had been torn from my memories. "Martin, that's not your name, is it?"

"Oh, my girl! I wanted to tell you for so long. But that's part of a curse, or at least mine. To be bound and forgotten, to be hidden from those I would protect."

Mars. Martin was Mars.

I started to cry as I held him tight, probably too tightly, but he didn't fight to get away. All this time, I hadn't known, but Mars—as Martin—was the one who'd saved me that night in the river. He'd brought the hunters to me and stayed by my side while I lay dying in the hospital. "Mars. How...I don't understand how you're here!"

"Denna," he said. "She found us and said you were going to head back this way. Knowing you, I figured you'd be at the hospital sooner or later. And I could sense you getting closer. The bond of father and daughter is always there. Love doesn't lie, my girl."

I laughed through the sobs. All along, I'd had him with me. Love didn't lie. Our bond had been there all along, lasting even beyond death. Or a strange shift of forms.

A paw tapped my calf, and I crouched to address Bebe. "This is Mars. He...I thought he was dead, but he was you know, cursed. Like you."

He dropped out of my arms to the ground and butted his head against Bebe's—cat greetings I supposed. "You've been looking after my daughter too. Thank you."

"She's my bestie." Bebe stared hard at him. "This is kinda weird. How did you get cursed by Petunia too?"

"It's complicated. Come, we have to get you to

Freya. Tyr spoke with me in a dream. He told me we need to get you there."

Tyr. The same man who'd been speaking to me.

"No." Havoc went to clamp a hand on me, and I scooted sideways, avoiding him.

Two cats at my feet, Havoc in front of me. "Why not?"

"Because she is not the answer, she will only complicate things," Havoc said.

I stared hard at him. I could lie. I could try to weasel my way out of this. But with him, I wanted to be...honest. Maybe it was because of the ties to me. Maybe it was because running from him was a lot of damn work.

I didn't want to admit that there were any actual feelings involved with this sudden need to be honest.

I held his eyes. "Sven told me to go to Freya. Did you know that? When I fought going to Juniper."

Havoc jerked as if I'd slapped him. "What?"

"Sven told me to get to Freya. So that leaves us with a few options—you help me get to her, you come with me, or I go by myself. Up to you. I've escaped you three times already; don't think I can't do it again."

What was I doing? This was insane. I didn't want him with me.

Fuck yes, I did. I mean, literally *fuck*. But I told myself it made logical sense too. If he was with me, I could keep one person off my ass.

Havoc took a step toward me, and I stepped back. "Why don't you want me touching you now?"

"Tried to cut the bonds to him, did you?" Mars chuckled. "That's going to be a problem. But she's right, boyo, she can slip away from you. I taught her every skill I could. You won't find another alpha female who's her equal."

Havoc looked over his shoulder at the hospital. His jaw ticked and that scar across his eye tightened. Would he leave his pack to come with me alone?

I didn't know if I should keep trying to convince him. Or just run.

"Let's go," he finally said. "I will take you to Freya, and once you see that she's not going to help, we will do it my way. We will go to Juniper and convince her to help."

Mars let out a pained meow at the mention of Juniper's name, but otherwise said nothing.

"She will kill me. Try to fuck and then kill you. Skin Bebe. Destroy anyone and anything that has any attachment to me." I spoke plainly in the hopes he'd understand. "Going to her is not worth it."

He took a step toward me, and I forced myself to hold my ground. "She won't hurt you."

A promise I was sure he wouldn't be able to keep. I shook my head. "You don't know her."

Havoc lifted a hand as if he'd touch my face, then

thought better of it. "I don't have to know her. She won't hurt you."

I didn't agree, and he took note. He motioned at the SUV. "Get in. The others will find a different way back to the pack."

The screech of tires behind us had me spinning around, two cop cars. But it was not cops inside the vehicles. No doubt they'd been stolen from the accident site.

The bonds to my brother lit up like roman candles on Halloween night.

"No. The car's not going to do much. We need something better." Which meant we were going with the escape plan I'd been turning around in my head, only now it involved Havoc.

I felt Mars turn. "They aren't the boys you raised, Mars. They aren't."

Maybe Richard. Maybe Shipley. My heart whispered that two of the brothers could be brought back.

Maybe.

The three vehicles that had slid into the parking lot, drifting around the corner, came to a stop.

My brothers stepped out of the trucks. Meghan was nowhere to be seen.

What was it like for Mars to see them after all these years? "Even if they could hear you, you won't get through to them. They'll never believe you are who you say you are."

"I know." The pain in those two words was almost more than I wanted to hear.

"Bebe. Go to Havoc." I bent and scooped up Mars, holding him in one arm as I took off running toward the hospital.

Havoc had no choice but to follow.

"They are coming! They have guns!" Bebe yelled.

That was what I was hoping for. The plan I'd put together for Havoc and his pack would work just as well on my brothers. I chose not to wonder where Meg was—had Han taken her to his side?

Was that who he'd been fucking?

I swallowed the nausea that rose with that thought. Not because I wanted him—fuck no—but because Meg didn't deserve to be cut up into pieces after he was done with her.

I squeezed through the automatic doors that led into the emergency room before they had time to fully open. Havoc was right behind me, Bebe clinging to his shoulder.

"You can't be in here with animals!" a woman yelled at us.

"Leaving!" I yelled back.

I caught a glimpse of Berek, saw Havoc motioning to him to stay with the others, protect them.

Protect those they loved.

I knew this hospital well. I'd spent a solid week here after the river incident.

Which made finding my way to the stairs that led to the roof no problem. Clinging tight to Mars, I hit the bar across the door with my foot in the hopes of leaving as few trails as possible for my brothers. The upside of the hospital was that it was full of scents that would mask my movements and irritate their noses.

Human. Body fluids. Astringent cleaners.

And hopefully that would work in our favor.

Of course, they were tracking us using a different method, one that Han had given them, that was still going to be a problem.

Screams lit up behind us as we slid through the doorway to the stairs. "Can you block it?"

Havoc flicked the deadbolt behind us. "That's all we have time for."

It shouldn't have been funny, but both Bebe and I were laughing as we raced up the stairs.

"Where are we going?" Havoc said. "I could kill them all right now."

Mars let out a pained meow.

"The roof. And not yet," I said with a grimace. Because...Richard. Shipley. If there was a chance, I had to try to reach them.

We flew up all the way to the top, where again I asked him to block the door after us.

While he did that, I ran to the only other thing on the roof that was of use. The helicopter.

It would suck for the hospital, but I knew that there

was a second helicopter the next county over. Besides, if I died, no one would make it through the next few days.

I jerked open the door to the big bird, and blessed be the moon goddess, the keys were in the helicopter. I started warming the flying beast up, waking the engine and getting the rotors going. It all took time. Which was something we didn't have.

Mars sat beside me and called out across the open space of the roof. "Denna, you should come out now."

With that, Denna slunk toward us from the shadows of the rooftop.

Bebe screamed for her. "Bad bitch! You came back!"

Grinning wide, her be-spectacled eyes filling with tears, Denna loped across the roof. "I'm sorry!"

"Don't apologize, it's been a ride." I laughed. "You found Mars!"

"Yes." She clambered into the helicopter. "Yes, I knew it was time to bring him to you."

I looked across to where Havoc stood guard at the door.

"Please, don't kill them," Mars yelled. "Please."

Moon goddess, how could I deny him a chance to save his sons? I couldn't. Not knowing what I did about Juniper warping their minds.

"Just throw them off the roof," I yelled at Havoc.

He gave me a backward wave that might have involved a single finger. I wasn't sure. Didn't matter because things came together faster than I thought they would.

I had the bird lifting off. "Havoc!"

He spun and bolted for the helicopter as I lifted it a few feet off the roof.

The door behind him snapped open and my three brothers spilled out into the open space.

Shooting. Richard missed by a mile, shooting into the sky. Not even trying to hit Havoc.

Havoc leapt for the passenger side of the helicopter and pulled himself inside as the bullets ripped through the air around us.

Behind my brothers, Berek leapt out onto the roof.

"No," I breathed the word as they turned on him.

Kieran shot him in the chest and dropped him right there.

That tie I'd cut to him? It flared to life, demanding that I protect him.

It was Havoc's hand on mine, steadying me, flying us away from the roof that kept me from scrambling out and taking a flying leap for my brother's heads.

"He's gone. You can't save him now."

Gone.

Just like that.

The one I would have followed, the one who seemed so like Mars, was gone. Bebe let out a yowl of pain and I couldn't even comfort her.

But worse was the shot of grief that flew from

Havoc to me. Berek was—had been—his friend in this fight with Han.

The loss had me bowing my head, struggling until Havoc pulled the emotions back, tightening his hand on my leg. "Fly."

17

CANADIANS AND THEIR SORRY APOLOGIES

Bebe let out the most pitiful mewl as we lifted off, her eyes on Berek. I didn't slide the headset on, so my ears could pick out words and noises even with all the rotor wash.

Benefits to being a shifter.

Handing my stolen phone to Havoc, I said, "Use my phone. Call the hospital, tell them there is an injured man on the roof." He did as I asked, though the operators probably couldn't hear him over all the noise of the helicopter. I just knew we had to try.

The guilt and grief I felt over Berek's injuries was intense. As if he were indeed still part of my pack. I clung to that bond between us even as I felt it sliding away.

Death pulling at it.

I let myself look inward and could have cursed.

From the ties I still had to Havoc, *all* the others had grown back.

"FUCK," I snapped. All that effort to be free and I was still bound to them.

I tried to tell myself I was pissed. The truth was, I didn't want to feel Berek die.

Bebe and Mars set themselves on my lap, curling around one another. Both hurting, but for different reasons.

Denna leaned forward. "I am sorry I left you, I was scared. And then I...I remembered that Mars said he would help me be brave. That he'd taught you to be brave in the face of fear, and he could do the same for me."

I blew out a slow breath, steadying the hurt in my body and the ache in my heart. "Where did you find him?"

"Taini and Copper had come back looking for you. They knew something was wrong when you didn't show up." Denna glanced at Havoc, and I knew there would be more later, when he wasn't around. "They actually went to Montana, thinking your family had you. They weren't far off. They're watching the pack now, and Mars and I came to the hospital. We figured you'd show here eventually. Or he did at least. I just followed."

Her words echoed what Mars had already told me. I wanted to hold him tight and ask him so many things, but I needed all hands-on deck for flying the heli-copter. I was more than a little rusty.

"Aren't you worried about the police?" Denna asked. "I mean, you stole a helicopter from the hospital."

"We'll land close to the border, take supplies with us, and then cross. By the time my brothers or Han catch up to the landing site, we should be long gone."

Havoc looked across at me as I flew. "You are...resourceful."

"She's my daughter," Mars said from his place on my lap. "She will survive this as she has survived every-thing else the world has thrown at her."

His faith in me buoyed me more than anything. And he hadn't even bothered clarifying that he was my stepfather...he was just my father. End of story.

"I believe you," Havoc grunted. "In all my years, I have not met another female of such irritatingly resourceful skills. It's enough to drive one mad."

"With worry?" Bebe offered as if he needed help finishing his sentence.

Havoc didn't so much as glance at her. "Yes."

Yes. He'd been worried for me.

Maybe he didn't want to kill me as much now?

The helicopter dipped a little. But Havoc ruined that little burst of emotion the next second by adding, "If she dies in the next week, the world as we know it is done. That is not something I'm willing to take a chance on."

So much for the warm fuzzies.

I made myself focus on what was important—and that was *not* the man across from me. "I want you to text my friends. Tell them to get away from Grayling."

I gave him Taini's number and he messaged them. It should be enough. They were like me, survivors in a world that didn't see any value in them. A warning would have them off and running again. Getting far away from Grayling.

They were better friends than I deserved.

I flew through the remainder of the night, getting close to the border as we neared dawn. Denna crouched in the back, hiding from the growing light.

Mars and Bebe slept soundly. I focused on getting as close to the border as I could.

The radio blipped to life, a static voice coming through.

"Pilot! You are flying a stolen helicopter!"

I grabbed the radio. "Roger that, I'm well aware. I stole it all by myself."

Havoc's lips curled ever so slightly.

Yeah, he liked the sass when it wasn't directed at him.

"We have an escort to guide you back—"

I clicked the radio off and just pushed the bird as hard as I could toward the border. Straight north. As close to where we needed to be for Freya's little get together as I could get us.

Until we were joined by two other helicopters, all dressed in black as it were. I waved to the one on my side and blew them a kiss. "Everyone strapped in?"

Havoc clicked on his belt and Denna squeaked in the back. "What are we doing?"

"Evasive maneuvers," I said.

Bebe and Mars both stuck me with their claws. I grunted as I tipped the helicopter into a nosedive. I didn't want to hurt the humans in the other helicopters, but I couldn't let them catch us either.

As we hurtled down, Denna screamed in the back.

"Regretting your decision to rejoin us?" I yelled as I banked us hard to the left, driving the helicopter flanking us on that side back.

"Incredibly!" Denna screamed back. "This was a terrible idea! The worst! I've changed my mind, I don't want to be brave!"

Laughing, I took us through as many maneuvers as I could, always veering north, closer and closer to the border.

"When we land, shift and run," Havoc bellowed as we buzzed the tree-tops, kissing the leaves and highest branches.

The border flashed along below us—the big sign saying welcome to Canada clearly visible. The two black helicopters peeled away, but I didn't let myself get excited about it.

That just meant they had friends on the other side.

There was a solid clearing in a field just ahead of us. "There."

"Good enough."

"Denna, you got something to cover up with?"

"I do." She yanked a body bag out of the back and settled it over herself. I mean...it was solid black and would keep the light off her.

"Here, take the phone." I flipped the stolen phone back to her. She caught it in one hand and held it tight.

Behind us there were two more helicopters, clearly marked as Canadian—the mark of the RCMP on the sides. We were going to have to be fast.

I took the bird down. "I'm out of practice, brace yourselves and be ready to run."

Out of practice meant we literally bounced across the ground, skipping like a stone across water, sliding sideways before we finally came to a stop.

I flicked all the rotors off, and then we were all out of the helicopter and running.

The Canadian helicopters landed behind us.

"Hey! Sorry, but you can't run away!" someone yelled.

I stripped as I ran, shedding clothes and then falling into my four-legged form. Next to me, Havoc had already shifted. The big black wolf glanced at me, arched a brow and then half crouched as if preparing to pounce on me.

Shit.

I bolted, tail between my legs on golden instinct alone before I realized that he was...trying to play with me.

His wolf liked me better than the human version of him did.

Barking, I bolted through the thick field, Bebe and Mars keeping up with us, no problem.

Denna...shit, if I'd been on two legs, I'd have peed my pants laughing. She'd ripped a hole in the bottom of the body bag and was racing along behind us, zipped up tight except for right where her eyes were.

I glanced back at the officers.

Pale as the snow on a fresh winter day, they pointed at Denna.

"Ha! They think a body just got up and ran from the helicopter!" I barked, dodging and diving around Havoc.

We ran until we found cover in an old barn about five miles from the almost-crash-landing site.

Havoc and I went in first, and I immediately sneezed from all the dust that billowed up with our entrance.

Denna was next in. Pulling her zipper down to peer out, she said, "I smell dead things."

Now that she mentioned it...I wrinkled my nose and picked up a whiff of rotting flesh. "Mice."

Bebe circled in and around my front legs. "Freya's cult meets tonight. Do you know how close we are?"

Question of the day. I shifted to two legs and crouched in the hay, ignoring the ache in my belly. The chicken last night had helped, but I needed more calories. At least I wasn't cursed anymore, so hopefully that would make a difference.

"I'll see if they have a cold storage. You both need to eat," Mars trotted away from me, searching the barn.

Denna handed me the phone, which I brought to life with a click of a single button. Not noticing that Havoc had drawn closer, or that I was shivering.

He pressed his thickly furred body to me, and I reacted on instinct, leaning into his warmth. Shit, so much for not touching him.

Sighing, giving up, I looped an arm around him and then worked my way through the phone to the website we'd found earlier.

That took me to a Facebook page. Which led to Instagram. And finally to a Tiktok where Freya herself smiled into the camera. Her voice low and throaty. Her eyes glimmering with power. Weirdly enough, she reminded me of Jor.

"Come see me. Little wolf." She already had over ten thousand views, and a hell of a lot of men offering to be her little wolf. But I had no doubt who she meant.

Fuck. She knew I was coming. Good or bad, I didn't have much choice at this point. I scrolled to the comment section.

"Tonight, eight o'clock, Building A, 4698 Worthington Street." I read the address out loud. "Maybe they're renting a place?"

"Must be, but it's kind of weird," Bebe said as Havoc leaned across me, trying to keep me close. Possibly to keep me from freezing to death.

I pulled up Google Maps and put in the address. "From here, it's about an hour drive."

Not bad, not bad at all.

Mars found an old pantry in the back of the barn. The food was...edible, but not exactly gourmet. I managed to choke some of it down. Knowing that I had to, made it only slightly more doable.

Once the food—and I use that term loosely—was in me, I shifted back to four legs. I shook my head and glanced at Mars. "Not wondering why I look like this now?"

He sniffed. "I can smell the magic on you, my girl. It's not pretty. Dark magic has a definite feel to it. Petunia's in particular."

Fair enough. I bobbed my head. "Bebe—"

Before I could direct her to hop onto Havoc, Mars did. "You take your friend," Mars said.

My guts twisted up. Goddess of the moon, was he going to try and have a talk with Havoc about me?

"Dad," I said. "It's not like that."

"I can smell exactly what it's like," Mars said.

Havoc didn't so much as flinch as Mars dug his claws into his thick coat, likely deep into the flesh.

I sighed. There were worse things than having my dad back and trying to protect me. The thought made me smile. I'd take this any day over not having him in my life.

Dad embarrasses daughter in front of hot hook-up guy. Oh yeah, that was one for the books.

"What about me?" Denna whispered. "I don't want to leave you, not again! I'm trying to be brave."

"Wait until dark," I said, bunting her with the tip of my nose. "You're fast in the dark, come when you can. You can do this, Denna."

She sighed and nodded. The relief on her face was real.

I didn't know if she'd be able to find us, but our paths would cross again. I'd find her again, somehow, even if she wasn't able to catch up.

With that settled, the four of us started out for the address where Freya's cult would meet.

I took note that Havoc had been rather silent through all this. I spoke to him as we loped along. "Why don't you think Freya will help me? I'm assuming Sven didn't tell you about this?"

"She might tell you that she can help you, but it would be a lie," Havoc said. "She's too busy trying to rebuild her fan base. Couldn't you tell?"

"Fan base? Like what is she, an Instagrammer?" Mars asked.

He shook his head. "No, far worse than that."

Bebe screeched a laugh. "Stop, are you saying she's TikTok famous?"

I thought back to how many views and comments she had on her short clip of a video meant for me. I hadn't thought to see if there were more videos. I'd assumed that it was just a one and done sort of thing.

He rolled his eyes. "Yes, that's exactly what I'm saying."

I barked a laugh, I couldn't help it. It was...ridiculous.

A Norse goddess trying to rebuild her cult via a social media storm...Actually, the more I thought about it, the less crazy it sounded. Some influencers had a maniac following, and online 'wars' had been waged over a few words slung in the wrong direction.

They were like dynasties, vying to be the best.

And it all fit in the palm of your hand.

I shook my head. "Well, let's hope we meet her standards for a selfie."

18

FREAKING FREYA

By the time we reached the address where Freya's cult was supposed to meet, it was barely noon. We had hours and hours to kill. But better than staying at the barn and getting caught or being unable to find the place at the last minute. I let Havoc lead the way into the back of a small mall down the street from the address. We waited patiently until a delivery guy opened and propped the door to receive multiple deliveries, and then we slipped through.

In a matter of minutes, we had clothing once more (stolen from the back rooms that were locked, and which Havoc opened with a flick of his fingers as soon as he shifted to two legs). I shifted too and quickly got dressed, but my stomach was tight with hunger.

Again.

Three shifts in one day were too much for me. "I need to eat."

Havoc slid his hand around mine, lacing our fingers when I tried to pull away. "I don't trust you," he said as he drew me after him, into the little mall. The smell of food—greasy, fat-filled food, no less—called to me like a siren to a sailor.

I don't know how Havoc had money. Maybe he'd conjured it with some form of old magic, the same way he'd opened the lock on that door. I didn't care at that point. I only cared that he bought us a stack of burgers and sat the entire thing down in front of me.

"Yes," I mumbled around the first burger.

Bebe gave a meep from under the table where she and Mars sat. "Girlfriend, don't get greedy now."

I slipped a burger down to them.

Bebe tore into it.

Havoc sat next to me and started in on the food stack. Did we get a few looks? Sure, but I didn't care. We had a stack of burgers and two cats with us. Life was good.

Mars seemed uninterested in the food. He leapt up onto the seat next to me and started to ask questions. Okay, he asked one question.

"What happened after Juniper had me removed?"

Removed.

"She used Petunia on you, too? I'm assuming anyway," I spoke around a mouthful of burger.

He bobbed his head and waved a paw as a signal to go on. Havoc sat on my other side, his thigh pressing tightly to mine.

I wasn't going to run from him. But I couldn't blame the guy for being concerned that I was going to take off. Our track record wasn't exactly stellar. I mean my track record was world-record breaking. His not so much.

Except in the bedroom. I'd give him 110% on that scorecard.

Mars sighed and swiped a paw over one ear. "Her two boyfriends took me down when I was on a hunt, pumped me full of silver, and stuffed me into a cave way up on Lone Mountain. Petunia found me when I was so close to death, I would have agreed to anything she asked of me. She said my wolf body was too torn up, too deeply poisoned to heal, but she could give me another. It would give me a chance to come back to my children. To make things right one day."

My heart ached at the choice he'd had to make. "Did you know what your new body would be?"

He shook his head. "Didn't matter to me. I didn't care so long as it gave me a chance to...to stop Juniper. When we'd been together, I'd been able to help keep her reined in. She knew it too, which was why Juniper had to get rid of me. What I didn't expect was for Petunia to take a liking to me and use me as a familiar. What little magic I had she wanted to use. But I finally pissed her off enough that she went to drown me in the river. My advice is don't point out her husband's infidelities. That will send her over the deep end."

"Juniper slept with her husband. That's how I ended up a part-time golden," I said. "So no surprise there. It is definitely still a trigger for her."

Mars scrunched his face up. "I'm sorry. I'm even sorrier that it took me so long to get back to you."

"Things happen for a reason," Bebe yelled from my feet.

"When Petunia went to drown you, that's when we found each other." I squinted as I chewed, thoughtful for a moment. "You think she knew I was going to be there?"

Mars swiveled his ears. "I hadn't thought about it. I suppose it is possible."

"She's Loki's wife," Havoc said slowly, folding up a bunch of the wrappers. "It's likely she knew exactly when—and even where—you'd be needed. She can see a bit into the shadows of the future. It's partly why Loki keeps her around."

That would have been handy to know before now. Like when Petunia had shown up with Loki.

I shot a look at Havoc. "So, you've decided to be useful?"

He grunted and tore into another burger. "You are dabbling in things that are so beyond you, Goldie. So beyond you. But...I can't deny that you've made it thus far on a rather...unusual path."

I snorted. "And yet, here I am. Still alive. Outsmarting you, Han, and a giant serpent destined to kill the world. I think I'm doing more than dabbling, big man. I'm going to break the fucking mold."

That slowed him. He paused long enough to meet my gaze, amusement dancing in his eyes. "What is your plan with Freya then?"

Havoc's eyes were all but swirling with darkness that I could fall into, that silver fleck otherwordly. I could easily believe he was a prince of the Norse pantheon. I opened my mouth to tell him my plan, but then a tiny pair of claws dug into my calf.

I let out a sharp hiss and smacked the table. "Bebe!"

"Sorry, claws slipped," she said as she cleaned off her little razor blades. "Thought you might need a reality check is all. A reminder of who is actually on your side and not just a good piece of ass."

Havoc looked under the table. "If she would share her plan with me, I could help."

"Or tell her it's useless. And try to haul her off over your shoulder like a caveman to face a woman who is bent on killing her." Bebe stood on her back legs to take a swipe at his face. He jerked back, dodging her blow.

"I know your type," Bebe leapt right up onto the table. "Good in the sack but a controlling bastard who thinks he knows everything. You don't. She's a rockstar at this surviving business. Not trusting her, that's your mistake."

My heart constricted. Bebe still caught me off guard here and there for how short of a time we had known each other. A friend who was fierce and loyal but also didn't try to manipulate me into being something, or someone, that I wasn't.

Havoc leaned in close to her petite face. "She hasn't trusted me."

It was my turn to laugh. "You are going to try and kill me, are you not? That's not trustworthy. Or was Jor lying about that? My death is *required*, regardless of which side I am on. Correct?"

I mean, yes, Loki and Petunia had told us to go to Juniper, and that if we did so, the threat of losing the sun and moon would end. But that didn't mean my mother wouldn't kill me. Or that some other awful shitty thing might not happen.

He didn't so much as flinch. "I have never tried to hurt you. Nor did I ever hurt any of the others who carried the sun within them."

My eyebrows shot up. "You left me to face Han alone at the vampire's house."

His jaw tightened. "You didn't carry the sun then—"

I held up a hand, stopping him. "Yes or no on the killing me question."

I honestly thought he'd say no. A deep part of me wanted...something...with him. I didn't even know exactly what it was, just *something.*

"Yes, I am supposed to kill you. To stop Ragnarök."

It felt like the wind got sucked out of the space around us.

I swallowed hard and leaned back in my seat. I had no words.

He'd fucked me—not once, twice—and there was still a hovering need between us. Should the option show up again, I was sure that we'd both indulge.

But he was going to try and kill me. Maybe not in the next week or so, but at some point in the future.

"I could have killed Soleil before the last solar eclipse, she was with me that day," he said, as if that made his previous statement better. "But I am trying to buy as much time to..."

"Find another solution?" Mars offered. "That is what my daughter is trying to do. She is going to appeal to Freya. And if that doesn't work?"

I had a Plan B, and Mars knew it. He'd trained me to always have a backup plan. I sighed and confirmed, "I have a backup plan if Freya doesn't pan out."

"And what is it?" Havoc asked. There was no ire in his voice, no anger or frustration.

Shit.

He was curious.

"Find a way to kill Han," I said. "That should end both the bond to me, and his need to kill me."

Havoc didn't so much as flinch. "You think you can do what no one else has in all these years? You think I haven't tried to kill him? Or that he's not tried to kill me?"

I frowned and picked up another burger. "I think... that maybe a new perspective can make a difference. I don't pretend to know for sure, Havoc. But what I know is that I am not going to run and run, because that's how you trip and fall."

"Well said," Mars murmured. "Now. How long before this meeting happens?"

"Another hour," I said. I could feel the sunset coming on outside. As if my transformations still depended on it.

I stood up and stretched, grabbing the tray, which now held nothing but wrappers. I carried it over to the garbage and dumped the trash, then walked away from Havoc. Of course, Bebe and Mars trotted alongside me, much to the delight of several kids. I didn't look to see if Havoc was following. Because just like the sensation of the night pressing in on us, there was a sensation of Havoc, coming closer to me.

That fucking bond that was tying us together.

A little girl squealed, startling me, as she ran for

Mars. He waited patiently as she scooped him up and squeezed him. Even if his eyes did bug out a little.

Bebe laughed. "Man, that is...I don't know that I wouldn't scratch her face off."

"She's a child." Mars butted his head against the kid's. "She's learning."

The mother arrived at the same time as Havoc caught up to us.

"What in the world!" She gasped and tried to pry her daughter's hands off Mars. "Why is there a cat in here? This is a food court!"

"Companion animal," I said. "And the food court is over there."

"I saw you with that animal under your table." She finally succeeded in forcing her daughter to release Mars, which caused nothing short of a Muppet-esque tantrum. Her little head tipped back, her mouth opened wide, and her arms and legs flailed independently of one another in a way that didn't make sense to me. I wondered if her head would begin to spin.

"You should keep your demon spawn better leashed," Havoc rumbled, his words echoing my own thoughts.

The woman gasped. Bebe laughed, and I couldn't help but smile as I scooped Mars up and out of the direct aim of the now unhinged child as she flailed about.

We left the mother there, the little girl screeching

obscenities that I wasn't sure I'd ever used in my life, and that was saying something.

Mars curled in a little closer to me, his heartbeat... slow. Sad, he was sad.

Juniper would have melt downs like that, with him. She would come completely unglued, nearly passing out from the screams she let loose, only to wake up and continue whatever tirade she'd started. Or a new one if we were truly unlucky.

"Do you miss her?"

"No. No. But I missed my children, every day. If I hadn't been imprisoned, I never would have left you alone with her, Cin. Never. I'd have tried coming back as I am now, even if it meant my death."

I knew it in my heart that he was telling the truth. We made our way outside the little mall and sat on one of the benches, waiting for the sun to finish its fall into the night.

"Berek is alive," Havoc said quietly. "I can sense him. The doctors were able to get the bullet out quickly, and he will heal."

Bebe let out a squeal and leapt about. "That's amazing!"

"It is," I said quietly. Now that he'd mentioned it, I could feel Berek's bond to me too. Simple, frayed, but alive. I couldn't help but send him a little burst of energy in the hopes that it would help him.

Bebe leapt away at the first sign of night bugs,

chasing them across the small courtyard, dodging and leaping as she tackled them from the sky. Mars joined her after a quick look from me to Havoc. Then he was gone.

"Your cat father gave me shit," Havoc said as he sat down.

I laughed. "He dug his claws into your flesh, did he?"

Havoc didn't look at me. "You aren't wrong. My job is to make sure that you die at the best possible time. I've held off killing any of those who carry the sun, because...I don't want to see the world come to an end."

"But you are still bound to."

"Yes." I was watching his face as he spoke, and I could see the pain that flashed across it. He didn't want to kill me.

Damn warmth slid through me again, and I leaned into him, absorbing some of his body heat.

"Is it like...a curse?" I offered. "Like you want to kill me, but you've held yourself back?" I wanted to understand not only him, but also what I was up against. Was it the same way for Han?

"Not a curse. It is a command I agreed to before I understood what was being asked of me." He squinted up at the darkening sky, maybe seeking answers from among the stars. "I don't..." He shook his head, shutting down what he was going to say. "If there is a way around this, I don't know it. But I have never looked for a way to circumvent the task I was given."

"Freya might help then," I said. "Sven seemed to think it was possible."

"He sees something in you." Havoc did turn to look at me then, lifting a hand to take my chin between his thumb and fingers. "You aren't like the others who have fallen to the curse. They were all scared. Terrified. As they should be. You...you are the first to fight back in all these years."

A terrible, awful warm glow rolled through me from his words and his touch. I told myself it was stupid and I didn't like it. Even though both my wolf and goldie were fucking basking in his touch and the words that felt so very much like praise.

"That's disappointing." I pulled my head slowly from his hand. I had to stay strong, I had to keep a distance between us. He'd admitted to needing me dead. Even though I understood he didn't want me to die.

Complicated much?

He smirked and took my chin again, harder this time. Holding me as he brought his head close to mine, his breath ghosting over my lips.

The urge to kiss him, to taste his mouth cut through me, straight to my lower regions.

"Behind you, there are three figures stalking close. I'm guessing your brothers."

Well, fuck me with a fork, so much for kissing. I tensed and leaned a bit closer to him, our lips almost touching. "Can you handle them alone?"

He raised an eyebrow. "You doubt me?"

"I've been disappointed by enough men that I doubt you all." The truth fell out of my mouth, and he caught it, snaking his tongue out and running it along my lower lip.

"I will handle them. Go to Freya. Find me after."

I couldn't breathe through the fire he'd sent racing through me with that single touch.

He stood and faced my brothers. "Hello, shit heads."

"Don't kill them." Mars ran between Havoc and Kieran, who stood at the front. He puffed up, facing Havoc. "They may have lost their way, but they're still my sons."

He'd done this before, standing between the boys and someone who would have hurt them. Protecting the boys from Juniper after they "dared" to stand up to one of her boytoys.

My heart twisted up, because for just a second, I could see my brothers as they had been before Juniper had twisted them into shallow shells of their former selves.

Scrawny and scared, but willing to protect one another. Willing to protect those that they were supposed to protect. Like me.

I hadn't thought it possible that I could still feel bad for them. Not after all they'd done.

I laid a hand on Havoc's tense forearm. "I know they've been a thorn in your side. Let me try to get through to them. One last time."

He took a half step back. "If they so much as try to hurt you, I'll destroy them."

I drew a breath, pulling in all the strength I had, asking my wolf and my golden to lend their aid. Because there was strength in that damn dog, no matter what it felt like when I was forced into that body.

Kieran was in the lead, but he was not the one I thought I'd be able to sway.

I looked to his right, to my oldest brother. "Richard. This is not who you are. It never was. You remember when you used to protect me and Shipley? Hiding us from her wrath? You remember when you stole food for us because we'd run away for so long? You were the strongest of us, you had the heart of a dragon, and you buried it—*they* buried it—under your ogre beer. But I always knew I was safe if you were there, because you stood up to her. You stood up to her and she didn't know what to do in the face of your strength. That's why she started you on the drink. To dull you."

I turned to Shipley next, but there was nothing in his eyes. I still tried. "You held out the longest, Ship. And you were my best friend. I thought we'd keep our backs together and face the world. We worked together, found ways to do...what she wanted, even when it cost us."

Kieran's face was hard, his eyes as dead as Shipley's. It was as if he wasn't even there. As if Juniper stared out at me from his eyes.

I shook my head. "I would have gone to war for any of you. I would have stood with you against her. Even if we'd died, we would have done it as a family. Not this broken, shattered mess that has no resemblance to family. A mess that doesn't even look like a pack. Look at the bonds between us? They...they are ugly."

And the bonds were indeed that, now that I paused to look at them. They were like open wounds connecting us, dripping with venom and putrescence.

Kieran's face didn't waver. Neither did Shipley's. That surprised me. I'd thought he might come around.

It was Richard who locked eyes with me—clear eyes. "We had no choice, Cin."

A funny pang happened around my heart. He hadn't used my name to my face in years.

"What...what do you mean?"

He tipped his head as Kieran growled at him to shut his mouth. "You think I wanted to throw you in the river? How else was I going to set you free? It was the last thing I could think to do, to get you away from her. From him."

Set me free.

"I told him where to shoot you," he said. "Had him hit you where I knew you'd survive. I called the hospital, tipped them off that they'd need to be ready for a silver poisoning. Sent those hunters toward you. Reached out to Petunia and asked for her help. I knew she had Dad."

My throat closed as my eyes filled. This...could not be. "Then why now?"

His smile was sad. "Too deep, kid. We're all in too deep. Her claws are sunk into our spines, spells woven around us to control us, and there is no freeing us. Not even for you, Dad." He bent and ran a hand over Mars.

Mars let out a low moan and bowed his head. "It cannot be too late, my boy. It cannot be."

Richard sighed. "It is. The demons she's attached to each of us...there is no undoing them now."

I wanted to grab him, hug him, scream at him that he was still my brother. That no matter what, I would fight for him if he wanted to be free of her too. That if he was in too deep, I was there, too. Even as I thought it, the bond between Richard and I shifted, changing.

Growing clearer. Richard let out a heavy sigh.

"Han wants you dead. He knows you carry the sun, even if that makes no sense to me," Richard said. Kieran snarled and Richard just held up his hand, silencing him. Telling me what I already knew.

Richard had always been the one meant to lead. "This is why she kept you drunk."

He nodded. "Nothing for me to drink out here. Not with Han running the show. First time I've been sober in thirty years. But even sober, I can only do so much, little sister. I got Meg out. She's on her way...somewhere safe. Somewhere far, far away. It was the best I could do."

Holy shit. Tears filled my eyes.

I took the chance. I pushed past Havoc, stood right in front of Richard and grabbed him in a hug.

He hesitated, then carefully hugged me back.

"I've missed you, the brother I knew before." I whispered.

"You too, Cin. Her magic never worked on you. It's why...you are the only one who could stop her. And it's why she hates you so much. She broke the bonds you were making to us, keeping us safe too." He pushed me back a little, then stepped back himself. "You understand? Juniper is the monster, but we can't stop her."

I stared at him, his words sinking in. "If I kill her, will it set you free?"

He nodded. "Yes. In simple terms. But she has her witch man now, and he will have tricks up his sleeve. And she keeps him well hidden away from the rest of the pack. She has us. You'd have to go through all of us to kill her. That's...a problem."

The shakes started deep in my core.

Everything was pushing me back to Grayling. Everything.

I made the decision quickly. "How much time can you buy us?"

Richard looked to Havoc. "You can help her?"

He let out a growl. "I will keep her alive."

Keep me alive. No more killing then? I looked at him, and he repeated it. "I am keeping you alive, Goldie."

Richard looked over his shoulder at the two brothers. Kieran snarling, spit dripping from his chin. Shipley just staring at me. His eyes unreadable. "I can hold them steady for maybe an hour. Maybe. We can track you. Han has given us that ability. It's more than just the pack bond—it's like a homing beacon." He paused. "An hour. Then you will either have to kill us or run to Grayling."

An hour.

I had a single damn hour to change the world.

19

FAMILY FEUD: NORSE PANTHEON EDITION

Mars and Bebe stayed behind to keep an eye on the boys. I'd love to say that I could trust what Richard was saying, but...let's be real. He'd given us a reprieve from their attack, but that didn't mean something else wouldn't change.

He might lose control of our brothers, and then we'd have Freya in front of us and the boys coming in hot from behind.

Havoc jogged along with me. "You used something on them, you broke through the control she has on them. How? I tried to break through that connection already, when they came over the garden wall back on the coast."

I winced a little. "I have some of the same abilities as my mother."

"She is a true alpha?"

"In power, yes. In control of herself, no. The only one she couldn't stop was Mars. I don't know why, maybe it was the mating bond?" I could see the unit number up ahead, and a few of the humans gathered around the still-closed door.

I didn't say more to Havoc because it was...awkward.

I didn't understand it myself. Apparently, he did.

"Most packs run on a hierarchy of alpha male at the top, working on down through those who were most submissive at the bottom. You know this. Mars was your alpha."

I nodded. "Yes, of course."

"What you likely haven't heard is that wolf packs in nature are matriarchal. The power of a true alpha female is something to be inspired by, but also feared. Because if the alpha misuses her control, there is only one way to stop her."

This was all new to me. "Okay, tell me."

He grunted. "A true alpha female is rare, Cin, but they hold the ability to bend males in the pack to their will, to impose on them any truth they want them to believe. I've only ever met one other alpha female, and that was almost four hundred years ago. The position requires a balance of control, power, and compassion. If that trio is not balanced, a monstrosity of a dictator is created."

Sweat beaded along the back of my neck and slid

down my back. "You said there was only one way to deal with an alpha female."

We'd almost reached the unit. "Another alpha female. Because as with Juniper, she could make most of the males who come into her circle bow to her within minutes, forgetting who and what he was. Maybe all of them if your brother is right and she has some sort of witch-man working with her. If you want to free them and that pack, Juniper has to die."

His words were like a gong going off in my head. But I had to focus on the here and now.

A few eyes swung our way as we approached the cloaked figures—yes, cloaked. They stood around the door to the rental unit, awkward as hell with their cosplay gear on. Most of it was well made, accurate.

I saw a few daggers hanging from hips. Foam daggers.

"Goddess save me," I whispered.

Havoc grabbed my hand and clamped down. "Don't invoke any goddess in front of her. Not one."

"New members, hello and welcome! I'm Rufus, I am the head of our little group." Rufus held out a hand as he approached us, and I shook it quickly and then let it go.

"Cin," I said. "And this is Havoc."

Rufus' eyes went up and down us both, eyebrows into his hairline. "Wow, cool names. Most of us here use pseudonyms too. Better that way."

"Is the meeting starting?" I asked, tapping at my wrist. "We're on a time crunch."

"Oh, well, we have to wait for our queen. Freya has the keys to the unit."

I shot a look at Havoc. "She has the keys."

His lip twitched. "Well, seems reasonable."

"I didn't think you had a sense of humor."

He smiled. Okay, it was his version of smiling, a bare lifting of his lips. "I have an excellent sense of humor when I'm not in the middle of saving you from a sea serpent, my psychotic family, your psychotic family, or chasing you across the continent so as to keep you safe from yourself."

I did laugh at that. "Please, you make it all sound so mundane."

His eyebrows shot up and he laughed with me. Damn it, he full on tipped his head back and laughed. Gods, that sound struck as much of a chord in me as his damn growling did, though instead of affecting my lady parts, it did something to a much more dangerous organ thumping wildly in my chest.

"Aww, a love story in the making!" a woman sung out. "Oh! And it's one of my family members no less!"

I spun around to the woman who was approaching the group. She wore a long tunic dress, a thick white fur draped over her shoulders, a crown on her head, and she even had a raven perched on one shoulder. The same woman from the Tiktok video.

She really was trying to go viral.

Havoc dipped his head toward her. "My queen."

Freya, it could only be her, stepped to the door and waved her hand at it. The humans slid through the now open door, moving now as if on auto pilot. Robots run by an overlord.

This was not a good start.

"Come, my court is meeting tonight." She motioned for us to follow her, and really, what choice did we have? None. Even though I couldn't see into the depths of the room. Couldn't smell anything.

Which wasn't right.

Even so, I was here for help. And I had to hope Sven was right about her and she'd be able to help.

Havoc went through the door first, motioning for me to wait.

So when he disappeared—*literally* disappeared— well, I didn't hesitate. I called for back-up.

"Bebe!"

She came running, only she wasn't alone. Richard was running ahead of her. "What happened?"

"I think Freya just took Havoc!" I peered inside, trying to see into the depths. "Hold my hand, let me lean in."

Bebe slid to a stop. "You really want to trust this one?"

I looked at Richard and gave him my hand. "Trust is earned. Earn it, Richard."

His eyes softened. "Hang on, little sis. I've got you."

He grabbed my wrist, and I clenched my hand around his arm as I leaned in through the doorway.

Immediately, I was yanked in as far as Richard could hold me, a sharp cold winter wind tugging at me hard enough that I fought to reach back with my other hand, to grab the edge of the door. Only there was no door left. Richard was all that was left between me and falling.

As my view cleared, I found myself looking out across a vast winterscape, trees coated in snow, mountains rising all around the valley beneath me.

Richard's grip never slipped. It didn't have to.

Laughter curled around me and jerked me forward, which in turn dragged Richard along with me.

And Bebe, who was hanging onto him.

"Son of a bitch!" he bellowed as we tumbled through the air, then down into the snow, bouncing down a slope as if we were children once more, playing on the edge of the Rockies.

There was no real slowing ourselves, we had to just let the fall pan out until we were at the bottom. Bebe popped up next to me.

"You know, that wasn't too bad. I would do it again." She shook her head, snow flicking off. "It's not even that cold."

"Because my humans would shiver too much if it

were a true northern cold," Freya spoke, her voice seemingly all around us. Richard and I stood, immediately putting ourselves back-to-back.

"Where is Havoc?"

"Oh. He's here." Freya materialized in front of us, Havoc kneeling at her feet. She had a hand in his hair and was gripping hard.

I started toward her. "Let him go."

"No, you see, there is no reason to let him go. He came here. You followed. I don't have to let either of you go." She smiled.

"Sven is so getting his ass kicked." I addressed the words to Havoc, ignoring Freya. On purpose. I knew how power-hungry women worked. "Do you think he knew she was going to be irrational?"

"I am not irrational—"

"He probably thought it would be funny," Richard drawled, rubbing a hand over his hair. As far as I knew, he'd never met Sven, but he was playing along like a champ. "You know how he is. Thinks it's funny to make people look stupid."

"Fuck," I muttered. "Okay, well, Havoc, let's go. Sven has obviously been smoking the wrong leaf."

From the corner of my eye, I saw her splutter. "I am a queen—"

"Maybe we can get that other Norse goddess to help." I scooped up Bebe. "What was her name? Was it Petunia?"

Richard bumped a fist against my upper arm. "You know what, she owes me one. I bet we can get her to help for nothing. She's good like that. Super helpful."

Had Richard and I planned this? No. But that was the strength of family, even when it had shattered apart. You knew each other. And this was a game we'd played before.

Working the crowd, tag teaming our mark.

I reached Havoc and physically pulled him away from Freya, who stood there stunned.

Until she absolutely came unglued.

Snow flung everywhere, melting until there was not a drop of it left. "Do *not* ignore me!"

"Easy to." I shrugged. "You aren't the goddess we were looking for. Because the goddess we were looking for would have been able to help us."

Her mouth dropped open; I clung a little tighter to Havoc. His fingers laced with mine and he gave me a squeeze. Keep going. That's what I took from it.

"Richard." I turned away from Freya, giving her my back. "Where do you think we can find Petunia?"

Before he could answer, the roar of two familiar wolves rippled through the air.

"What in the hell is this?" Freya screamed, her fists at her side.

Shipley and Kieran had found us.

I reached for Richard, and he held my hand as if I were a lifeline. "I can't stop them. Whatever you did for me, stripped me of Juniper's madness. But it's still heavy on them."

I knew he couldn't. He'd held them for as long as he could, just like he'd said.

Havoc was at my back. "*You* can stop them, Cin. Just like you broke through to Dick here."

"Only Dick when he's a dick," I whispered. I couldn't take my eyes off my two brothers as their wolf forms raced toward me.

Deadly intent, it was all over them.

"Richard, pin Kieran. I'll take Shipley. Just pin him."

He gave my hand one last squeeze and leapt toward our brothers. Intercepting.

"ENOUGH!"

Freya roared the word and her magic slid around all of us, pinning us down.

"Good job, you have her attention now," Havoc whispered, and there wasn't an ounce of sarcasm in his voice. He was actually praising me.

We were lifted and spun around. Bebe sat at the feet of the Norse goddess. "I explained everything to her. Girl to girl."

I stared at my small friend. "You are most awesome, Bebe."

She grinned up at me and stuck out her tongue. "I'm a woman trapped as a cat. The two most awesome beings mashed together."

"She has explained the issue. You are being hunted by Han in his quest to fulfill the prophecy. And you seek a way around it?" Freya flexed her fingers, curling them, which pulled me toward her.

"Yes. I need to find a way to stop him."

There was a little pop, like a balloon being stabbed with a pin.

Another woman, one I recognized, appeared from behind Freya. "No, there can be no changing things!"

"Oh, you bitch! *I* am helping them now!" Freya spun, and we were all dropped to the ground while Freya and Petunia launched at each other like a pair of hissing cats.

Which left Shipley and Kieran to their own devices as Freya's magic slid from them.

Kieran came for me, and Havoc slammed into him, grabbing his throat. "Rich, get the other one!"

Richard snarled and had Shipley by the scruff in a matter of seconds. Shipley hung from his grip, his tail tucked between his legs as he twisted and fought to get away.

I got to my feet and went to where Richard stood. "Ship, you've gotta come back from this. You held out the longest. I know you can do it."

He whimpered and tried to look away from me. Shame rolled off him, shame and guilt.

I put all the strength of my wolf, bound up with the compassion of my golden, into my next words.

"Please," I whispered. "Please come back to us. Be the man that Mars taught you to be."

Our eyes locked hard, and in him I still saw the boy who had been my best friend. The one who'd snuck out at night with me to steal food from the kitchens. Run through the woods at night chasing fireflies.

Hidden from Juniper when Mars wasn't around to protect us.

"Come back," I said, not with power and thunder in my voice, but with all the love that I'd thought was buried and dead. The boy I knew, I'd thought he was dead, but I could see him there, hiding behind the man he'd become.

I put my hand on the side of his face, the sibling bond between us flaring to life, burning away the control Juniper had laid on him. Tearing away the darkness she'd bound him up in.

His eyes rolled in his head, and he slumped in Richard's hands. Richard laid Shipley down.

I shook my head.

Havoc held Kieran down while my brother thrashed and fought to kill him. I opened my mouth to tell Havoc to let Kieran go, so I could kill him myself. Because the bonds there, between him and I were...he still wanted to hurt me in the worst possible ways.

"No."

We all froze as magic settled down on us, holding us in place once more.

I could only move my eyes, and what I saw sent chills rippling through me. Petunia and Freya stood side by side.

Freya stood a little taller and Petunia rolled her eyes. But it was Freya who spoke. "We have come to an agreement. You must go to your pack, and you must deal with your mother once and for all. That is the way to the path you seek."

Fear sliced through me. "No."

"Yes." Freya dipped her head in my direction. "After discussing the matter with Petunia—honestly," she turned to Petunia, "—you could have picked a better name—" and then back to me. "Anyway, I see that she was correct to put you on the path toward Grayling. I did not realize...certain things."

"No," I said again, unable to do much more.

Freya smiled and the snow swirled faster around her. "I will help you. I will send your last brother back to your mother. There will be no one hunting you. But you must arrive in Grayling before the night of the dead moon. And I will give you this."

She flipped something toward me. I caught it in my hands. The stone was square, a dark aged green as if it had sat in a watery tomb for a thousand years, cool to the touch, and hung from a thin, iron chain. "What is this?"

"An amulet of protection. The runes on it will fade as you draw close to the night of the dead moon. On that night, you must face your destiny. For good or for ill, you must see that night through to the end."

She clapped her hands and Kieran disappeared. Richard and Shipley did not.

Petunia sniffed. "Your mother has the answers you seek. How to stop Han and free yourself and save our world from Ragnarök. Juniper is the key."

20

COUNTDOWN TO BITCH-TOWN

The party was over after that little announcement. Freya wiggled her fingers and Havoc, Bebe, Richard, Shipley, and I were thrown up the mountain, out the door, and across the pavement of the mall parking lot to where Mars stood, pacing.

"Are you okay?" He raced to each of us, touching us with his nose as if to be sure. "I couldn't get through the door!"

The panic in his voice, the pacing...I scooped him up and squeezed him tight. "We're okay."

He breathed out a sigh and I handed him to Richard. Until he'd been held by each of us, only then did he calm.

"Don't do that again," he muttered. "I thought my heart would burst."

I saluted him. "You got it."

There was no sign of Freya's followers. But then again, they were drinking deep of that particular Kool-Aid.

Havoc was on his feet first, putting himself between me and my two brothers. Couldn't blame him for that.

But even as I sat up, I could feel that the bonds between me and the two of them had changed. They were steady. Calm. Quiet.

"They're okay, Havoc."

"They've been trying to kill you for years," he said. "And rape you, correct?"

Richard sat with his elbows on his knees. "Trying to hurt her, yes, but not by choice. Kieran...he...wanted other things from her."

No explanation other than that.

Kieran was the one who wanted to start his own little dynasty with me. There would be no coming back for him from the darkness that I'd pulled Ship and Rich from—I'd seen it when the bonds between us had flared for a moment.

And even that, we—Richard, Shipley, and I—would still need a hell of a lot of time to rebuild what had been lost.

Mars sat next to Richard, one paw on his leg. "You came back my boy."

I stood, Bebe pressing against my calf. "How do you know you can trust them?" she asked. "I mean really?"

I looked inward, not trusting what I was feeling. "Because they are no longer tied to Grayling or Juniper." I paused. "Havoc. Check your bonds."

Havoc took a breath and then grunted. "Shit. They're with us, not Grayling."

Us.

Yup, my heart might have flip-flopped a little there. "They are tied to me, and as such, they are now tied to you, who I am also tied to."

"A lot of tying up going on," Bebe muttered. "Kinky group."

Havoc grunted, walked over to Richard. They sized one another up and I could see the tension there for just a moment. The two male wolves checking one another out. Then Richard dipped his head, ever so slightly. Second to Havoc, who held out his hand. "Come on."

Richard took his hand and let Havoc help him up. They weren't far off in size, Richard only a little smaller than Havoc.

"Thanks."

Havoc turned to Shipley, who stayed on his belly, eyes closed. The bonds between us thrummed with the same hot shame I'd felt earlier. I went and crouched down in front of his face.

"New start, Ship. I...didn't realize that Juniper had that kind of control over you. I didn't realize...that she'd done what she'd done. Used magic and spells to control you."

I mean, how could I?

I thought they'd chosen to follow her because... because she was a scary bitch. That was why I'd stayed so long. I hadn't realized they'd been forced to do her bidding. They'd had so much power within the pack, the possibility had never occurred to me that they had been bound up with spells and whatever else it was that I'd ripped them clean from.

Richard stood with a grimace. He limped as he turned to look at Shipley still lying on the pavement.

"Are you going to kill us?" He directed the question not at me, but at Havoc.

Havoc let out a sigh. "That is not up to me. Your life is in her hands."

And then everyone looked at me. Three were-wolves, two of them strong alphas, were looking to me to decide their fate.

"Don't be stupid," I snapped.

Richard lifted an eyebrow. "What are you going to do with us then?"

I knew what he was asking. They'd tried to kill me —multiple times. By all rights their lives were mine to take.

I didn't look at Havoc for help. Didn't even look to Mars, who'd been incredibly quiet through all this.

"I am not her," I said softly. "And I'm not going to demand your lives."

Tension I hadn't realized Richard and Ship were holding slid out of them. I held out a hand to Richard, expecting a hug.

He went to one knee and took my hand. Like a knight of old. Shipley slunk forward on his belly, his snout at the tip of my foot.

Richard held tightly to my hand and lowered his eyes. "I will follow you, Cinniúint. Until the end. You should have been our alpha."

Until the end. My throat tightened. "No. We aren't seeing the end of anything. We aren't done yet. And I don't particularly want to be alpha of anyone."

I looked at Havoc as I pulled Richard to his feet. "We need a place to hunker down. I'm not rushing into Grayling."

Bebe pressed herself harder against my leg. "I can feel you shaking just talking about going into that place."

"Yup," I said through gritted teeth.

Havoc reached out and took my hand, clamping down on it. "I still don't trust you not to run."

I laughed at him. "Because now I have more people to help me run?"

Richard gave a low warning growl. "Why would you run from him if he's on our side?"

I sighed. "It's complicated. I'm not running, not right now."

Havoc led me—and thus everyone else—away from the small mall. "Sven is on his way. We need to find an abandoned house, building, something like that."

"We saw an old church on the way into town," Richard said. "It was south of here, behind a couple of suburbs."

"That would work." Havoc started in the direction that Richard had pointed. "You two go ahead to check it out."

Richard shot me a look and I nodded.

"Mars," I said. "Why don't you go with them?"

Mars trotted after Richard. "You can hear me?"

Richard nodded. "I can. Always could. But I couldn't let Petunia know that I knew. When I came to her house."

Secrets and games, it was all about survival.

And Richard had made sure that he survived.

As soon as my brothers and Mars were out of earshot, Havoc spoke. "Do you trust them? Or could they be playing you?"

I tried to untangle my fingers from his, but he hung on tight. "Look, I get why you'd say that, but they were wrapped in some sort of spell, I saw it. I don't know if it was Juniper or her witch-man, but it coated the bonds they had to Juniper, and when it came off...they could make decisions on their own. When we were young... Rich and Ship, they weren't bad."

I couldn't say the same for Kieran. There had always been darkness in him.

But now, Richard and Shipley, they'd decided to face her down with me. I knew that she scared them. I knew there was a chance her magic could wrap them up again. But for a little while, I had two of my brothers back.

And I wouldn't give that up, not for anything.

Havoc loosened his hold on me, but I didn't pull away. I let my hand rest in his. "I don't expect anyone else to understand why I'd give them a chance."

He was quiet a moment. "I do."

I sharpened my gaze. "You tried to reconcile with Han?"

He stared out ahead of us. "I went to Han, tried to make him see there was another way. That was the first time he ran me through. Not the last. And not the last time I tried to get through to him."

There was a flash of images in my mind, memories not my own.

Havoc holding his hand out to Han.

Han spinning around with his axe and burying it in Havoc's heart, dropping him.

Blood everywhere. A woman screaming.

Then I saw that same woman at Havoc's feet, her eyes lifeless. A ring on her finger.

Pain shot through the connection that bound Havoc and me together and I gasped. That was the woman he'd loved, the one who'd carried the moon the first time.

Havoc had been married to her, and Han had cut them both down.

"Did he know that he couldn't kill you? That you wouldn't die?" I asked quietly.

"You saw?"

"Yes, I saw."

Havoc let go of me completely. "Then you understand why I won't trust your brothers not to try and kill you. Even now."

I didn't feel like arguing. Didn't feel like trying to point out to him that he was also on that do-I-don't-I trust you rollercoaster. He said he'd keep me alive.

But he also said that he was bound to a command that would mean he had to kill me.

The silence held between us as we left, following my brothers.

We reached the abandoned church just after midnight. Shipley was back on two legs, and he and Richard waited for us outside of the two-story building.

Havoc went ahead of us, and a pointed glance from Bebe, who was trotting along next to me, slowed my feet.

"Listen," she said. "Can I tell you what I think?"

"Advice?" I asked.

"Yes, my advice is this—don't trust anyone."

"Not even you?"

"Well shit, I'm not just anyone, am I?" Bebe flicked her ears and tail rapidly. "Don't trust those who've proven they are in this for themselves. That's the difference. You know, everyone who's been really difficult has a penis. You notice that?"

I laughed. "Yes, I did notice. But you haven't met Juniper yet. And there was Meg. And Petunia."

"Shit balls, how do I forget about her, when it all started with that witch didn't it? Okay, fine. Maybe testicles aren't the only problem," Bebe muttered and then she went still. A figure had stepped out of the church, moving a little slowly. "Is that Berek?"

And she was off, running flat out for the werewolf. And then she leapt into his arms.

I followed more slowly, letting myself feel all the connections to those who were inside. It wasn't the whole pack, but Berek was there, along with Claire and JJ. Sven was inside waiting for us too.

Richard shot me a look. "You sure, sis?"

Was I sure it was safe, that was what he was asking. I put a hand on his arm as I passed him. "It's what it is, Rich. It'll be okay."

Shipley stood to one side, wearing just a pair of shorts he'd scrounged up somewhere. "I'm sorry. For everything. I wish...I wish I could take it all back."

I pulled him into a hug. "I know. But we have a chance now at a family that isn't so fucked up."

He hugged me back, tentative at first, and then leaned in and gave me his weight. A sob rattled through his chest. Just one.

I pushed back the emotions that noise stirred inside of me. "Let's see what Sven's done to this place."

And when I stepped in, it was nothing like what I'd expected.

21

THE CALM BEFORE THE TWISTER

Sven had turned the abandoned church interior into something out of a fairy tale. Trees and plants grew along the edges, the floorboards were thick with moss, and there was a small creek flowing down from the second floor, through the middle of the room, dipping down out of sight at the far end of what had been the pulpit.

Lights twinkled overhead.

A fresh breeze blew through the space, as warm as an early spring wind.

I introduced my brothers. "They were wrapped in a spell that we were able to break. And they are here now to help." I looked to Berek, who had Bebe wrapped around his neck.

He gave me a look. "It was the other one who shot me. I saw you," he tipped his head at Richard, "shoot into the sky. And you," he motioned to Shipley, "You didn't shoot at all."

Shipley looked at his feet. Richard grimaced. "It was all I could do."

"I believe you. We have Sven here to keep us from being tangled up with magic that would warp who we are." Berek sighed. "I would like to talk to you though. See where we can fit you in."

And just like that, some of the tension rolled away.

"I smell food," Richard said. "Please tell me I'm not having a hallucination."

Sven stood in the middle of the space. "There is food. Go to the second floor, there is plenty for everyone."

No one else waited for him to say more. I waited till it was just him, me, and Havoc.

"You sent me to Freya, but you didn't know if she would help?" I asked. "Thanks for that, really good time we had there."

Sven grimaced. "I suspected there might be a fight between her and Petunia. But if they could work together, I believed their advice would be closer to correct."

Closer to correct. "You mean they could still be dicking with us?" I asked.

Havoc stepped up behind me, the heat from his body warming the space between us. "They both want her to go to Grayling now. To meet with Juniper, to beg for her help."

"What does that mean though?" Sven asked. "What will begging require of our sunshine?"

Our sunshine.

Something about how he'd said it felt...strange. How long had it been since I'd truly been a part of a pack? Maybe not even when Mars had been with us in Grayling. So maybe that was why it felt strange, because it was the first time a pack had truly claimed me as their own.

The tightness in my throat took a moment to swallow down. To go back to the question Sven had.

What would it require of me to deal with Juniper? I hadn't wanted to think about it. Because I suspected it meant I would have to challenge her.

And a challenge would mean one of us would die —and while I'd had some pretty good bravado back in Alaska, I really didn't know if I could beat my mother. Add into the fact that if she had a mage or witch-man working for her, that was a whole other problem.

"A fight," I simplified. "That's what it means. Because no matter what those two goddesses think, Juniper will not help me for any reason." Which would mean I would have to force her to help.

I started toward the curved, wooden steps that led up to the second floor. Voices floated down to me. When we reached the top, it opened into a wide space with a massive table down the center. Bench seating ran all the way along both sides.

Shipley was talking with Claire. Richard and JJ were discussing silver poisoning as if it hadn't been one of my brothers who'd shot JJ and Berek. Mars sat with Richard, just with him, saying nothing.

Berek sat quietly, eating slowly, with Bebe right next to him.

Sven followed me up, passing me and sitting. I stood for a moment, taking it in. Almost like a normal pack if you discounted the talking cats, tree king, and... "Denna. You found us."

She sat in the shadows of the window, barely visible. "Are we safe?"

Of course, she'd had her own run in with my brothers. Both Richard and Shipley had treated her...well... like trash.

I went over to where she was crouched and sat down next to her. "For now, yes."

I gave her a quick rundown of how things had gone down with Freya, including how I'd broken my mother's control on two of my brothers.

I touched the amulet that Freya had given me. "This is hiding me from Han for the next few days. I have to go to Grayling by the night of the dead moon."

Denna gave me a sharp look. "The night that Han has to kill you by to set Ragnarök in motion?"

"That's the one." Bebe joined us. "Seems rather coincidental. Don't you think?"

I did. But for right then, we needed to rest. To recoup from the damage done to Berek and JJ.

And maybe I needed it too, for myself.

I sighed. "I need to eat. Denna, you are safe here."

"There is a basement," Sven rumbled from the table. "For the morning."

Denna reached over and grabbed my head, pulling my ear to her mouth. "I need to speak to you."

Privately, she meant. I nodded. "Outside."

I stood and went to the table, scooped up a plate that Havoc had just filled, and turned back toward the stairs. "Thanks."

He didn't so much as pause, just took another plate and filled it for himself. He didn't seem worried that I'd make a run for it. And I knew why.

Because my brothers were here.

No utensils, but that didn't slow me. I picked up the steak and tore a bite out of it before shoveling fluffy mashed potatoes in my mouth with my fingers. By the time I reached the bottom of the stairs, I'd finished the plate. Bebe was at my heels, following me out.

"What do you think is wrong?" Bebe asked.

"No idea," I said quietly.

Hurrying outside, I found Denna waiting on a gravestone that was positioned about fifty feet from the side of the church. "What is it? Are you okay?"

"I am fine," she whispered. "I reached out to Grant when I went to find Martin. Mars, I mean."

Grant, my geeky looking vampire friend in Alaska. He'd always had a bit of a crush on me, but I'd never returned that kind of affection. But he'd been good to me, given me a job even at the bookstore where I'd met Denna.

"Is he okay?"

She grimaced. "He said that the vampire we went to see near Portland—"

"Theodore," I said.

Denna bobbed her head. "Yes. Theodore. He read that book we gave him. The journal. It belonged to Han. At least originally."

I remembered the murderous thoughts that had been scripted onto the pages. "I'm not really surprised."

Denna bobbed her head and shuffled along the top of the gravestone, balancing like an oversized praying mantis. "There...there were other things written in the book. Grant wanted you to know that the book was easily five hundred years old. And multiple people had written in it. Like it had been passed around."

I frowned. "None of this is surprising. What was he worried about?"

Denna swayed a little. "One of the writers talked about a pack of werewolves hidden near the mountains in Montana. Whoever the writer was...wrote about Juniper. About how she would be the one to save the world. That she would be the catalyst for peace, healing the wounds that would bring about Ragnarök."

A sucker punch wouldn't have done a better job of knocking the wind out of me. "Are you...sure?" My knees wobbled. Juniper, the savior of the world? No way. She was too much of a selfish narc to even consider lifting a finger to save...well, anyone, never mind the whole world. She never did anything without getting a benefit out of it.

"Yes. That's what had Grant so fussed. It said she could stop the two wolves chasing the sun and the moon."

The two wolves were Han and Havoc.

This was why Petunia had been sending us to Grayling then. To stop Han's mission.

Denna shriveled up on herself. "I'm sorry. I know that she was terrible to you."

I put a hand on her shoulder. "No, no. You were right to tell me. I don't know what to do with this. But you made the right call."

Bebe hissed, low and long. "So your bitch of a mother is going to save you?"

That was how I was taking it. That I would have to convince my mother to stop Han and Havoc.

But how could I convince a woman who'd wanted me dead for so long to keep me alive? And just how was she going to stop them when no one else had been able to?

That was the question of a lifetime.

"Goldie." Havoc's voice echoed from the church. "Inside."

"He's bossy," Denna whispered. "Is he safe?"

"Safe is a relative term at this point," I muttered. "Safer than his brother. Safer than my mother."

"I'm going to stay outside." Denna touched my arm when I turned to leave. "I don't like being close to the other ones. They all look at me funny."

I put a hand over her long skeletal fingers. "Is there somewhere you can hide when the sun comes up?"

"I'll just pick a grave." She shrugged. "I'll sleep easier out here."

"Thank you, Denna. For coming back. For being brave." I gave her hand a squeeze and then started back toward the church turned pack sanctuary. How upset would the priest of this place be to know it was currently full of supernaturals, a couple of Norse gods (assuming Sven fit into that category somehow), and some possessed animals?

"What are the chances," Bebe said, "that your mother will protect you?"

"Not good," I said. "Not good at all."

It was hard to feel anything about what Denna told me. I mean, the bigger concern was that the Grayling pack had been on the radar of someone in the Norse pantheon for five hundred years. Long before Juniper was born. At least as far as I knew. She was closing in on a century. Nowhere near the five hundred years the journal seemed to be.

Had Han written that part? No. I didn't think so. Nor Havoc. He didn't seem to know much about my family pack. So where did the Grayling pack tie in?

"Petunia and Loki," I breathed out. "I'd lay my money on them being behind the Grayling connection."

The smell of wolf tickled my nose as I stepped through the door and into the church. "And what connection is that?"

Richard was waiting for me on the first floor.

"One that is going to get me fucked over," I said.

Because if my life, and the survival of the world, was dependent on Juniper protecting me, we were all dead.

22

THIRD TIMES A CHARM

The night of the dead moon was seven days away. A week before I'd have to go back to Grayling and somehow convince my mother to protect me.

Which was the biggest fucking joke of my life.

"She won't save anyone, least of all...." Shipley said quietly. I'd pulled him, Richard, and Mars outside to have a chat. I noticed that Havoc hadn't interfered with any of my private discussions. Maybe because he already knew what was freaking me out. He did however seem to be giving me time limits to my private discussions.

Was he trying to show that he trusted me to make good choices? Maybe.

"Yeah, least of all you," Richard added. He ran a hand over his head. "Havoc and that tree beard dude explained what was going on. We only got whiffs of it from Han. And in the beginning, he wanted the other girl more than you. That Soleil woman that he killed. Going back to Grayling is a terrible idea, Cin. Probably the worst idea."

It seemed like forever ago that I'd watched Han cut Soleil's head from her shoulders. Seen the light dim from her eyes.

That would be me if I was not very, very careful.

"Do you have a plan?" Bebe asked. "A way we might be able to force her to help?"

I grimaced. "Not yet. We have a few days to figure something out."

The door to the church opened and Havoc stood in the doorway, silhouetted from the light behind him. "Inside."

"Maybe we're having a private conversation!" Bebe yelled at him. "That doesn't include *you*!"

Richard shot a look to her. "You have got serious balls, cat."

She blinked up at him. "You can hear me?"

He nodded. "I can. Just like I can hear Mars."

Mars had been quiet through this. "I don't know what would have been written about our pack in a journal that old. But I agree with the boys. Juniper will not care if you live or die. So we must find a way to make her care."

"Even if you explain that it will save her own hide?"

Bebe asked quietly. "I mean...wouldn't playing along be the smart thing to do?"

It would be smart. But I wasn't sure her smarts outweighed her hatred of me.

I started back toward the church. "Tomorrow. We'll discuss it with everyone tomorrow."

Richard and Shipley fell in beside me, and Mars and Bebe shot ahead of us, back toward the warmth and comfort of the church.

Havoc was waiting for us, just inside the door.

"I'm tired," I said, the words no sooner out of my mouth before a wave of sheer exhaustion hit me. For the first time in what felt like forever, I believed that I was safe. Even if it was just for a moment. My knees tried to buckle on me, and I would have dropped right there if not for one thing.

Havoc.

He scooped me into his arms and carried me across the fairy-tale space to a doorway covered in long vines and flowers. He pushed through, and on the other side there was a thick cushion that looked to be made of flower petals wrapped in a sheer gossamer cloth. He laid me down on it, and I sunk into the softness with a sigh.

"Get some rest."

"Stay," I whispered as sleep dragged me down, making my tongue loose and the filter in my head gauzy. Moon goddess, I did not just ask him to stay with me, did I? Please let that have been an inside voice.

His hand slid from my upper arm down to my hand and then my fingertips as he let me go.

I closed my eyes. Bebe didn't join me.

I was alone.

Which meant that I was no longer tired. No, not true—I was still wiped out—but my mind wouldn't slow. My heart picked up speed and I felt like I needed to move. To run.

I forced my eyes shut. "Go to sleep you idiot," I muttered.

The bed was warm and comfortable, but I lay awake a long time. Long enough that the others in the building went quiet.

Except for one.

Havoc.

The bonds tying us together jangled with his unease. Maybe he thought I was sleeping, and so he didn't try to keep his feelings in check.

Fear was at the forefront. Fear and rage.

I sat up. I could go find him.

Or I could bring him back to me. The need to soften all the chaos in his head was strong, and I didn't want to think about the why of it.

"Havoc." Just his name, that was it, and a moment later he stood in the doorway. I crooked a finger at him. "You need sleep too."

"You should be asleep."

"Can't sleep when a giant Norse Prince is thumping around, his emotions flicking between fear and rage. Rather disturbing."

I shimmied to the side of the mattress. "I won't touch you. Your virtue is safe with me."

Amusement flickered through the connection between us. "Perhaps, but I cannot guarantee the same in return."

My mouth went dry, and the fatigue and exhaustion disappeared in a flash of heat.

He stepped into the room. "Neither of us will sleep if I lay down with you."

"Well. Hopefully I don't fall asleep in the middle. That would be embarrassing. For you, that is." I smirked up at him as he moved to the end of the bed and slid out of his shirt and then his jeans.

I still had all my clothes on, but I wasn't worried.

He dropped to all fours and crawled up my body, pulling my clothes off as he went until I was naked under him. His hand ghosted over my arm, collarbone, and across my breast, sliding further south to settle on the curve of my waist. I let my hands travel too, touching his face, feeling the scar. Wondering about it.

Knowing that he'd probably never tell me.

Because this was not love, this was not two people who'd come together with a pledge to share their darkest secrets. This was just...need.

He dropped his head, pressing his lips to the underside of my jaw and working his way along my neck.

I arched my back, silently begging for his touch in other places. A low, throaty rumble slid out of him as he pressed his body down onto the bed and slid down, his mouth leaving a trail of hot branding marks.

Mine.

The word echoed between us.

Not love. Possession.

The feeling was echoed from my wolf. She'd claimed him.

Mine.

I'd take it.

His mouth latched onto one of my nipples, sucking it in deep, rolling the nub and then growling as he drew it out, the sound vibrating through me as if I were a tuning fork. I struggled to breathe as he let go and slid further down my body, biting, marking my skin up as he went.

Possession.

Mine.

I dug my nails into his shoulders, drawing scores across his broad back.

I couldn't reach him as his mouth settled at the apex of my thighs, still marking me. His teeth grazed the sensitive flesh, gentler as he sucked my clit in and out of his mouth. Pulsing. Demanding. Pushing me to the edge.

He looked up at me, his eyes blazing with a heat that should have melted the ice. Instead, those dark flames pinned me down as his mouth and touch drove me away from this world.

I struggled to breathe, gave up entirely as he slid his fingers into me and began to pulse in and out, demanding that I give him control.

I grabbed the edges of the bed as the pressure and pleasure built in waves that drew so close to ultimate satisfaction and then receded.

Need and desire, that's all I could feel. My body was taut with it all as he kept me there, on the edge of pleasure that called to me. I'd get close and he'd pull me back from that cascading pleasure until I was slick with sweat, my body humming and shaking with every lazy lap of his tongue.

"Close?" He murmured against my inner thigh.

I gasped as he blew a breath across my clit. It throbbed, aching for him.

He slid back up my body, every bit of his skin touching mine as he pushed his cock into me slowly, inch by inch. I hooked a leg over his hip and tried to pull him in faster.

I arched my hips up, and he went to his knees, grabbing my ass with both hands.

"Look at me," he growled.

"You first," I whispered.

His eyes locked on mine as he pulled my body to his, sheathing himself as deep as he could.

Using my ass as a handle, he began to slide in and out of me. Tipping my hips, he made sure the tip of his cock slid over my clit every time.

I wanted to writhe and thrash. But I held still, eyes locked on his as he moved faster with each stroke.

Faster. Deeper. Harder. The friction of our bodies, wet and on the cusp of coming, was the only sound outside of our breathing.

The pleasure he'd started with his mouth grew again, slipping up and through my body until every part of me was tingling with the expectation of what he was promising me.

He groaned, his eyes flickering to half-mast.

"Eyes on me," I whispered, and his dark eyes opened wider. I could see he was straining to hold this all together. To keep us both balanced between pleasure and the crashing orgasms that were building. To demand we give this moment everything.

I slid my hand between us, and he pushed it away. "Your pleasure is *mine*."

I didn't understand how he was going to... "Oh fuck."

I whimpered as he stopped pumping and held me tightly to him, filling me up while his hand went to my clit, his head dropping to my breast.

With his mouth and hand and cock, he drew me back to that sweet and spiced edge, my body humming and struggling to hang on as the need built and built.

And he held me in that place again, hovering over an impossible space—right at the brink in a place that begged me to leap for him.

"Please," I whimpered, writhing under him, my body no longer my own.

Only then, once I'd begged, did he do as I'd asked, then I could feel his smile against my skin as he began to slide his cock in and out, his finger moving faster, his mouth on my nipples, dragging me to the precipice.

He lifted his head, eyes alight with heat. "Come."

One word and I crashed over the edge. I didn't know if I screamed, didn't know if I stopped breathing.

Shit, I might have died for all I knew as the orgasm took me. I mean, could I even call it that? Because it was more than any orgasm I'd ever experienced.

What I did know was that he hadn't come with me.

We'd see about that.

As my tremors eased, he began to fuck me in earnest, and all my ideas of making him beg at my feet as I sucked his cock fled from my mind.

The second orgasm roared through me, matching his as we rode the second wave together, his face buried in my neck, biting down hard as I dug my nails into his back, my legs wrapped tightly around his waist as if I could pull him deeper.

As his shudders eased, he slumped across my body, his breathing slowing.

I closed my eyes for just a moment.

When I opened them again, I was alone in bed, the smell of Havoc everywhere.

23

THE PLAN BEHIND THE SHIT PLAN

Six days left until the night of the dead moon. We planned our way into the Grayling pack territory. No one could agree about anything. Shocking.

Five days left until the night of the dead moon. Richard, Shipley, Mars, and I tried to figure out how to convince Juniper to protect me. No one could agree about anything.

Four days left until the night of the dead moon. Havoc called the remainder of his pack, and they arrived. No one got along with Shipley or Richard. Fights broke out between them.

Three days left until the night of the dead moon...

"We leave tomorrow morning," Havoc announced to the group. Richard, Shipley, Mars, and I sat at one end of the large dining table. "Get some rest, be ready to leave at first light."

Havoc's pack sat at the other end with a definitive space between the two packs. Not because we weren't getting along—but because no one could agree on how to deal with Juniper.

Not ideal, seeing as we were going into enemy territory together.

I had my own idea of what I needed to do. How to ensure we all survived Juniper. It wasn't something I'd run by my brothers, Mars, or even Havoc. I wasn't sure they'd agree with me.

Because if I wanted her help, and didn't want to fight her, I had only one other option.

A trade. And she would not do anything without a trade that favored her heavily. Unless she was getting something from this exchange, there wasn't a dog's fart chance in a windstorm that she'd help.

Bebe sat with me. "You haven't slept with Havoc since our first night here. Why not?"

Richard choked on his drink—water—and shook his head as he stood and walked to the other end of the room, muttering to himself, "I do not need to hear this. Bad enough I heard you that night."

I glanced at Bebe, seeing the space that had opened around us. "Wanted to talk, did you?"

"You're hard to get alone, everyone wants your thoughts on what to do, only to tell you it won't work.

What are you really planning? What are *we* going to do?"

I laughed and shook my head. *We.* It was always 'we' with her. Still, I got up and led the way to a corner of the room where my back would be between two walls. We could have gone outside, but I had someone watching me at all times now. Protecting me.

Smothering me.

Bebe squinted up at me, and I scooped her into my arms so my mouth was close to her ear.

"When we get close," I said, lowering my voice, "I need to go to Juniper on my own. If she sees all these people...she'll attack first, ask questions later. And then we'll have nothing. No hand to play."

"Hmm. And what are you offering her?"

This was where it got tricky. "My mate bond with Han. She will want him because he's powerful, and even more so because he's supposed to be mine. It is something she's stolen from others before."

She jerked back and looked me in the face. "Then he won't be able to track you. And she's stealing your mate...oh, that's good. Two birds, one big rock."

I gave her a wink. "I know. But I have to make it look like I don't want her to have Han. It's the only way."

Because she would only want to take something that I truly wanted. Which was why I had to talk to her without Havoc there.

There was no way she wouldn't sense the bonds between us. Or scent each of us on the other, even now, a week later.

Or my fear that she'd take him from me. "I can't let her near Havoc."

"You love him?" Bebe asked quietly.

I rubbed a hand over my face. "No, of course not."

"Smells like a lie to me," Shipley said as he walked by. "Whatever you are denying."

Fuck.

I waited until he was gone, then I addressed Bebe in an even quieter voice. "There is...something between us. I don't know. He's possessive. So am I. Feelings for him? Yes. I'll bend to that."

I didn't want to fall in love with him. Not when I knew he had no love for me, and likely never would. Did he want me? Sure. Absolutely he wanted to fuck me. He wanted to keep me alive.

Neither of those things equated to love.

He'd lost his wife to the brother that was hunting me. I doubt he'd ever open up to anyone again, after the pain that I'd felt from just his memories.

And I couldn't really blame him. I'd hidden for years, not letting anyone in because it was safer for my heart.

Bebe butted her head against mine. "Claire and Berek fucked last night. So that's out for me."

I grimaced. "I'm sorry, Bebe. I really am."

She shrugged. "Not like I had a chance, not like this. And it wasn't love."

I sighed and held her a little tighter. "I'm looking forward to strippers and ice cream at this point."

She gave a muffled laugh that had a distinct hiccup on the end of it. "Yeah, me too."

I barely slept that night. I partially wondered if Havoc would join me. And when he didn't, I struggled to keep from pacing the room. Because I knew that it was the last night before I'd slip away to face Juniper on my own.

Even so, my mind kept circling back to Havoc.

I definitely didn't love him. I knew that.

I grimaced, not liking how my wolf or my golden reacted to that sentiment, and made my way through the church, past my sleeping guard, and out to the cemetery where Denna had been staying. I'd barely seen her over the last few days. With all the added werewolves, she'd been even more unwilling to come out.

The cool air wicked away the sweat that had been beading along my spine and the back of my neck.

"Denna," I whispered into the night.

She crawled up and over one of the headstones. "Cin. Are you okay?"

I shrugged. "I'm here. Alive."

"Better than me." She smiled and laughed a little. "You're really going to Grayling?"

I nodded. "No choice now. But I have a plan."

Denna's already big eyes widened further. "Am I a part of this plan?"

"Think you can get a message to Grant?" I asked quietly.

I bent close and whispered the message into her ear.

"Oh." Was all she managed. "Yes, I can get that to him. But...you want me to send it now?"

I nodded. "Go to another graveyard tonight, Denna. I don't want you coming with me to Grayling. It's...it's not going to be pretty."

Denna looked from me to the church behind me. "The other werewolves would try to hurt me."

I nodded. "Even if they didn't know you were with me, my mother will try to hurt anyone who stands with me."

Which was the other reason I needed to slip out on my own. I could keep them all safe if I could manage this without a whole pack behind me.

I watched as Denna slipped into the night, taking my message with her. It wasn't a message of any importance. But I'd gotten her out of here. She'd be safe, and she still felt like she was a part of helping me. Double win.

A crunch of boots on the grass had me slowly turning around. Richard stood behind me, his eyes tracking Denna as she bounded away.

"You always had weird friends."

I laughed. "At least I had friends."

"Touché." He gave a flash of a smile. "So, when are we leaving the rest of the group behind?"

My eyebrows shot up. "What?"

"Don't even pretend you aren't going to slip away when we get close. You and I both know that if you go in with all of these people, she'll use them against you." He scrunched his face up as if he smelled something rotten. "So, when are we going?"

We.

"You think she already knows you defected?"

He shrugged. "Doesn't matter. She's gotten away with too much, for too long. If I don't stand with you now...what's the point of going at all?"

There was a huff of air and we both turned toward Shipley as he crept through the graveyard. "You know that Havoc's plan won't work. She won't bend to him. So, when are we leaving?"

I rubbed a hand over my face. My brothers were finally standing with me, after all these years.

And I wasn't going to turn them away when we had a chance to stand together.

"Tomorrow night, we'll be close enough then to go on foot."

Havoc's plan had been to go in and surround the Grayling pack and hold them hostage unless Juniper agreed to protect me. Which would never happen. No matter how we'd argued, he'd refused to see sense.

To be fair, she might have bended had the exchange been for one of my other siblings, or for some other thing that she loved.

But not for me.

"We wait till everyone is asleep. Then we'll slip away, and be back before Havoc realizes. Hopefully no one will notice we're gone. I'll offer her my mate bond with Han."

Rich gave my knuckles a tap with his own as Ship gave a low whistle. "Think you can make her believe you care about that fucker?"

I nodded. "We learned how to lie from her. Time we turned it around on her ass."

Richard reached out and pulled me into a one-armed hug. "It'll work, Cin. It'll work."

"It better," Shipley said. "Or we're all going to die."

24

THERE'S NO PLACE LIKE HOME

The next night we stopped at a small, abandoned farmhouse ten miles from the Grayling pack border. It hadn't been abandoned when I'd left Grayling all those years ago. A young family had lived here with two small children, a border collie, and a herd of cats to keep the rat population down. Their possessions were still here, as if they'd left in a hurry.

"Lots of blood," Berek said, Claire all but clinging to his arm. "There was a slaughter here."

Bebe sniffed at them both and stayed close to my leg. "I don't know what I ever saw in him."

I didn't mention the magic fingers she'd raved about. No need to rub salt in the wound.

I sniffed the air, my golden coming forward to breathe it all in.

Blood. Fear. Rage.

The family had been slaughtered, down to the last animal. A whiff of Juniper in the air had my belly tightening. I dropped to a knee and touched a small shoe that had belonged to one of the children.

My mother had done this. All by herself. There wasn't a single whiff of any other wolf. I looked up at my brothers, both of them tight with the same horror that roiled inside of me. She had never been a child killer before I left.

"She's been getting worse." Shipley said quietly. "This was not the last time she did something like this, all on her own."

Havoc had no idea what we were walking into. He had no idea how bad Juniper was, even though we'd told him. He wouldn't understand until he saw. Until he experienced her for himself.

Bebe shook her head. "I don't like this place." Then, in a smaller voice, she added, "I don't want to listen to them...together."

I scooped her up and held her tight. "I know, Bebe." I didn't say out loud that we'd be gone in a few hours. Because of course I was taking her with me.

Truthfully, I had my own tender heart wounds to deal with. Havoc hadn't so much as looked at me for the last few days.

I understood on a logical level—I was a potential liability to him, so pushing me away made sense. He'd lost his wife to Han. Why would he want to put himself out there again, on another woman that Han was hunting no less?

Let me get to that part in a minute.

"Set up camp," Havoc said. "Sentries on shift."

The others did as he asked, and I followed him around to the back of the farmhouse. "Havoc, I want to talk to you."

He went still, keeping his back to me. "What is it?"

I wasn't sure I had the right words. I wanted to say goodbye—just in case. But I couldn't let him know what I was planning.

He turned. "What is it, Goldie?"

Goldie. He'd never used my name. I was just another carrier of the sun. Maybe I'd been hoping he'd say something to change my mind, to make me believe that I was wrong to leave him and the others on my own.

I shook my head, retreating from what I would have said, from what could have been. "Nothing. Thought you'd want a blow job before we went into battle. But I changed my mind if you can't even be bothered to say my name."

He sucked in a sharp breath, but I was already turning away from him. Turning away from the almost, from the maybe, from the never gonna happen.

I went and found a spot to the side of the farmhouse, so everyone could see that I was very much sticking around.

Everyone needed to think I was staying.

Especially Havoc, who joined the group a few minutes later. He didn't so much as look my way.

Fucker. I locked down all the bonds I had to him and his pack as tight as I could.

There was not much talk. Even though Havoc believed that his strength as an alpha, as a prince of the Norse Pantheon, would be enough to intimidate Juniper into working with us, there was a strange quiet over the camp, and it was not long before everyone turned in as the sky darkened.

Richard, Shipley, and I had to wait until everyone else was asleep. Richard was on his shift for guard duty on the south side of the camp, near where Shipley and I were pretending to be asleep.

The night was familiar here, filled with the call of nightbirds flitting through the air, the whoosh of bats as they scooped up bugs and insects, and the smell of the wind. I knew all of it as if I'd never left this place.

Mountains and wildness, a crisp tang of frost in the air, the smell of a distant river. This had been my home, and I knew it inside and out.

Bebe and Mars lay next to me and Shipley as we waited for Richard to give us the signal. I knew both of them would be coming, whether I liked it or not. Mars wasn't about to stand down from a confrontation with Juniper, not when he was finally with us.

And there was no way Bebe was staying behind. She was the jelly to my peanut butter, the Snoopy to my Charlie Brown, the cat to my dog. I was lucky to have her.

Near midnight, Richard stopped at the foot of our bedrolls and tapped the bottoms of our feet. On our bellies, we crept out past the sleeping bodies and were into the tree line in under thirty seconds, the sound of our steps muffled by the long grass. Moving swiftly, we made our way deeper into the trees until we'd put a solid mile between us and the camp.

Only then did we speak.

"That...that seemed easy." Bebe squinted up at me in the dark. "Didn't it? Like not one person flinched."

A trickle of unease rolled through me. We'd never been able to just slip away from Havoc and his pack without *someone* noticing. "Yeah. I don't like it."

"Take it," Richard said, keeping his voice low. "Luck turned her face our way, don't spit on it."

I put a hand on his shoulder, unable to ignore the unease that was tugging at me. "Hang on. Just let me check my bonds to everyone. To be sure."

I needed to make sure that they were okay. Because no matter what, there were bonds between all of us, and they'd been growing with each passing day.

I centered myself and reached out to the bonds I had to Havoc and the others.

Quiet, peaceful.

A sigh of relief slid through me. "Sleeping. They're just sleeping."

Shipley grinned. "See? Rich is right. Luck is on our side."

I smiled, but honestly it still felt off. Even so, we didn't have time to sit around and debate it. We moved on, Mars trotting along next to Richard, keeping pace with his oldest son. Here and there, I thought I saw a shadow of the man he'd been. He'd looked a lot like Richard when he was on two legs, and they would have been hard to tell apart had they been standing next to each other.

It was easy to tell myself I was just seeing things. That it didn't mean anything.

By early morning, the sun still below the horizon, we were well within the pack lands and moving our way toward the center of Grayling. The amulet around my neck felt heavy and cold. A quick glance showed the engravings on it were fading—just as Freya had said they would.

My protection from Han was running out. It would be gone by the end of the day, if not sooner.

Juniper would still be asleep. She rarely rose before noon—dependent upon whatever male she had in her bed.

Richard led the way, so we avoided the sentries easily. "They've gotten sloppy since we left."

Shipley nodded. "Kieran will be a problem if we run into him."

"Take him together, if he finds us," Mars said. "Pin him, and Cin will try to reach him, just as she did you two pups."

I wasn't sure that would be possible, or even that I wanted to try. He was more like Juniper than he was like Mars. There'd always been a mean streak in him, from the time that he was young.

Sure, Mars had helped keep it in check, but...that check had been gone a long time.

Kieran had seemed to revel in Juniper's wickedness. He'd been more than eager to try everything she wanted on for size.

Slipping through the forest of my childhood, I struggled with the memories that washed through me and fought to put them out of my mind.

Because I was here to strike a deal with a devil who would want me dead. I had to be smart. I could not, under any circumstances, let myself get distracted.

"I will go in first, right to her room. Try to reason with her in private." I grimaced as I spoke the words, my brothers already shaking their heads.

"She'll raise an alarm," Richard said. "You know it."

"Eventually. But I am banking on her wanting what I have."

We'd talked about it, and the boys agreed it was the best plan we had.

She would want Han and the power he represented. I just had to spin it right. I had to set the bait in front of her so carefully she wouldn't even know it was bait.

Bebe butted her head against my leg. "Are you sure?"

I gave a quick nod. "I have to. You four keep watch. Don't follow me in, Bebe."

What I didn't bother telling them was to run if it didn't go as planned. I didn't have to say it—I saw it in Richard's eyes that he would get the other three out of here, back to Havoc. That was the deal with our family...you got left behind if you were stupid enough to put yourself in danger.

I touched my knuckles to my brothers', then gave Bebe and Mars both a head pat before I was off, ghosting around the edge of the pack's central home.

Juniper's home.

My childhood home.

The smells of the forest whispered to me that this land would always be my home, even as my mind reeled at the stupidity of me being in this place.

Danger, danger, danger!

My survival instincts demanded that I get the fuck out of there, but I had to do this. I had to try and make

Juniper see that protecting me would both benefit her and save her.

I paused at the back side of the house that I'd grown up in, nervous sweat sliding down my spine. Timber framed, the wood was gray with age and weather, the windows dark like the eyes of a long dead creature. Despite the wood and the smoke curling out of the upper chimney, there was no warmth.

No movement anywhere that I could see either.

I blew out a slow breath and waited another beat. Mostly because I did not want to face Juniper. Even knowing that I had to, that it was going to save us all, I struggled to make my feet move.

Two guards slept around the back side of Juniper's house, doing a piss-poor job.

Creeping out of the trees, I passed them in a few strides and opened the back door on silent hinges.

Neither of them stirred.

I shut the door behind me, holding the handle so there would be no click of a metal latch. I stood in the kitchen, breathing in smells that left me shaking.

The scents of magic and wolf, of the forest and Juniper with her constant rage, which smelled of wood ash and a thick cloying vanilla. I swallowed hard and made my feet move through the house and up the stairs. My breathing was shallow, as memories stormed me with each lungful of scents.

The stairs that led to the second and third floor

were dark, hidden in shadow. I took them quietly, evading the fourth step and the seventh for the creaks that lay in the wood.

A low moan whispered on the air. The hitch of a sigh.

The sound of flesh on flesh.

Shit.

I'd have to interrupt her.

Just what I wanted, to see my mother naked with some idiot who had no idea what kind of snake he was in bed with.

I reached the top of the stairs, wrinkling my nose and trying to focus on wood polish, cleaning astringent, and anything but the smell of what was beyond that door. Let me tell you, smelling your mother's... desire...is atrocious.

I made my way across the landing to her door, cracked open an inch. I did not look in.

Nope, I knocked on the door edge and then took the next set of stairs up to the third landing, where her office had been before. She'd smell me and follow me up, I was sure of it.

What I found was not the office I remembered.

She'd converted it to a torture chamber.

Fuck my life.

25

READY FOR THE PLOT TWIST?

F uckity fucking shitty shits. Of all the shittiest gods-be-damned things to walk into, my mother's torture chamber was one I hadn't expected.

There was a werewolf strapped into a contraption that held his body tightly to the wall, pinned down with silver stakes. I didn't recognize him—how could I when his face was covered by a metal mask, his mouth stuffed with a metal gag. I drew a short breath.

"Pluto." One of Juniper's favorites before I'd left. I moved toward him and stopped.

Because she was right behind me.

A groan, that's all he could utter before I had to turn to face the woman who'd stepped into the room in nothing but a silken white robe. She hadn't even both-ered to tie it at the waist, leaving her body bare to me.

Her eyes widened as they landed on me. "I thought I was smelling things. I'm surprised to see you still alive. How have my sons not killed you yet?"

"Juniper." I didn't bow to her, didn't drop to my knees as she made the pack do. "I have a bargain for you."

She laughed, her power circling around me like a wolf on the prowl. "You are not wasting words, Cinny. No hello? No you missed me?"

I fought not to flinch at the nickname only she and Kieran used. "I would make a bargain with you, fair for fair."

We'd all agreed it was best if we didn't tell her the whole truth. Some things were better kept back from her cunning, dark mind. Keeping the words short and simple, that was the way with her. The more you gave her, the more she could figure out.

Her dark red eyebrows lifted. "You...would bargain with me? Why? You do know I want your head on a pike, yes?"

"You are my mother." I wanted to vomit the words. "Is that not enough of a reason to ask you?"

She stood there, bared to me, the evidence of her lover all over her pale skin. "I am not your mother."

I sniffed. This wasn't the first time she'd said so. "Blood says otherwise."

Her smile was slow and...hard. "Blood is fickle. I am the one who birthed you, yes. But you are not mine. Nor was I ever yours. So why are you here when you know I wish you dead?"

Dead, because I could match her strength for strength. Realization hit me square in the chest.

That was why Meg had been the favorite. Why she'd been safe.

Meghan was no threat to Juniper.

I couldn't believe I hadn't seen it before.

Freya and Petunia had said I needed Juniper, that she held the key to stopping Han. I didn't understand why, but I was here to figure it out. Why did I need her?

"You don't even want to know what my request is?" I tipped my head to the side. "No curiosity?"

Juniper narrowed her eyes. "Speak."

Time to set the bait. I'd need to be slick as eel snot.

"You are key to saving the world, Juniper."

Her eyes didn't so much as blink, but I could see her mind working. "Go on."

Her enormous ego drew her in more than anything. Something I'd been rolling the dice on.

I didn't move, though I wanted to pace. "For some reason, the Norse gods have decided to dabble in our world. Petunia is one of them. Her husband is Loki. The man you fucked is a Norse god."

Juniper's face didn't change, but I knew her. I had no doubt that it pleased her to no end that she'd been fucking a god. Even if it was a little g.

"Is she still angry about that?" Her smile was slow, sultry.

"Probably." I shrugged. "But that is not the point. I want to know if—for a bargain of fair and equal trade —you will help us find a way to stop the Norse Ragnarök from coming down on all of us."

Behind us, Pluto shuddered in his chains, whimpering.

She ignored him. "To put my life on the line against a pantheon of gods? No, I think not."

I shook my head. "No, not to put your life on the line...the gods seem to believe you are the key to all this. That you have a power or knowledge that will help us stop what is coming. I honestly don't even know why. But somehow, it will be on you to bring peace."

Her smile didn't change. "And what do you think, Cinny? Do you think I am the hero or the villain in this story?"

Games, it was always games with her. "You know what I think of you."

"I want to hear you beg for my help, little Cinny. I want to hear you cry for me to save you. Like you used to cry for me as a child. But I know you won't, you never would let yourself beg me, even when I let *them* take you."

Her words made my gut tighten. I would not go to that dark place. I refused to let what had happened have power over me. She kept going. "When that pack came in, and those men took you, after Mars was gone...you didn't even beg then." Fuck her for going there. "And even if you did beg and cry now, it is not enough to make me turn my head and save anyone, least of all you. That you had the nerve to come speak to me, here...for that I will let you go. I will let you have a head start on my wolves."

Her wolves.

Mars's wolves.

This was where the games she'd taught me would help. I had to lead her nose to the treasure I was hiding —the thing I knew she would want. If I offered it outright, she would never bite. She had to think she had the upper hand. Not that I believed she would have let me leave. Not for a hot second was she just going to let me walk out of here.

I was a threat to her power.

Even now.

I moved toward the window. It wasn't barred, but open wide. A temptation to those chained within the room—false freedom, if only they could get loose. "It would save you too, Juniper, is that not reason enough?"

"I am safe." She smiled, her teeth perfect as always. Why she would think she was safe was beyond me. Her ego knew no bounds.

I slumped. "Then my mate and I will go. I will see if there is another way to save the world."

She held up her hand, stopping me. "Since when do you have a mate? Is it a true mate bond?"

Funny that was what she reacted to, not the end of the world comment. I let my shoulders slump further. "He rescued me from the shelter. Drawn to me, even... trapped as I was. His magic found me. Healed me."

The hook was baited and set so carefully, I had to keep from congratulating myself, because the hook still had to settle in her gut. I paused at the window, gripping the ledge as I prepared to throw myself out. I could see Richard and Shipley waiting in the shrinking shadows between the trees. I shook my head.

"Wait."

I turned, keeping my hands behind me as I flashed Richard a single index finger to wait. "You have changed your mind?"

Her smile was icy cold. "I want something of yours. You said your mate has magic?"

I nodded. "He does. He is one of the Norse pantheon. A prince."

The bait just got bigger, and the hitch in her breathing said it all. "He is not strong enough to save the world?"

I frowned, baring my teeth slightly. "Saving the world is no small thing. Even for a hero like him."

If I baited the hook much more, she would choke on it as she swallowed.

She held up her hand, fingers curled toward me. "Perhaps there is one thing I'd like from you. One small thing. In the scheme of saving the world, it would cost you almost nothing."

I let relief flow over my features. "Anything. Name your price."

Her smile widened. "Your mate bond."

Even though I'd known what she would ask for—even though I'd planned for it—I'd worried that I might not be able to respond with the appropriate amount of revulsion. But what I saw in my head was her hand on Havoc.

My wolf roared to the surface, and I launched at her, driving her back onto the third-floor landing.

"You will never touch him," I snarled the words.

Seeing Havoc. Just Havoc was enough to make my reaction believable.

Her smile widened as she backed up and gave me room. "That is the deal. I'll give you some time to think about it. Come back tonight. Come for dinner with your mate. And then you will give me his mate bond, because you and I both know that you are the good one. You are the one who will break herself apart to save the rest of the world."

Funny how she thought that.

Maybe once, a long time ago, it had been true.

But now?

Havoc in bed with her. Her hands on him. The thought was enough to send me into a tailspin that I wasn't sure I could control. Even though he was not my mate, my wolf refused to acknowledge that fact.

And I knew in my heart that to keep him safe, I would let the world around me burn.

I left, leaping out the window, across the roof, and then down onto the hardpacked earth. I was in the trees and running, Richard, Shipley, Bebe, and Mars leaping along to catch me.

We ran until we were clear of the edge of the pack lands, and only then did I slow.

"She took the bait," I said. "She wants me to come back tonight at dinner, to give her the mate bond. It'll be cutting things close, but...if there is a key in her, then we will find it. She wants my mate with me but we can fudge it. Use one of the other wolves."

Not Havoc.

Richard grabbed me by the shoulder. "Good job. And you didn't get killed in the process. Even better."

I grimaced. "She was fucking someone. I interrupted."

That was likely all that had saved me. For her, sex was...well, it was everything. Because to her, sex was control and power.

We were almost all the way back to Havoc's camp

before I realized we'd lost someone. "Wait, where is Mars?"

"He wanted to stay behind," Shipley said.

I'd just assumed he was following us. I'd seen Bebe and hadn't thought that Mars would want to do something as foolish as staying behind when he'd be a mouthful for some pissy werewolf.

I turned as if I would go back, but Richard touched my arm. "He has his own things he needs to do, Cin. Let him."

My guts churned with fear for him. Fear that he would get eaten, killed, snapped in half. His death—supposed death, whatever—still haunted me. To have him dropped back into my life, only to be stolen away again would be nothing short of torture.

We slowed our steps. I had to prepare myself for Havoc's wrath. Defying him had become a solid pastime for me, but I wasn't stupid enough to think that he'd be happy to see me. At least not at first.

Maybe he'd spank me for leaving without him. A smile slipped over my lips.

I blew out a slow breath and stepped out of the last line of trees before the camp.

Which was completely empty.

Richard and Shipley stepped up beside me. "What is this?" Richard said quietly.

"Did those fuckers leave without us?" Bebe shouted as she raced through the space, sniffing at the bedrolls, sniffing at the embers that were no longer glowing in the fire pits.

The space felt...empty.

There was no answer to our questions.

"What the hell happened?" I whispered as I did a slow turn, searching the ground. There was no blood that had been spilled. It was as if they'd just been scooped up and floated away. Not a footprint, not a scuffle, no fighting had occurred that I could see.

"Magic," Shipley said. "Juniper has her court wizard, or whatever you want to call him. He could have done this."

This.

Taken my pack from right under my nose.

Anger snapped through me, and the world around us seemed to dim. I closed my eyes against the onslaught of the weight of what had happened.

A creaking of wood spun me around.

Sven stepped out from the far side of the camp. "You...were not here when the spell was cast?"

I drew a deep breath, calling my golden up to help me out, her nose stronger than my own.

Magic, it lay very, very subtly on the edges of what I could smell.

And that magic was familiar.

It smelled of living things, of an atrium where the ferns were so soft that they were like velvet under my fingers. "No." It was a pitiful denial. I took a step back. "Sven. He thought you were his friend."

Sven spread his hands wide. "I am in many ways like Jor. Neutral."

"Bebe." I stared at her, on the other side of Sven. Too close, far too close to him. "Get back here."

Even as I said it, Sven spun and scooped her up with a wave of his long-fingered hands. "No. I want to make sure you will be there tonight. You need to be there."

She screamed and thrashed, hissing as I leapt forward, trying to cover the space before he...disappeared. With Bebe.

"No!" I screamed as I fell through the space he'd been standing in, landing on an empty bedroll.

"Shit." Richard let out a low snarl. "Shit. She knew...Juniper knew they were here?"

Shipley kicked something, sent a backpack flying. "He was working for her. Sven was with her, all along."

Only I knew the truth. Sven wasn't working for Juniper. "No. He was still working for Han. He never stopped working for Han."

But then why heal me when I'd been so close to death? He could have killed me then. Unless I had to die by Han's blade.

A memory flashed through me—Soleil's head rolling sideways off her neck as she fell to the ground. The blood glittering on his axe.

His eyes as he'd looked at me.

Then Sven's words to Havoc. *Look at her! How could he not see the glitter on her skin?*

He'd been trying to tell Havoc that Han already knew the truth. I reached for the bond, oily and dark, that connected me to my fated mate. It shimmered there, under the weight of all I'd done to dampen it down.

He was waiting for me, back the way we'd come.

On the pack lands of Grayling.

26

WHO'S YOUR DADDY?

"Where are you going?" Shipley called after me as I ran from the campsite, my mind racing.

Sven was working with Han. But he was working with Havoc too. Or maybe he was forced to work with Han? I didn't know. What I did know was that Sven had looked hard at me when he'd said he was neutral.

Like Jörmungandr.

"Going for clarification and help!" I yelled back, racing toward the river. The river they'd dumped me in, the river that I was betting would hold a rather large serpent now if what he'd told me held true.

I ran for all I was worth, sliding to a stop at the bank of the river, stones and debris falling in.

"Jor! You must be here, on this last day before the

night of the dead moon, wondering if my death will free you." I scooped up a stone and flung it into the river, toward the eastern bend.

Nothing.

I turned to the west to see the scales of the Midgard serpent roiling under the water, flashing and sparkling in the sun. Relief is not something one should feel when staring down a creature large enough that its coils could wrap around the world one day.

"Well, well, golden wolf, what brings you here..."

I held up a hand. "Nope. You don't get to play stupid."

His head rose out of the water. "You think that I would play games?"

I barked a laugh. "At this point, I have to assume everyone is playing games."

His grin was wide, showing off his teeth. "Then what game am I playing, golden one? One of glittering skin, one of all the sunshine in all the worlds?"

I put my hands on my hips and narrowed my eyes at him, assessing. "I think you're bored, so you will do whatever you can to make life interesting. Like saving me one minute. Trying to fuck me the next."

He rumbled in the water, wiggling with what could only be called happiness. "Oh, I knew I liked you. I would really prefer it if you didn't die. You are *interesting*."

"Then you will help me?" I asked.

"What will you give me?"

I looked around the space, because I had nothing of value. Except...he thought I was interesting. It might work.

"What if I gave you a coffee date, one a month, for as long as I live? An hour to talk. To be interesting. And that will cover the previous favor too."

His head shot out of the water. "That is...intriguing. Make it longer. A day. And I still get my original favor."

I shook my head. "Two hours, no additional favor."

"Half a day, plus my favor."

"Three hours, that is my final offer," I said.

His head whipped side to side, then he slowly nodded. "Done. Now...ask me the questions you have, interesting one."

I could feel Richard and Shipley behind me. It felt good knowing they had my back, although they probably couldn't do much to help me if Jor decided we were no longer friends. "Freya and Petunia have both said that Juniper is key to stopping Ragnarök. To saving the world, bringing peace. How is that possible? What do we have to get her to do?"

Jor's eyes widened. "Is that what they said? Oh, that is a tricky thing. Tricky indeed."

"Why?"

He lowered his head to rest it on the bank next to me. "Because she both is *and* isn't the key. She is part of the puzzle to *you* saving our world. Just as Havoc is the key and not the key. Just as everyone here has a part to play."

"They invited me to dinner to kill me," I said. "Her and Han, I'm sure of it. She took my pack, she took Havoc."

"Then I suggest you get them all back." Jor blinked up at me. "I suggest you take every bit of whatever strength you have within you and do what you must. Unless you are ready to die and let me be free?"

I frowned. "That didn't sound neutral."

"I'm looking forward to our coffee dates." He grinned. "I think it will make Havoc shit a brick, as they say."

Richard snorted behind me. "I don't want to like him, but that's funny."

Jor turned his head toward my brothers. "Interesting. I see you pulled them out of the darkness."

"Out of Juniper's hold."

"That is its own kind of darkness, Sunshine." Jor squinted at me. "Don't be too hard on Sven. Or any of the pantheon. They don't want Ragnarök. But they aren't very good at this game of survival anymore. They've lost their touch. You on the other hand, are very, very good at it."

I sat on the edge of the sluggish river, staring into the water that had nearly been my end. I reached over and put a hand on Jor's head. "So you're saying that I have to go have dinner with my mother, and what will be will be?"

"Yes. But for what it's worth, I believe you *do* need to be here. Your path has brought you full circle, Sunshine. That is rather fitting, don't you think?"

"I'd rather be in Mexico, enjoying a margarita and lying on the beach," I muttered.

He grunted. "I am trapped to whatever water is near those two boys. Perhaps you should go to Mexico. I would like that."

I patted him on the head. "Let me survive this. I'll go to Mexico. Bebe can have her ice cream and strippers while you frolic with the dolphins."

He lifted his head. "I like you."

Richard crouched behind me. "What do we do between now and then? We have hours."

We didn't just have hours; we had a whole fucking day ahead of us.

"May I suggest a nap?" Jor offered.

A nap.

It was the slow wink that tipped me off. He was trying to get me to go to sleep. "Someone wants to talk to me?"

"Just a suggestion for my new coffee friend." He grinned. "I like my coffee with equal amounts of cream and sugar, and a shot of whiskey wouldn't go amiss."

I laughed. "Okay, nap time it is."

"Good luck tonight." He slid back into the river. "Try not to die."

I backed away from the river. "Okay. Let's get some sleep. We'll take shifts."

Richard gave me a nod.

"They'll look for us back at the camp," Shipley said. "So where are we going?"

I grinned. "Remember that cave we found? We hid from Juniper there a hundred times at least. She never found it."

Shipley grinned back. "Perfect."

He and I led the way, Richard following. Because this was a place that Richard had never found either, all the times he'd looked for us on Juniper's orders.

West of the pack lands, we found the rocky bluffs, the waterfall that spilled into a shallow pool.

"We'll dive down first," I said to Richard. "At the bottom, there's a rock set in front of the opening. I'll get it open and go through. Richard, you come through next. Shipley, you go last."

Richard ran a hand over his head, a sheen of sweat on his face. "You know I don't like tight spaces."

Juniper used to lock him in a small crate wrapped with silver chains as a punishment.

"Give me three minutes' head start. I'll get the lights on." I gave his arm a squeeze, turned and dove into the water, straight to the bottom of the pool. It looked shallow but went twenty feet down. At the bottom, I gripped the smooth flat rock and shifted it to the right, continuing on down into the slight curve of the tunnel before swimming forward and then immediately up.

I broke through the surface of the water into the cave. Pitch black had nothing on this place, the only light coming from the tunnel I'd left behind.

I lit the old lanterns Shipley and I had left there... illuminating the place. For good measure, I tugged on my bonds to my brothers.

Fear raced through them.

Richard all but shouted down the length of the bond.

Kieran found us. We'll lead him away. Do what you've got to do, little sister.

And then, because he too was an alpha, he shut the bond down between us, blocking me from sensing where they were going. From what was happening to them.

I slid off the ledge, feet in the water, but someone grabbed me from behind and threw me away from it.

"Girl, that is a terrible idea."

I spun around in a crouch to stare up into the face of the man who'd been visiting my dreams.

Tyr, of the Norse Pantheon.

He grinned at me. "How are you faring, Sunshine?"

27

IS THAT A SNAKE, OR ARE YOU HAPPY TO SEE ME?

I scrambled back from him and up to my feet. Just like in my dreams, he had long braided hair on one side and a short shave on the other. "What do you want from me?"

"I'm actually trying to help you survive all this." He waved his hand in the air around us. "Freya, Petunia, Juniper...they are all going to manipulate the ever-living fuck out of you." He sighed and sat on a stump that Shipley and I had dragged in here one summer as a seat.

"Yeah, I've already figured that part out. How about telling me something useful, like what exactly I need to do to get Juniper to do her part."

"You have to fight her, but you already figured that out," he said, and I could have sworn his voice dipped into sadness.

"That's it?"

His jaw ticked. "No. No it's not it."

I narrowed my eyes. "You aren't supposed to be helping me, are you?"

"I am the only member of our council who can help you without repercussions." He smiled, but then sighed. "I am hopeful that you will be able to do what you must."

"You said I had to challenge her."

"You have to kill her."

The air whooshed out of me. I'd told Denna once that I could take Juniper. I'd told her that I was stronger.

Truthfully, though, I wasn't sure. Telling myself that I was stronger was how I'd slept at night without constantly waking and looking over my shoulder.

"She is afraid of you." Tyr raised his hand and the lantern rose in the air between us, our figures dancing in the shadows. "Because you carry a power that even she cannot touch. But it must be unlocked."

I frowned at him. "I am an alpha female. That is power enough."

He shook his head. "Not in this case. To ensure the world is safe from Ragnarök, you must become more than you are now. You must change the game."

I raised my eyebrows. "How?"

"Find your heart, Sunshine. Are you the wolf? Are you the golden? Which of those will come to aid you when you face Juniper?" He stood and the lantern began to spin slowly in revolutions that threw light across the damp walls. "You must dig deep. For she is not just an alpha female, any more than you are."

I blinked and he was gone, the lantern at my feet nearly out.

When I looked back toward the water, I saw the light was fading.

Impossibly, the day had already passed.

Juniper had my friends. She had Havoc. And likely she had Richard and Shipley now too.

I dove into the water and swam out to the small pool.

The time of reckoning was approaching, but I wasn't going to Juniper alone. I made my way through the forest, my mind ticking over what Tyr had said. And what he hadn't said.

Powers that were beyond that of an alpha female.

I paused at the river. "Jor, perhaps you'd like to watch me fight for my life? It will be interesting, I'm sure."

His head popped up out of the water. "An invitation to come on land? Oh, you are a good friend."

He slid from the river and onto the bank, making his way through the woods next to me. Of course, I had my reasons for bringing him along.

One, to show I was not afraid.

Two, because it was badass to walk into the Grayling pack lands with a giant snake.

I felt more than saw the sentries take off as we approached, running ahead to tell Juniper I was on my way, with company.

Jor was quiet until we were almost to my mother's home. "What will you do?"

That was an excellent question. "We'll all find out once we get there."

Tyr had said I needed to fight and kill my own mother.

Freya and Petunia had said my mother was the key to saving the world.

And that bitch had my friends.

I was inclined to kill her and deal with the fallout later. The amulet was cold now, and a quick glance showed there was a single rune etched into the square stone.

One rune. One hour left before Han would be able to seek me out. Even though I'd sensed him somewhere on the Grayling pack lands, he wasn't on me yet.

I drew a slow breath, the brilliant light ahead of us drawing my eyes.

Of course, Juniper had known I'd come.

"Cinny," she called to me. "Come out, come out, Cinny. I have all your friends. And I have a special surprise for you."

Fear lanced through me. I blew out a breath and

kept walking, pushing through it. Because I could feel them on the other side of that fear.

My pack.

Havoc.

Bebe.

Richard and Shipley.

I steeled my spine and kept moving.

"Well met, Sunshine," Jor whispered. "I knew I chose my coffee buddy wisely."

I stepped out of the shadows of the trees and into the brightly lit center of the pack. A clearing with houses all around the edges, the pack center was used for meals, for grievances, and for challenges.

Havoc was bound in chains to a post. I frowned as if it did not send me into a rage that wanted to burn it all to the ground.

Sven stepped out beside Juniper. "Cin. It is the night of the dead moon and...goddess, what is that... you brought Jörmungandr with you?"

I smiled and my wolf crawled up through me, smiling with me. "His fate is twined with mine. He deserves to be here if I am going to die. Or if I'm going to live."

Havoc let out a low snarl, his anger circling around me. Not at me though, at the others. I gave him a quick nod.

Juniper sighed. "You offered me your mate bond in

exchange for helping you figure out the key to saving this world. What have you decided?"

Ask for her help or challenge her to a fight to the death?

"Would you actually give the help I asked for?"

She snarled at me. "You think I would not honor a bargain made?"

I laughed, threw my fucking head back and howled to the sky. "Oh, I have not heard something so funny in such a long time." I wiped at my eyes, noting that the pack was circling in tighter.

I blew out a breath. "I challenge you, Juniper of the Grayling pack."

Her smile widened. "A fight for dominance? Oh, I like it."

I shook my head. "A fight to the death."

Havoc lurched in his chains. Richard and Shipley shouted at the same time as did Bebe.

"No! No you can't fight her, you don't know what—"

Sven snapped his fingers and silence flowed around us. "The challenge has been issued. Will you accept, Juniper?"

Her smile widened. "Yes. I accept."

That was too easy. Which meant it was exactly what she'd wanted.

Fuck. She'd set the bait, and I'd been hooked.

I glanced at Jor, whose eyes were wide as he

watched us. "You might be free by the end of this after all."

"Only if she uses...well, shit. You're in trouble."

I turned to see Juniper holding a double headed axe in her hand. Havoc's axe. Like Han's, it was designed to kill me and bring on Ragnarök. A dog's ass on fire couldn't have stunk more.

I'd been thinking we'd do battle hand to hand in a proper fight.

I had to think fast, the idea flowing to me in a single flash of either brilliance or stupidity. I wasn't sure which. "As challenger, I have the right to set the terms for our fight."

Juniper laughed. "And what will those be."

A hand settled on my shoulder, shocking the shit out of me. "That she also has a weapon."

I turned to see Tyr on my left, a weapon I didn't recognize in his hand. It was a short spear but had curved blades on either end, balancing each other out. He tossed me the spear, and I caught it in mid-air, the metal of the handle etched with something that felt like vines.

"You..." Juniper breathed out. "I thought you were dead."

He smiled. "You can dream about my death all you wish, but that does not mean I will die."

Jor gave a shudder. "This is amazing. Much better than reality TV. I wish I had popcorn."

A blink of light burst into being to our right, and Freya stepped out of the darkness. Another burst of light, and Petunia arrived with Loki.

"Is that everyone?" I muttered.

Havoc grunted where he was, and I realized he was gagged.

Why...unless he knew something Juniper didn't want me to know. I reached for the bond between us, pulling the blocks I'd laid on it away until the golden thread buzzed between us.

His thought was singular and terrifying.

Han is here.

28

MOMMY DEAREST

I put the pieces together fast, feeding them to Havoc as I saw it all in my mind.

I'd felt Han fucking someone—vigorously, but it had been far to the north. And I'd ignored his bond since.

I'd interrupted my mother in bed with a new friend.

Sven had helped her—because he was also helping Han.

I made myself smile as I hefted the spear. "How is Han in bed? Has he tried to kill you yet?" Juniper's eyes narrowed ever so slightly. I laughed. "You thought I didn't know?"

She did a slow roll of Havoc's axe. "Just have to take that pretty head of yours, and I will be queen of this world."

I snorted and put an elbow to Jor's side. "She thinks Han is going to share space with her. That's amusing."

Jor chuckled. "Yes, that is funny, even to me." And then he shoved me with his nose into the ring. "Now fight, Sunshine. I want to get to our first coffee."

I spun the spear in a slow circle, feeling it out.

Wondering why Tyr was helping me so much.

My thoughts wanted to wander to Mars, to Bebe and Havoc. But I had to survive Juniper first. And if I so much as blinked at the wrong time, she'd lop my head off.

With a scream she came at me, swinging the double-headed axe over her head toward me. I stepped back, ducked, and used her momentum against her, only she wasn't there.

She spun, letting the weight of the axe pull her out of my reach.

I didn't jab the spear straight at her. I crouched and stayed put, watching as she slowly circled me.

"All the questions you must have for me," Juniper whispered in a teasing voice.

I smiled. "Like how you haven't contracted the clap yet? That is a mystery for the ages. I doubt there will ever be an answer."

Her face twisted. "Vulgar bitch."

I bared my teeth at her.

Bebe shouted from the sidelines. "Tell her she smells like rotten dick!"

I grinned. "Good point, Bebe. Especially if it was Han she was fucking."

Very few people could hear Bebe, but those who did laughed.

Richard tipped his head toward me. "Fucking hilarious, if only she could hear what was said first."

Kieran was close to him. He cuffed him on the back of his head as Juniper and I tested each other and our weapons. The clang of steel on steel filled the air, accompanied by the screech of metal as we slid the blades across one another.

Back and forth we went, over and over, until we were both slick with sweat. Matched in speed and strength.

Like mother, like daughter.

I caught glimpses of those watching. Of Sven, his eyes full of worry.

Of Havoc on his knees, focusing intently on us.

Of Bebe bouncing on her toes as she shadow-boxed with herself, screaming insults that buoyed me.

But it was Han stepping out of the shadows who made me falter. He tugged hard on the mate bond, freezing me in place. Trying to steal my energy again.

No. Havoc's voice slid through me. *You have to fight!*

Juniper caught me in the gut with a foot as I stood there, frozen. She drove me backward, bending me at the waist, and the crowd screamed as my hair fell forward. Baring my neck.

I dropped to the ground and rolled as the axe swung straight toward the ground. It didn't get my neck, but it did go through my spear, shattering it.

I was still on my belly, crawling away, fighting for air, fighting to get to my feet.

"Finish her off, my queen," Han purred.

Fucking *purred* at her.

Juniper's eyes never left me. They glittered with rage and blood lust.

I didn't have time to strip. I shifted on the ground, knowing that I was not going to be a wolf when I came out on four legs.

The laughter that filled the crowd as I stood there, golden as the day Petunia had changed me, echoed through the clearing.

"Look at her!" Juniper screeched. "A dog!"

She turned her head from me, dismissing me.

Dismissing loyalty. Protection. Fierce love.

I shot forward and sunk my teeth into her calf, breaking through the skin as I dragged her to the ground. She hit face first, her hands loosening on the axe. The minute her fingers left it, it disappeared.

Gone. No more weapon for her.

I circled around her.

Shot in and snapped at her face. She screeched as I raked my teeth across her cheek.

The crowd wasn't laughing any longer as the golden that I was embraced that wolf that I had been.

For my family.

For my friends.

For the future that might be, if I could only hang on.

Juniper shifted on the ground, her deep red wolf snarling and leaping at me. I took the hit and rolled with it, flipping her over my head.

My tail was not wagging.

I was half the size of Juniper as a wolf.

I didn't care.

I trusted the golden, just as I'd trusted my wolf.

A snarl slid out of me, my body bracing as she raced toward me. We went up on our back feet, clawing and biting at one another.

Her teeth clamped down across my muzzle, cracking the jawbone. I yelped and screamed, tumbling with her on top of me.

I kicked and fought with everything I had.

"Don't give up!" Bebe yelled. "Keep fighting!"

"You can do it, Cin!" Ship screamed from the sidelines.

Havoc's voice was quiet, inside my head. *Call your wolf. Call your wolf now.*

I scrambled under Juniper's bigger body, blinded by her fur.

My golden was scared but fighting for our lives. But it wasn't enough. Except...somehow I knew I couldn't just call my wolf. I needed...I needed them both.

Juniper grabbed me by the throat, her teeth crushing my windpipe before she threw me across the space. My body rolled and tumbled through the dirt. I came to rest with my back to her, pain lancing every part of me.

Mars pressed through the crowd and pressed his nose to mine. "Daughter. Rise up. Call your wolf. It is time to end this. Protect your pack. Protect your mate. Do your duty."

His words echoed through my very soul.

I closed my eyes, fighting to breathe.

Seeing the golden on one side of me and my wolf on the other. Both, I needed them both to do this.

Thunder rumbled in the sky above us as I held a hand to each of my two halves.

Loyal.

Fierce.

Compassionate.

Deadly.

Lighting struck the ground near me, the heat of the electrical current throwing everyone near me backward as I pushed to my feet, my body shifting once more, although not to two legs.

I stood and faced my mother.

Golden fur rippled across my body still, but I was no dog. I tipped my head back and howled, calling my pack to me. Calling their strength to me so that I could save them all.

Juniper spun around, but I was already on her. Tackling her to the ground, my teeth tearing holes in her hide as I fought to get to her neck. I would not make the same mistake that she had.

I would not let her lie on the sidelines to find a new rush of energy.

No one shouted at me now, not to kill her, not to finish it.

Sorrow filtered through the bonds from my two brothers.

I clamped down on Juniper's neck as she tried to get away, shifting at the last second back to two legs.

"No, Cinny! You're my daugherrrr—"

I crushed her neck between my teeth with a hard snap, jerking violently to the side, snapping the remaining bones.

She went limp.

Lightning crackled around the camp, dancing in the spaces where our blood had spilled.

I had time to hear Jor say, "This is far more interesting than even I could have hoped for."

And then half of the spear that Tyr had given me... was driven into my side.

I screamed as I fell, my body shifting back to two legs as I stared up at Kieran. He held an axe above his head. Not Havoc's axe. Han's.

"That was for Juniper." He hefted the axe a little higher. "This is for me."

29

SAVE THE CAT

I couldn't move.

The world was going to end.

Only I hadn't banked on so many things happening at once.

Richard burst up and toward Kieran, tackling him to the ground as Shipley ran for me. He scooped me up in his arms. "Let's get you out of here!"

I clung to him. My brother, my best friend, once upon a time.

He gave me his grin that he'd always saved for when he'd known I was scared. The goofy grin. A wink.

And then he stiffened, his eyes widening as he stared down at the blade pushing out of his chest. "I'm sorry," he whispered as he began to slump, still holding me tight. "Run, Cin. Run."

Only there was no running from the monster behind him.

Han looked down at me, ignoring the snarls from Richard and Kieran battling it out. "Oh, that was fun, mate. Don't you think?"

The spear wound had gone deep, the blood spilling out of me too fast. I had to give the sun to someone else. But who would take it willingly?

Shipley went to the side, and I rolled from his arms.

I lay in the dirt.

I breathed out. Bebe stared across the clearing at me, her eyes widening in understanding. If I died, everyone died—unless someone took the sun from me.

She shot across the space, between Han's legs and landed on my chest. "I'll take it. Just promise me you won't die."

"I promise," I whispered, even as the blood poured out of me. Kieran was no amateur. He'd cut a major artery in my belly.

I felt the sun slide away from me and into Bebe, because she was taking it willingly.

"Run." I pushed her aside as Han lifted his axe above his head. Bebe shot off, straight for Havoc.

"Any last words?"

I stared up at Han, his golden boy good looks so terrible in this light. "You won't win."

"I have already won." He smiled down at me.

I tried to push away from him, but he put his boot on my belly, pressing it into the wound. "There is no escaping me."

The bond between me and Havoc glittered bright. I couldn't look at him, but I could feel something...he was fighting something that was not tangible.

Magic.

Magic was falling over him, dulling something in him. But whose magic?

"I'm sorry," I groaned the words. "I'm so sorry, Jor. I...wish I could have that coffee date with you."

"Me too, Sunshine," Jor said. "Damn it. What the hell, why not?"

Han shouted as Jor's tail snapped across him, sending him flying through the air. "You have about five minutes before he comes back. The night of the dead moon will be over, but you'll still have Havoc to contend with by the looks of things. So I suggest you run."

The two packs around us erupted, not all fighting, some just trying to get away.

I couldn't blame them.

Strong hands scooped me up. I thought it would be Havoc, *wanted* it to be Havoc, but it was Richard who held me. "Time to go."

The bonds between us tightened. "Shipley."

"We got him. He'll survive. It wasn't a silver blade," Rich said as he ran.

"Bebe!" I screamed her name. And then there she was, bounding through the forest ahead of us, glowing like a tiny star racing across the ground, the tips of her coat glittering bright with the sun she carried.

"Here! Let's go!"

I didn't see where Petunia, Freya, or Loki had gone, and that made me nervous. So very nervous. "Havoc."

"No, he's not coming with us." Rich breathed. "One of those others, they did something to him. Something bad, Cin. I don't...I don't think he's himself."

I floated in and out of consciousness as Richard got us back to one of the SUVs that we'd driven in with.

In the SUV, Bebe crawled up onto me, and I held her close as someone stitched me up.

"I've got the bleeding stopped. She'll make it. She's healing already."

I didn't recognize the voice. Didn't know whose steady hands had stitched me.

"We've got to get them far, far away. Where?"

I said the only place that I knew better than Montana. "Alaska."

Richard reached back and grabbed my hand. "You got friends there?"

"Some." I whispered. Grant would be there, he would help. And he had connections. Lots and lots of connections.

"Havoc," I whispered his name again as the bond between us glowed, glittering and strong. He wouldn't hurt me. I knew it to my bones that he was not the villain. He was the mate I should have had.

Run. His voice caressed my skin. *Run. Because now I will hunt you, I can't stop what they are making me do. And I am not Han, Goldie. I am the monster you believed me to be when we first met. I am the wolf who will devour you whole.*

DON'T MISS WHAT'S COMING NEXT

BOOK 3 OF THE GOLDEN WOLF WILL BE OUT
IN 2024

Sign up for a release day email from

www.shannonmayer.com

Or scan the code below

ALSO BY SHANNON MAYER

FOR A COMPLETE BOOK LIST VISIT

www.shannonmayer.com

Made in United States
Troutdale, OR
08/27/2023

12396480R00201